KILLING HURT

KILLING HURT

Will Thatcher

Tampa, Florida

Killing Hurt

Published by Gatekeeper Press
7853 Gunn Hwy, Suite 209
Tampa, FL 33626
www.GatekeeperPress.com

Library of Congress Control Number: 2022951285

ISBN (paperback): 9781662935633
eISBN: 9781662935640

1

When I cut Andy's throat on Guacalito de la Isla in Nicaragua it wasn't out of anger. It didn't even feel like a violent thing to do. I stood over his back in the heavy mid-day rain and held his head up with a fistful of his wet hair. His hands were zip-tied behind his back. I switched off my mind and just let my body cut him from ear to ear with a rubber-handled utility knife.

One of the things I've noticed in sobriety is that when other people do terrible things I think of them as terrible people, but when I do terrible things, I have lots of explanations and reasons. Yes, I have an excellent explanation for killing Andy, and no, I don't think I'm a terrible person for doing it. I had policemen and a gangster pointing guns at me, instructing me to cut his throat. What else could I have done? There were three of them. Two wore the short-sleeved blue button-down shirts of the Policía Nacional, while the third was shirtless and covered from the forehead down in ragged prison tattoos. The shirtless one had a shaved head and a thin mustache. The look in his eyes said that he really wanted to kill me. The other two were all business.

They looked like they were just following orders and didn't really care what happened. I wasn't sure which was more worrying, but the point is that my life was on the line, and I wasn't about to die in the mud trying to protect Andy.

At that point I wasn't thinking about him at all. I was thinking about my daughters. They grew up with a drunk, angry dad for most of their lives. After I finally got sober and was able to be the father I always wanted to be, I knew I couldn't fuck up their lives further by getting gunned down in the street in Nicaragua.

As much as this was Andy's fault, I had to look at my part. I wouldn't have been in that situation if I hadn't fallen for his con. For reasons I'm only now beginning to understand, I wanted and needed him to be a savior. I let him play that role despite the advice of good friends and people who knew him. I had expectations for him and when he failed me, just like he failed everyone else who knew him, I became resentful. No, it wasn't my fault that Andy got his throat cut in the street, but I accept responsibility for getting mixed up with him in the first place.

Unfortunately, as you'll find out soon enough, I had to kill some other people in Nicaragua as well. The truth is that I had no choice, and the truth is also that they completely deserved it.

Andy was a very charming, friendly guy. He was rugged, a little rough around the edges, and handsome in an offbeat way. He looked like he was a couple of bad facial features away from being movie star-level handsome, but I couldn't pin down which ones. His skin was pockmarked and damaged from decades of drinking and drug abuse, but overall he looked good for fifty-five. He was tall and athletic-looking. He had had his teeth reconstructed years earlier in Costa Rica, so he had a hundred-watt smile that looked a little weird because it was too perfect and too white for a guy his age. He had a mop of wavy salt-and-pepper hair that always looked two days removed from a shower, as well as the kind of bushy surfer beard that had recently become fashionable. He always wore cargo shorts, work boots and t-shirts with some kind of spiritual message. The day I cut his throat his shirt said: *Expect Nothing, Appreciate Everything.* It had a picture of the Buddha sitting in meditation in the middle of the text. He wore rings on every finger and lots of those beaded bracelets on both wrists. I think the whole getup was supposed to be "spiritually fashionable."

He told everyone he met that he was sober. At first this seemed like a noble thing to do. Some guys do that, so they can help as many people as possible. In Andy's case, after I got to know him and saw the way he operated, it started to seem like it was part of the con, a way to establish credibility and draw people in. Don't get me wrong, he really was sober for over eight years. Actually, in his case, I would say that he was dry rather than sober, meaning that he was abstinent but didn't practice the principles of the program in all his affairs.

He was a useful guy. He had gone to a technical high school in LA, studying to be an electrician. He then worked as an electrical assistant in the Army for two years, long enough to qualify for the GI Bill, which paid for his associates degree in electrical technology. He never finished and never got licensed, but his knowledge was better than almost anyone else you could find in Nicaragua, and he had a brisk business there since you didn't need a license . . . or at least nobody gave a shit if you had one. He had built relationships with all the local tradesmen because of his business.

The "gold coast" of Nicaragua had been booming for several years by the time Andy got there. Houses were popping up everywhere. Expats from all over the world were drawn to the great waves, two decades of relative political stability, and the fact that they were now largely priced out of surf towns in neighboring Costa Rica. It was an opportunity to get in early. Housing lots that had been selling for five to eight thousand dollars in the '90s were selling routinely for fifty to a hundred thousand by 2015. Andy and his buddies could slap together a nice, simple cinderblock and rebar house for $75 per square foot and you'd be off and running.

I got my first glimpse of the way Andy operated a few days into our surf trip. My friends and I were hanging out on the beach after the 1 p.m. Popoyo AA meeting. We were chatting with a bunch of people from the meeting who were smoking cigarettes and drinking coffee when I overheard an argument between Andy and Gary, a French-Canadian senior citizen. I had heard Gary share a couple of times by then. He seemed like a smart, mellow old guy who knew a thing or two about life. I was surprised to hear him raise his voice, so I started paying attention to their conversation.

"No!" Gary shouted, and then with his finger pointed in the air as if to punctuate, he said, "It was *not* a favor. Tell me this, Andy. Did you make a commission?"

Andy guffawed as though he found the question offensive. "What does that have to do with anything?" he said with a look of disbelief on his face. "Am I supposed to work for free?"

"No!" Gary shouted again, fitting a remarkable amount of French accent into such a small word. Then, in a lower voice, he explained very succinctly, "This is the point. It was not a favor. It was work. Work that you profited from, which makes it *not* a favor, and that makes you responsible for the result."

Andy had a look on his face like Gary was being crazy. "Listen, Gary, I can't control every aspect of every introduction. I don't appreciate you getting all huffy with me. Next time do it yourself. Leave me out of it."

The following Wednesday, we arrived at the AA meeting in San Juan Del Sur just in time to see Andy fending off a physical attack from a red-faced middle-aged woman. She was dressed in a crisp white sundress that had a yellow and red flower pattern. As we entered the restaurant, she was throwing punches wildly, trying to hit his face. Her pocketbook hit the floor, makeup, sunglasses and wallet exploding out. Her hair was working its way out of a bun and flying around as she kept winding up and throwing bombs. Some of her punches missed badly and the rest were deflected away. "You're a disgusting fucking liar!" she yelled.

"Jesus Christ," I said to my friend Jose, who stood frozen with shock. "Should we do something?"

"Like what?"

Later, Andy explained to me that she was upset about a real estate deal. "Around here, it's pretty common, unfortunately," he said. "After you buy a place, you find out there are multiple parties making a claim for the same property. I helped her and her husband buy a small farm on the hills outside San Rafael. Unfortunately, three other people claim to have purchased the same property."

"Wow," I said. "That's insane."

"It's a disaster," he explained. "It's bad for them and it's bad for my reputation." "So how does something like this get resolved?" I asked. "What's going to happen?"

"Once these property disputes get into the court system down here, all bets are off. It's really just a matter of bribing the right people to make the judge's decision go your way. That was what I was explaining to her before you guys got here. I told her I could help her out. If she gave me ten grand, I could spread it around to the right people. That's when she flipped out and started throwing punches."

This is how he managed to make enemies with just about every "favor" he did. I don't know if he even understood that the same thing was happening over and over. It was just his modus operandi. There's a phrase that people in AA quote a lot. It comes from the ninth step promises: "constitutionally incapable of being honest." I think this applies to Andy. I think he *wanted* to be honest; he wanted to think of himself as a good guy, and he certainly wanted other people to regard him as such. He just wasn't built that way.

He meditated every day, he went to lots of meetings, but I don't think he was ever really sober. There was always this impermeable barrier of dishonesty between him and the world. The bottom line was that he had to get over on everyone he knew. He had to come out on top in every relationship. The impulse was just as undeniable as the bottle was when he was an active alcoholic.

—

Six Weeks Earlier

We arrived in Managua on a Saturday night. We had flown from Miami to San Jose in Costa Rica, and then connected a few hours later to a twelve-passenger puddle jumper. It was one of those flights where they ask you to weigh yourself and then assign you a specific seat on the aircraft so they can balance the load. It seems like a hazing ritual to the uninitiated. My friends Jose and Rob had never been through this before, so they laughed anxiously and told bad jokes to shake off the nerves.

Jose Perez grew up in Venezuela, where he had surfed almost every day with his pack of seven brothers, so he was by far the best surfer of our group. Jose is super chill, has a great sense of humor, and is fully bilingual, so he's always a huge asset to travel with, especially in Central America. He was one of the kindest and most generous people I knew when he was on land. In the ocean he was a different person. He yielded to nobody. If Jose had already caught ninety waves, he would cut in front of an old lady for number ninety-one. He was a complete savage, whether the swell was two feet or eight feet, whether he was fresh or exhausted. He let zero makeable waves pass. Ever.

He was also a huge part of my sobriety. He was one of the recovery counselors on staff at my rehab and guided me through my first few steps. Jose had been kind of like a de facto sponsor until I got on my feet.

Rob Hernandez and I got sober around the same time. We belonged to the same home group, went to the same meetings, hung out with the same guys, and so became close friends. Rob had a similar ethnic background to me—his father was Latino, and his mom was a Jew from Queens—so he walked around with a Latino name but wore a Jewish star, which rarely failed to confuse people.

Rob worked in commercial real estate and had only started surfing when he got sober, so the sport was newer to him. He was a good athlete and he picked up the basics quickly, but he was used to the two-foot wind swells we surfed in Florida. Nicaragua was a big step up, so he was a little nervous coming into the trip. We trained together for three months prior to ensure he was going to be safe in the water even if his surfing skills weren't top-notch.

We were met outside Sandino International Airport in Managua by a chubby, disheveled local guy with bloodshot eyes and a sign that jumbled up all of our first and last names. Rob nudged me in the ribs and said, "Hey Troy, do you suppose he's looking for us?" We all laughed. He strapped our boards onto the roof of a late-model sedan that had dents in most of its fenders. I'm kind of a car guy, but I had no idea what make and model this thing was. In any case, we crammed in and headed for Playa Gigante. All of us spoke pretty good Spanish and Jose is fully bilingual, so we had a little chit-chat with the driver in the halting "Spanglish" spoken all over around there.

We asked him how long it would take to get to Gigante. "About two hours," he said. I know I shouldn't judge any city based on the area around the airport, but the ride through Managua was really sketchy. All the strung-out and busted-up-looking locals were attracted to the surfboards on the roof. While sitting at traffic lights they came over to beg for money, offer us any and all forms of sin, or just take a closer look. "Wow," Rob said. "We're not in Kansas anymore."

We made it through the city in less than twenty minutes, then headed out on a long road that led to the coast. The roads got narrower, darker and bumpier as we went along. The last forty-five minutes of the drive was a real test of fortitude, both for the sedan's suspension and my stomach. Finally, we drove through the town of Rivas, which stood out as the first outpost of civilization we had seen for a while. The driver explained that this was "the city." Rivas looked to have roughly the same amount of commerce you would find in an average strip mall in South Florida.

Around midnight, we arrived at the front gate of Dale Daggers Surf Lodge in Playa Gigante. The owner, an expat from Georgia named Mike, came out to greet us and help with our bags and boards. Mike was skinny and even taller than me. He had long blonde hair that was pulled back into a ponytail and a neatly groomed brown beard. His blue eyes seemed to tell you everything you needed to know about his mood. At that moment, they were saying that he was genuinely stoked to meet us. He carried a couple of suitcases up to the front porch with his wiry, muscled arms and chattered. "It's great to have you guys," he said. "We're stoked to have you here for a nice long stay. The forecast looks stacked. You're going to score!" He laughed and patted us on the back. We felt comfortable before we walked through the front door of the lodge.

It was late and I was ready for bed, but Jose and Rob agreed to take the tour of the house and hear the story of the history of the place. I was impressed that they gave a shit, but I guess they were excited to arrive and had early surf trip adrenaline that for whatever reason I was lacking. Anyway, the story was pretty interesting. Dale Daggers had been a renegade surfer/ musician/sailor/all-around weirdo badass who actually shipwrecked in Nicaragua on his way to Costa Rica in the early '70s. He found virgin waves and a sleepy, warm, family-oriented culture, and soon made himself welcome in the community around San Juan Del Sur— not an easy thing to do, considering the strong anti-American sentiment that was almost universal around the country at the time.

A few years later he built a house on the beach in Playa Gigante and started running surf tours in his motorboat, mostly for Australians at first, up and down the coast to the many surf spots. The lodge had changed hands twice since Dale's death in 1991. Mike, the current proprietor, also owned an ecolodge in the Mombocho Volcano National Reserve, on the opposite side of the peninsula and about two hours' drive north. He lived there with his family about half the time. When he was back on the Emerald Coast Mike lived in Rancho Santana, a nearby gated community pretty much exclusively for expats. The grounds included a private beach club, a couple of nice restaurants, a boutique hotel, high speed internet and paved roads.

The surf lodge was simple, comfortable and clean. It had four sparsely decorated bedrooms, each with its own bathroom, two on each side of a common area that included a kitchen and a couple of sofas facing a TV, playing an endless stream of surf videos backed by rock music. The four bedrooms each had their own split AC unit. The main room had no air conditioning, but it had a giant ceiling fan which pulled cool sea air in from the windows and kept the place comfortable on all but the hottest days. There was an awesome backyard, with a big covered patio and a huge covered outdoor kitchen. To the side were racks for surfboards and wet rash guards. The yard was shaded by mature palm trees, and was either fenced or walled-in all the way around. A big wrought-iron gate opened out onto the sand of Gigante Beach.

Playa Gigante was not that different from the way Dale Daggers had found it thirty years earlier. There were two large homes down at the northern end—one built by a French guy who owned a nearby café, the other a boarding house where people could rent bedrooms on Airbnb for forty dollars per night. Other than those and the surf lodge, the rest of the beach was lined with simple shanties in various states of disrepair with lots of open space in between. Wild dogs ran the beach looking for fish scraps.

The bay was calm outside the lodge, since Gigante was well-protected to the north and south by steep rocky cliffs. This is what made it a great place for fishermen to launch for the past two hundred years; there was pretty much no surf. Occasionally, though, when the biggest swells came through in the summertime, the bay would produce a little peeling A-frame.

The local fishermen launched at first light and would return around the same time the afternoon surf session was coming back in. Mike described the scene that we would see and he was downright romantic about it. "You'll jump off the boat and paddle your boards into the beach as they're pulling in their nets, all tired from your second session of the day. I'm telling you, it's about as peaceful and beautiful as anything you've seen." I was certainly down for that.

2

Long Island
1978

I was sitting on my bed in our house in Manhasset, assembling Mr. Potato Head's facial features in a funny way. He-Man and the Masters of the Universe played quietly on the nineteen-inch color television on my dresser. Our five-bedroom house was in Plandome, one of the fanciest parts of Manhasset, Long Island. Manhasset was known for its great train service to Manhattan, its colonial-style mini-mansions, and lacrosse.

I couldn't tell from her demeanor, when my mom came into my bedroom, that anything was wrong. She brought with her a roll of thick industrial garbage bags. "Hello, baby," she said as she peeled one off the roll and shook it open. She went over to my dresser, beneath He-Man, and started emptying my clothing into the bag, drawer by drawer. When that one was full, she tied it off at the top and opened another one. "Honey, help Mommy," she said. "Go get your laundry bag and empty it into one of these."

I looked out the window and saw a white and orange moving van parked in our driveway. "What are you doing, Mommy?" I asked. "Why is that van here? Is Daddy coming home this weekend?"

"I'll explain later, sweetie," she said. "Help me pack this up now."

Reluctantly, I put down Mr. Potato Head and went to get my laundry bag off the hook in my closet. I came back and took another bag from the roll, opened it and dumped my clothes in. That was my contribution. My mom packed up the rest of my room while I watched. It didn't take long. Lastly, she pulled the sheets and the comforter off my bed, stuffing those in a bag. "Help me bring these downstairs," she said.

"Where are we going?" I asked on the way down, carrying a bag of my belongings. I followed her out to the driveway and handed her my bag after she had thrown hers in the back of the van. The interior looked like a small, dark, dingy copy of our house. Our furniture, accessories, small appliances and a bunch of cardboard boxes looked sad and defeated back there. They looked like they wanted to go back into their beautiful house where they belonged.

"We're moving to a new house," she said as she closed one side of the barn door and then slammed the other one shut.

"What? Why?" I asked.

She drove the U-Haul fifteen blocks to the apartment complex. When she parked on the road in front, took out the keys and got out of the van I just stayed in my seat. I was still wearing my pajamas and slippers. "Come on, honey," I remember her saying. She was standing in the road with her door open in traffic, talking to me across the front seat of the van. Cars were passing behind her.

I started crying. "I don't like this place, Mom," I said. "I want to go back home." I didn't want to take off my seatbelt because if I opened that door and stepped out, it would be like officially agreeing to start a new life in this place. I really liked my old life. I had a big bedroom with my own bathroom. I had a drum set in the bedroom next door, and a second TV and an Atari video game console. I had a big playroom in the basement. The house was beautiful and bright with sunshine. It had a swing set in the backyard. This place was dark. The buildings were covered by big old oak trees. The grass was patchy in the shade and tree roots were growing above the surface. It was scary.

She came around and opened my door. She put both of her hands on my arm and she explained to me how it was going to be from then on. "Now listen to me, Troy," she said as she stood inside the open door of the moving van. "Your dad isn't coming back to live with us, and he's not going to be able to visit us for a while either. He got in a lot of trouble with the law. Do you understand what that means, honey?"

I held onto my seatbelt. I could barely see her through the tears, but I wouldn't let go of the seatbelt to wipe them away. I was holding on to my old life with both hands. She moved a little closer and I could smell the coffee on her breath. "We can't count on Joe for money anymore," she said. She turned around and looked at the apartment complex. "I know that this place isn't as nice as our old house," she said, turning back to me. "But it's going to be warm in the winter and cool in the summer. Okay? It's going to be clean and we're going to be just fine living here. We're going to have everything you need. I promise, honey." She stopped and wiped my eyes for me. I saw that her eyes had some tears in them also. "It's not fancy, Troy, but it's our home now. We're going to make the best of it. Do you understand?"

I definitely did not understand. I got out of the van and helped her carry some of the smaller items inside, but for a long time I was angry with her for changing my life, and I strongly suspected she was the reason my dad wasn't coming back to live with us. I knew, sure as shit, that I did my best every time I was with him to make sure he wanted to come back, so it must have been her fault.

We moved into a ground-floor two-bedroom unit that had linoleum floors and Formica countertops. It looked clean but it smelled musty. She opened the windows when we walked in for the first time and then stood in the den with her hands on her hips, looking around. She held her hands up and said, "Ta-da!" as though she had just performed a magic trick. I guess that was supposed to be funny.

To be honest, I don't think I ever really forgave her. I came to understand later that she did the bravest and most honorable thing I've ever seen a person do, but even after I learned to respect the choices she made, I resented the shit out of her for decades.

The following week, she had a closet full of cheap business suits and she started riding the Long Island Railroad into Manhattan to her job as a legal secretary at a big law firm. My grandma Rose came to stay with us during the week. She got me on and off the school bus until I was old enough to do it myself. She slept on our sofa. We had become people who sleep on sofas.

3

Nicaragua
2020

The next morning, I examined my face in the mirror while I was brushing my teeth. The cheap fluorescent bulbs were harsh and I looked a lot worse than I did in my bathroom at home. The amount of lines, scars and discolorations were alarming. My skin didn't look healthy, either. Traveling always dried me out, and I never slept well. I spit and rinsed for the second time as my alarm went off on my phone. 5:30 a.m.

I went back into the bedroom to turn it off and tried to identify the feeling in my stomach. Nervous, excited. There was dread and fear in there, too. It felt like the first day in a new school. A new world . . . endless possibilities for good and bad experiences. I took off my sweats and grabbed a pair of board shorts off the pile of clothing on the shelf. They were new and expensive, made of the latest and stretchiest technology, with no seams that could cause rashes after hours of surfing.

I tore off the tag. Standing there naked, I realized that the bedroom was freezing, so I poked the power button on the remote control for the air conditioner. The last thing I wanted was for someone to walk in there and think I had been wasting electricity like a selfish *gringo*. I'm sorry, but I like it cold when I sleep. I wear thick sweatshirts and sleep under two blankets so I can breathe cool, crisp air. It's ecologically insensitive, but sleep is important.

The smell of freshly brewed coffee came under the door, so I pulled on a t-shirt and went out to the main living space. I thought I would be the first one, but Rob and Jose were already sitting on the sofa drinking coffee. "Yo," Rob said.

"Hey," I answered.

"Morning," a voice said from the kitchen.

"Hey," I answered, surprised.

"That's Kai," Jose explained. "He's gonna be our main surf guide."

Kai leaned against the counter and picked up a mug of coffee. He managed a very tired smile and gave a thumbs-up with his other hand. He was a tall, skinny kid with short curly blonde hair that used to be brown. He stood shirtless and shoeless in a pair of worn-out board shorts that had probably been red with a pattern at some point but had aged to a solid faded pink. His blue eyes were bloodshot and it was possible he was either high already or just tired.

"Have a bite before we go," Rob said. "We're not going to be back until nine."

There was a spread out on the counter of cereal, fruit and yogurts. I poured out some coffee and mixed a bowl of yogurt and granola. "Where you from, Kai?" I asked.

"I grew up in South Carolina," he said. "Like the Outer Banks. Around there."

"Nice," I said, taking a sip. "Damn, that's good coffee."

Jose chimed in from the sofa, "Hey, it's pretty sharky up in the Outer Banks, isn't it?"

"Nah, man," Kai said, tossing a handful of granola in his mouth. "It's cool." The Outer Banks has the highest rate of shark attacks in the world, but we all seemed to decide at the same time not to argue with a half-asleep twenty-something who would have our lives in his hands shortly.

I took my bowl and coffee mug back over to the sofa. "Shit, man, I'm nervous," I admitted.

Jose laughed. "Nobody in the history of surf trips has been more prepared than you, Troy. Fucking chill." He had been making fun of my preparations for months. He didn't understand the significance of this trip. I tried to explain it to him once, but it sounded too ridiculous when I said it out loud, so I stopped. We had been out on long boards on a typical two-foot day in Boca. There was a long lull between sets when I started to confess,

"Dude, I've been surfing shitty little Florida waves for fifteen years. I've only been in 'real waves' on vacation maybe four or five times in my life. The first time I went to Nosara, the size and the power of that wave scared the shit out of me. I thought I was gonna die."

"Yeah, bro, it's a different scale," he said. "But you get used to it pretty fast."

That had not been my experience. I did not get used to it pretty fast. In fact, I didn't get used to it at all. I had survived it, and managed to paddle into a few big waves, but I also wimped out of ten times as many. I paddled in, looked over the edge, and every fiber of my being said, *Fuck that. No way.* "I'm going to be forty-six years old," I tried to explain. "I can feel myself getting stiffer and slower and less athletic." I could've added that I was also getting more fearful, but didn't. "I really feel like it's now or never, you know? I always imagined myself surfing in retirement... living somewhere where there's real surf . . . surfing serious waves every day. That idea's kept me going through a lot of bad days."

Jose wasn't listening. He was watching an outside set and checking to see what the surfers down the line did since they had a better view. When they turned and paddled out, he went in the same direction.

In preparation for this newest trip, I did everything I could think of to stack the deck in my favor. I surfed as much as possible to build up my paddle strength. When there were no waves, I swam laps at the pool.

I started doing yoga and Pilates to build core strength and flexibility. I did all kinds of high-intensity interval training to build cardio endurance. I bought every piece of gear I could think of: a fancy new mid-length surfboard, two different sets of fins, all kinds of hydration products and electrolytes, cutting-edge shorts and rash guards.

Still, I was concerned. No, I was afraid. What if I couldn't do it? I had been practicing martial arts for twenty years and lifting weights all my life, but those weren't part of my identity the way surfing was. The truth was that I had been kind of a fraud in that sense for a long time. I needed to clean that up or else I would have to reimagine my retirement, so the stakes seemed high.

—

At 6:00 we heard the boat pull up. Kai went over to the windows and said, "There's Walter. Let's go, guys. Grab your shit." Rob guzzled some water, which seemed like a good idea, so I quickly poured another big glassful from the cooler, pounded it down and met them on the back patio, where our boards were waiting for us. We walked out the back gate and across the beach.

There were four fishing boats on the shore. Fishermen were loading the boats with nets and other supplies as the sun came up over the cliffs and created a light show across the bay. "Fucking spectacular," Rob said as we waded into the sparkling water. We walked out past the shore break and then dove forward on our boards and paddled the rest of the way to the boat.

Walter waited by the ladder. "*Hola, hermanos.* Hand me your board," he said. He placed my board carefully on the bow and then jogged back to give me his hand to help pull me onto the boat, which was not necessary. He pulled me up and then started to laugh. "Oh shit, I got a big fish here," he said. He pretended to strain to reel me in with his other hand as he pulled me on board. He slapped my shoulder and laughed some more. "Welcome aboard, big guy. I'm the captain. I am Walter." He said this as though it was really funny and gave him enormous pleasure. I couldn't help but laugh.

"Great to meet you, Walter," I responded. "I'm Troy." I pointed to the other two floating beside the boat. "That's Rob and that's Jose."

Once the other guys were on board, we sat down and Walter went over to the captain's chair. "Okay, let's go have some fun!" he announced.

"Walter's like our camp counselor," Rob said and we all laughed.

Kai sat on the cooler wearing a pair of cheap green sunglasses. "Walter's the fuckin man," he said. "Total waterman. He was a fisherman out here for forty years before Mike hired him on." We all nodded in appreciation. Walter was a little guy, not more than five-five, but he was shredded with muscle from a life of physical labor. With his hand on the steering wheel, I could see the cords of muscle in his forearms and some serious biceps under his t-shirt. His head had probably been shaved into a crewcut a month or two earlier, but had grown out into a helmet of straight white hair. His face was deeply lined with the ruts caused by a lifetime of huge smiles and working in the sun.

"His wife is Maria, the lodge's cook and cleaning lady," Kai continued. "She's an amazing cook. Not the friendliest person in the world. Walter's the warm and fuzzy one, you know? Maria's cool, but she's a pretty serious lady. You can try to chat her up and shit, but she ain't gonna go for it."

Walter turned around and yelled, "Hey Kai, the wind and the swell are both out of the south. Let's check Colorado."

We headed northwest across a glassy Pacific, three middle-aged dads grinning like five-year olds walking through the gate into Walt Disney World. The morning air raced by, drying the warm sea water from my skin and giving me a chill that added to the excitement. Along the coast were beaches and jagged rocky cliffs, backed by tree-covered mountains. "This is awesome," someone said. We all agreed. My nervousness was momentarily replaced by gratitude for such a beautiful experience.

Playa Colorado is one of Nicaragua's most famous beach breaks. Walter stopped the boat about fifty yards behind the lineup. We all stood up to watch as a set of waves rolled past the boat and toward the beach. It was hard to tell how big they were from behind because I couldn't see the faces, but I could tell they were perfectly shaped, because they peeled from the apex right down the line each time. Although I couldn't see them break, I could hear them. When the first one detonated, I said, "Holy shit."

"Let's go, guys," Kai said. "This looks perfect."

Walter walked up to the bow and took the bungee cord off the surfboards. "Okay, Troy, here you go!" he called, and then laid my board gently into the water. It was my new seven-foot Rob Machado Sunday. The gray resin tint with a fresh coat of wax looked great laying in the turquoise water. It looked fast. I had set it up as a thruster (three fins) for the session, which would give me more stability in bigger waves. I jumped off, swam over to her, and strapped the leash to my ankle. "Hello, baby," I whispered as I climbed on and waited for the other guys. Kai paddled ahead from the other side of the boat, and we followed him toward the lineup.

There were only six guys in the water, which seemed crazy to me. On a day half as good as this in Boca there would be fifty in the lineup. There was a light offshore breeze that kept the water as clean as glass. Kai said hello to a couple of guys and introduced us to help break the ice. Tourists paddling in from a boat are not a very welcome sight in these parts, but there was hardly anyone there yet, so there were plenty of waves for everyone and the guys were cool. There were four young white dudes on tiny high-performance boards, and two local Nicas.

A set came through and, true to form, Jose paddled for the first wave ahead of everyone and took off down the line. We could hear him screaming as he pumped for speed and then made a couple of big turns. I tried to exercise proper etiquette and let the local guys take waves before I looked for one for myself. That turned out to be a good strategy also, because I got to watch what they did. I watched the speed of the takeoff and how the wave broke.

I asked the blonde kid next to me in the lineup where he and his friends were staying. He said they were renting a condo in an apartment building. He pointed to the beach and said, "Right back there." That seemed like a great setup—they could walk down and surf whenever they wanted. The downside was that they surfed Colorado or Panga (the surf break at the other end of the same beach) every day. I explained our setup at Dale Daggers.

The conversation settled my nerves a bit and gave me a chance to watch a set pass. By the time Kai called out to me, I thought I understood how they were breaking. "Hey, Troy!" Kai yelled out. "This one's coming right to you. A nice right. Go get it!"

I laid down on my board and started to paddle, looking backward at the wave. It looked like a mountain coming at me, but I could see I was in the right spot. It started breaking down the line to my left when it got to about ten feet behind me. I gave it three or four hard, deep paddles to catch up, arched my back a bit to get the nose of my board out of the water, and then felt her plane. *I'm in*, I thought. I set my hands and popped up to my feet. It was clean. It peeled open in front of me perfectly. I rode it down to the bottom for a moment and ran my hand across the face, which was taller than me. I threw my hands forward and to the right to turn back up the face. I did that two more times before it closed out ahead of me and I turned off to paddle back out.

"Thank you, God," I said. "Thank you so much for that." I was so happy. It was a nice wave. There were hundreds of them that morning all across the beach, but it meant a lot to me. I didn't have to reimagine my life. I could do this.

"Nice one," Kai said when I got back.

"Yeah," I answered. "That was fun."

Jose was carving up the waves like it was his job. He was in his full glory, pulling out his entire bag of tricks. I saw him pull a couple of floaters, lots of huge carves, and even a big jump off the end of a closing-out tube. He was thrilled, but by the time we left he had managed to piss off everyone in the lineup.

Rob held his own. He got smashed a few times, but he got a few good ones, too.

Most importantly, he was having a blast. Kai was something to behold in the water. He was a gifted surfer. He generated more speed down the line than anyone else I had ever seen, and then pulled big air maneuvers over the lip, landing them gracefully on the face of the wave or into the white water. The water temperature and air temperature were about the same, both around eighty degrees. It was delightful. The sun was in and out of the clouds, and the wind stayed light offshore for the couple of hours we were out there.

When we got back to the lodge, Maria was putting the finishing touches on a plateful of breakfast burritos. We sat down at the outdoor table and talked about our waves, laughing and carrying on like kids. The breakfast burritos were the best I had ever had. I was about as happy as I had been in a very long time.

Kai sat with us and seemed to be having fun also. Eventually he slipped into the conversation that he could probably get us some weed, if we wanted. "It's not that easy to get around here," he said, "but I know a guy in town here who grows his own, and it's pretty solid stuff."

We all laughed. He laughed along but was also eyeing us for clues into what we were laughing about and looking a little confused. "Sorry, Kai, but we're all clean and sober," I explained.

He shrugged, then waved it off and insisted it was "totally cool" and "not a problem in the slightest," but it was pretty clear he was disappointed. I guessed he liked to get high with the guests, that he preferred to get high for free off their weed, and that he made kickback money on each new batch of guests he hooked up with his guy. Three weeks with sober guests would be bad for Kai's bottom line.

As this realization seemed to be settling on him, I gave him some potentially good news. "Listen," I said. "We're going to need a ride to AA meetings in Popoyo and San Juan Del Sur each day. If you're game, we'd be happy to pay you to run us there and back."

The fake half-smile he was using to try to hide his disappointment turned into a real smile. "Stoke," he said, and I was pretty sure that meant that we had a deal. He texted with Mike, who agreed to let us use his Toyota Hilux pickup as long as we filled the tank.

We all showered and took naps for an hour or two before heading south to our first AA meeting in San Juan Del Sur. Kai drove slowly, trying to steer Mike's truck around the deep ruts and potholes. Jose sat shotgun. He turned to Kai and asked, "How did you end up in Nicaragua?"

Kai turned down the radio a bit and said, "I left USC a couple of years ago. I just really wanted to surf and travel. You know?" He was obviously high, but we didn't mind too much. Watching Kai operate was like a time machine for us. He was in that fun phase of substance abuse where the side effects didn't yet outweigh the effects. It was still working okay for him. I hoped it would never turn on him like it had on me.

"So, what made you pick this place?" Joe asked.

"I went out to San Diego first to visit with some buddies. I was there for a few months and we met this dude, this like really rich dude. He had a forty-foot Cat Ketch sailboat he wanted to take down to Baja, so my buddy and I said we would crew for him. You know, we both had lots of sailing experience. So the guy—his name's Rich Bates, he's like a tech millionaire type of guy, you know... good dude too—he takes on a fuckload of booze and food and weed and we set sail. We surfed pretty much every spot from San Diego down to Cabo and then around the Sea of Cortez. It took us like five months. It was sick. We met all these people and we had guests traveling with us half the time. Some hot chicks and some really cool people, you know."

We were mesmerized. He paused the story as we drove past a shack on the side of the road. "That's Walter and Maria's house," he said. "Up there is my buddy Rigo's house. See, there's his cows. I helped him fix that fence last week."

"So what happened when you got to Cabo?" Rob asked from the back seat.

"Yeah, so we ended up hanging out in San Jose Del Cabo for a few weeks and things got weird with some of the guests. Kind of aggro, you know. So we ditched them and set sail for the mainland. We cruised down the Pacific coast of Mexico, hung out in Sayulita for a while, and then my buddy from school called me. He had a deal to work as a surf instructor for the summer at this sweet spot in Mentawai. He said they needed two more guys...." The more he talked, the more I liked him, which is not the norm for me.

"Oh, so, here's the main church right here," he said when passing by a local cathedral. "There's another one back in Gigante, but this is the main one for the area. This was built in like the 1800s when some missionaries brought Catholicism to the area."

That didn't sound right. Rob and I traded sideways glances in the back seat. "What was Mentawai like?" Rob asked.

"It was fuckin' dope, man," Kai said. "We worked at this surf camp like right in front of Pitstop, one of the funnest A-frame breach breaks you'll ever see. And then right down the beach a couple hundred meters was E-bay which is this, like, left-hand reef break that throws off the most perfect hollow tubes. *In*sane. The whole place is a magic factory. The water looks fake. The sand is white powder."

"Sounds like heaven," Jose said.

"Why'd you leave?" Rob asked.

Kai shrugged and scrunched up his face. "I don't know, dude. It was just done, you know?"

Kai played an interesting mix of hip-hop from his Spotify playlist. It was mostly stuff my girls would know better than me: Nas, Chance the Rapper, etc. But he also had some Lauryn Hill, which I appreciated. About half way through the ride, DJ Jazzy Jeff and the Fresh Prince came on and our crew went off. We rapped in that special way that middle-aged white dudes rap. Kai cranked the volume and laughed his head off.

I'm always interested in how music holds times and places in my mind. I pictured myself, years later, hearing that song and remembering the ride in Mike's truck in Nicaragua. It was a good musical bookmark.

Jose asked Kai about Kandui and Hideaways, surf spots in Indonesia he had recently read about in a magazine. Kai gave us a ten-minute recitation on how he got there, who he was with, the conditions, rundowns on the best and worst handful of waves he got while he was there, the girls he met, the vibe of the locals, the food, the weed, how much it cost to stay there, how he managed to pay his way, why and when he decided to leave. Listening to most people talk non-stop like that can be tedious, but Kai was very entertaining. He was like a human podcast. He had a great sense of humor and he mixed in quick, funny stories.

San Juan Del Sur is about forty-five minutes from Gigante because there's no road that goes straight up the Pacific coast. We had to go across to the other side of the peninsula, through Rivas and then north and

back to the coast. The AA group there met Wednesdays
and Saturdays at noon at Josseline's Restaurant. We
walked into the restaurant about fifteen minutes
before the meeting started and were greeted by Dom
G. I never found out where Dom is from, but he's a
huge Midwestern farmer-looking type with a full beard
grown down to his stomach. Dom was around my age
and had a quiet, kind demeanor. He did a ton of service
in AA, in addition to running the SJDS meetings. He
sponsored three or four guys I knew of and was always
inviting people over to his apartment for fellowship
(AA-speak for hanging out with other sober people).
He lived above some galleries and boutiques in a nice
part of town.

Dom and Jacq were the co-chairs of the San Juan Del
Sur group and they ran all the meetings. He called Jacq
over to introduce us. Jacq is a Nica who speaks better
English than most *gringos*. I would guess she was in her
late twenties. She had short dreadlocks in her hair and
two full sleeves of tattoos, mostly Polynesian patterns.
The ones on her left arm continued across her shoulder
and onto her neck. She usually wore tank tops, cargo
pants and combat boots. I remember thinking that
the pants and boots were a big commitment to a look
when it's ninety degrees outside. She smoked a lot of
cigarettes and kept mostly to herself, but I think that
was because the group was made up of mostly middle-
aged men.

There were about a dozen other people in the meeting and we had a chance to meet them all. We were the only tourists in attendance, but they were obviously used to welcoming guests into their group. They told well-rehearsed jokes about how nice it was to have some new people to listen to because they're sick to death of listening to each other. Since we were the fresh meat in the room, they asked if any of us would like to speak. Rob volunteered, so I heard his story for the hundredth time, but it was cool to hear him deliver it to new people. I don't know if he did it intentionally, but he seemed to emphasize different parts of his story. He got sober at thirty-nine, midway through an extremely successful career in real estate development. His firm, in which he was one of three partners, built and managed some of the premier office towers in South Florida. The way he told the story on that Sunday afternoon made it sound like his professional success was the biggest impediment to his sobriety.

"I really believed," he said, "in all parts of my heart and mind, that I needed cocaine and booze to be successful. They were my secret weapons for many years that made me able to overcome my anxiety. They enabled me to think creatively, and probably most importantly, they enabled me to act the part. I felt I had to be a big shot, that I was expected to be a big shot. How could I do that without booze and cocaine? Everyone would know I was a fraud. That I was afraid.

"And then one day, they turned on me. My secret weapons, my best friends, my solutions to life. They fucking turned on me. They stopped working and they started demanding things. They demanded that I focus just on them. They were like insanely jealous lovers. They wanted all of me. They wanted all my time and money and they made me give up everything for them. It was a real 'deal with the devil' situation, and the devil called in the debt and sent up the hounds of hell to collect. We had such a good thing going, and it flipped totally around and turned into a total living nightmare." It was interesting; a new audience had brought out a new aspect of his story I had never heard before. I enjoyed it.

On the ride back to the lodge, Kai regaled us with more of his adventures. I had no problem picturing him living on the beach in Jeffrey's Bay, South Africa, or selling weed in Oahu to earn plane fare. It all seemed totally organic for Kai. One thing led to the next, and he followed the will of the universe until he sensed that it was time to move on. "Yeah, but how do you know when it's time to move on?" Jose asked him.

Kai thought about it for a moment. "It's kind of like just done, you know. Once I feel like I've actually lived in the place, not just visited it. You know ... I have relationships with people, not just get to know them. Once I've been stoked, bored, angry, tired and sad ten times each—you know, just kind of well and truly done.

I think the place has to become a part of me and I had a place and a part in it. Then I can go."

We all nodded thoughtfully. "Or it just sucks," he added with a laugh. "You know? Sometimes I'm just like 'fuck this place' and I'm out."

We laughed with him. I'm pretty sure we were all dead jealous of the life this kid was living. I know I was. I remember wondering if I would be okay with my daughters taking that kind of path. Kai made it seem okay. My general sense was that he was learning, growing and developing as a person as he traveled and surfed. He couldn't smoke enough weed to kill all the growth; some of it had to sink in. It seemed like a life well-lived and he seemed happy. What else could I want for my kids? Shit, what else could I want for myself?

By the time we got to Nicaragua I was at a real crossroads in my life. I was really impressionable for the first time in a long time, and this twenty-four-year-old stoner vagabond had become my role model for a moment. God abhors a vacuum.

4

New York
1982

Every few months, when she was in a pinch and working double shifts at her weekend restaurant job, my mother would drop me off at my grandma Leticia's house in Whitestone, Queens. I enjoyed hanging out with her and my grandpa Jose, and I liked to snoop around their house to find little clues about my dad. One rainy Sunday when she dropped me off, I went up to my dad's old bedroom, which is where I slept when I stayed over. As soon as I dropped my bag, I started rummaging through the same six drawers I had already been through several times. I examined the same old rusted Zippo that had "Play Baseball Later" engraved on one side, the same pair of silver cufflinks, the same gold skull-and-crossbones ring, the same subway and tunnel tokens, and the same old pair of sunglasses. Not much to build a profile around.

I sat on the edge of the bed and imagined my dad as a teenager, coming and going in this room, sleeping in that twin bed with that comforter, waking up in the morning and walking down that hallway to the bathroom. I breathed in deeply. The room smelled exotic. I looked out the window at the house next door and walked over to see what he would have looked at. I wondered if there were kids who had lived next door, imagining a pretty young girl on the swing in the yard.

Grandma stuck her head in. "Hi, Troy Boy," she said. "Come downstairs. I have some things to show you." From the staircase of their split-level house, I could see that she had piled a short stack of photo albums on the coffee table in the living room. We sat on her sofa. The backs of my legs stuck to the clear plastic cover that protected the cushions. She opened one of the books and placed it on my lap. "These are some of your father's newspaper clippings," she explained. On each page there was an article, held in place with sticky adhesive and protected with cellophane. At the top of each page was the masthead of the paper it had been cut from. As I turned through the pages, she told me who the people were in the pictures with my dad. It felt like he was a real celebrity, and my pride built as she started to narrate the stories.

One of the articles I remember included a picture of him and Kareem Abdul-Jabbar (then known as Lew Alcindor). Kareem, a head taller, had his arm around my dad in front of a row of lockers. My grandma explained to me that my father and Lew Alcindor were the only two *Parade* All-American basketball players from New York in the entirety of the '60s.

My grandpa came in and out of the room to offer commentary in his heavy Spanish accent, usually one-liners that supported what Leticia was telling me. "The moment your daddy walked in the gym, they used to yell, *He's in range!*"

Leticia giggled. "Yes, he sure could shoot," she agreed. "But do you know what he loved, even more than basketball?" she asked. She closed that book and pulled a thick green one from the stack. With a little bit of wonder in her voice, she said, "Baseball." She flipped past the first few pages of articles until she got to one from the *New York Daily News*. The headline was "Martin Rewrites the Record Book." The article went on to catalog all of the school, city and state records my dad broke at the plate during his junior year at P.S. 141.

"He was the best!" Grandpa yelled out from the kitchen.

One way or another, they worked this sales job every time I slept over. I was an eager customer on that rainy Saturday morning, eating up every statistic, image and anecdote. When my grandma finished with the baseball album, I asked her, "Have you heard from my dad lately?" It wasn't meant as a loaded question. I was excited about this superhero we were talking about, and I was trying to pull that image into the present day.

My grandma's face shifted as her thoughts moved from the wonder of a beautiful fairytale to the complicated, unfortunate reality. Her cheeks twitched a couple of times as if she was thinking about, or trying to, smile. "Oh, sure," Grandpa bellowed as he walked into the room. "He's doing great. Your old man is just as busy as a person can be. He only has about a minute to talk when he calls here, and do you know what he only wants to talk about?"

I didn't.

"You," he said, sitting down next to me. The plastic creaked loudly and he ruffled my hair. "All he wants to know is, how is Troy? What is Troy doing? Troy this and Troy that." My grandma's eyes told another story. They were watery, but she smiled and nodded at me. That was far as she was willing to go when it came to lying.

"Hey," Grandpa said. "Do you want to see something great?" I was kind of tired of looking at albums, so I shrugged my shoulders. I would've preferred to go back up to my room and get in bed for a nap, or maybe read a book. I didn't want to play this game anymore. "Wait here," he said, and he slapped my bare knee as he stood up. "I'll be right back." As he walked out of the room, he yelled behind him, "You're gonna love this!"

My grandma and I sat silently waiting for him to return. She held her hands on her knees, sitting with perfect posture and a faint smile. I looked out the casement window across from us. It was raining hard. My mom wouldn't be back for me until the following afternoon. Grandpa came back in, carrying a small wooden box covered by a worn-out tin American flag. He handed the box to me with both hands, so I took it carefully and put it on my lap. "Go on," he said. "Open it."

Inside were some medals and ribbons. He pointed to each one and told me what they were. "That yellow, green and red one is the Vietnam Service Medal. You see that red and blue one with the star, Troy? That one is very special. That's called the Bronze Star. That one is only for real heroes." He looked up to check my reaction. I sensed that I was expected to nod and smile. "The green and white one with the bronze star is the Republic of Vietnam Campaign Medal, and that is his Honorable Discharge Ribbon."

"Your dad fought in the Vietnam War," my grandma clarified.

"Wow," I said. I was starting to feel like they were ganging up on me.

Eventually, I asked if I could be excused so that I could go upstairs and do my homework. I just wanted to get out of their crosshairs, but they both seemed impressed. "Yes, of course, sweet boy," Leticia said. "So nice that you're conscientious about your work. Just like your Aunt Mary. She was in the honors program at school. She was always coming home with awards." I got up and headed across the room and up the stairs as she went on. "Everybody in the neighborhood always said she got all the brains in the family, but I didn't think that was fair. Joe was very smart also. He just had ants in his pants. He was always *zooming* here and *zipping* there. You couldn't keep him still for a minute to sit in front of his schoolwork."

"But he was very smart!" my grandpa called out as I closed the door to the bedroom.

I laid down on the bed and crossed my arms. I thought about the pictures in the green baseball album and remembered the day my dad told me his baseball story. It was a few years earlier. My mom had just signed me up for first grade little league, so he took me to buy a glove. I sat next to him on the red leather bench seat of his Cadillac as we drove to the mall. He turned down the radio, which was tuned to the local rock station. For whatever reason, I remember that "Light my Fire" by The Doors was playing.

"By the time I got to my senior year of high school," he explained, "the only question was whether I was going to play college ball or enter the pro draft." He glanced over to me to check my reaction. "Your grandma used to tell the pro scouts who came to my games that she wanted me to go to college." He laughed and looked at me. "Can you believe that? Typical immigrants, right?" I laughed too, because it seemed that he wanted me to, but I had no idea why that might be funny.

"Thankfully, Coach Bryant told them all I would go pro. I was no student, Troy. The last thing I wanted was more school. I just wanted to play baseball. I wanted to play every day and get as good as I could."

My dad was living in Florida at this point and he was coming home to visit my mom and me every few weeks. It was confusing. I remember that I always wanted to be with him, but when we were together I felt like I had to perform for him. I had to laugh at his jokes, even though I didn't understand them. I had to be really good and act happy. I had to make sure he had fun when we were together, so he would want to come back to see me more often. I can remember asking my mom, when we dropped him off at LaGuardia Airport, "Do you think Daddy had fun with us?" I wanted his approval, but more fundamentally I was desperate for his time.

Before telling me the next part of his baseball story, he took a deep breath and closed his eyes. He said that Grandpa Jose had a stroke at the end of his senior year of high school. This made him push everything back a year while he worked at my grandpa's bodega. Later that year, he was drafted by the U.S. Army instead of any baseball team, and he spent the following year in Vietnam. When he got home, he was eager to restart his baseball life, so he called the scouts and the colleges. Several of them expressed interest, but nothing ever materialized. They seemed to be hesitant to take a kid straight off the killing fields, even if he had been a top prospect two years earlier.

I later found out that he came home from Vietnam addicted to heroin. Sitting in his Cadillac, he left that part of the story out. Joe received a Bronze Star in Vietnam for his ability to run across lines and shoot the enemy, but he was shooting up two to four times every day.

Once he got home, he had to kick heroin before enrolling at Nassau Community College, which at the time had one of the best junior-college baseball teams in the country. He laid in his bed in Whitestone sweating profusely, shivering and hallucinating in the days before classes started.

"I made the team and I was the starting right fielder in maybe two or three weeks," he said. Again, he checked for my reaction. "My freshman year, we made it to the semi-finals of the NJCAA World Series." We were sitting at a traffic light. He tapped a cigarette out of the opening in his soft pack, lit it with a Zippo, and then rolled down his window. "That's the World Series for junior colleges. Troy, let me tell you, I had a great season, but when we got out to Colorado to play in that World Series tournament, I tore the cover off the ball. In front of a bunch of pro scouts I hit .647 during the playoffs with three home runs and six RBIs. I stole five bases. Shit, I even had three outfield assists. You know what that means?" he asked, as a way of checking in on me again and making sure I was paying attention.

I couldn't have looked away if I wanted to. He was great to watch when he told stories. He was animated and his voice jumped and dove with all different types of emphasis. He reminded me of an actor in a movie. He was wonderful looking—tall and tan with a thick mustache and his chiseled features, underneath a pair of stylish sunglasses. His hair was cut like Han Solo in Star Wars, but it was darker.

"That means I threw three guys out from right field. That's crazy. I had a cannon for an arm." Again, I didn't know what any of that meant, but it sounded wonderful. I nodded and smiled. He grabbed the bill of my Mets cap and pushed it down over my eyes. "That *finally* got me drafted into professional baseball. You know the St. Louis Cardinals?" he asked. I didn't, but it seemed like I was expected to, so I nodded and smiled again, opening my eyes wide. "They drafted me in the sixth round and sent me to Lewiston, Idaho to play for the Broncs, their short season A ball affiliate." My dad flicked the cigarette out the window as we pulled into the mall parking lot. He rolled up his window and ended the story there.

It took forty-years for me to learn the specifics of how and why his baseball dreams went up in flames.

5

Nicaragua
2020

We paddled out to the boat and handed our boards to Walter to secure them on the bow. Kai put down the cooler and sat on top of it, directly across from me. "So, what made you decide to come to Nica?" he asked.

"I don't know," I answered. "A lot of reasons, I guess." I tried to think of a way to summarize. There were too many to fit into a casual conversation with a stoned kid at six in the morning. "My birthday was last week, and my four-year sober anniversary is next week, so it seemed like a good chance to celebrate both."

Kai nodded. I couldn't tell if he was encouraging me to continue by staying silent or if he was just zoned out. In any case, we had time to kill, so I went on. "My youngest daughter, Ceci, left for college a few months ago, so I'm an empty nester. Also, I just retired from my career as a police officer, and I'm starting up a new job in a new industry next month. The company I'm going to work for sells electronics and equipment to police departments around the country. I'm going to be a product manager. I'm still not totally sure what that means, but it'll be nice to work with professional people for once. I did twenty years with the city of Fort Lauderdale, so they owe me a full pension. Plus, I had seven years with Broward Sheriff's office, so they owe me a partial pension. But neither one of those kick in until I turn fifty-five, so I have a little window to try out a second career." Kai nodded.

"Also, I ended a five-year relationship with my girlfriend Michelle a couple of months ago." I looked out at sea and continued, "To be honest, I'm not totally sure what happened there. We had a conversation about getting married, like six months ago, and then that was it. Two months ago, she said she wants to move out and get on with her life. She's crazy about my girls. I think she was just waiting for Ceci to head off to college." I watched a gull gliding along behind the boat. The day before, Walter had explained that they follow the boats because the fishermen often throw them scraps. This one gave up after a few minutes and swooped out to sea. "She moved the last of her stuff out last weekend." I shrugged and smiled at Kai. "So, it was a clean sweep–I was at a crossroads in pretty much every aspect of my life by the time we got on the plane. You know, the truth of the matter is that I'm glad to be out of law enforcement. I don't think I enjoyed ten days of work in my whole damn career."

Kai kept nodding. Or maybe it was the movement of the boat. I was on a roll and maybe I needed to say this stuff out loud anyway. "Honestly, the only part that really hurts is that my girls are all moved out. They're grown up and off at college. Roxy left two years ago and Ceci left last month, and it still feels like a big, painful, open wound."

Kai nodded some more. I think he sensed that I was done, because finally he spoke as the boat pulled up to Panga Drops.

"Stoke," he said.

Panga is along the same shore as Playa Colorado, but it's a point break at the other end of the beach. It was a really interesting setup because you could walk from one break to the other in twenty minutes, but it was a totally different wave. The swell was bigger that morning, so Walter and Kai figured that we were better off at Panga. When Colorado gets big it's a different animal. It drains from the top down, producing powerful, hollow, spitting barrels. You have to be an expert surfer to handle a wave like that. At the other end of the beach, Panga might be the same size, but it's a much easier, gentler shape. It breaks on a deep-water reef, which creates a more open wave face, easy to paddle into and less punishing if you fall.

"Alright, let's do it, guys," Rob called out, clapping his hands a few times to get himself pumped up. "Unless,

Troy, there's anything else you want to confess to Kai before we go."

It took me twenty to thirty minutes for my brain to adjust to the scope and size of the surf. I'd only been in surf that big a couple of times before. I stayed on the outside for a little while and tried to get in early on a few, but they kept passing me by. Still, I got close enough to the edge where I could look down and say, "Holy shit, that's a big wave."

I watched Kai and Jose to see how they approached it. Then I started watching a small group of old dudes on long boards paddle into these things effortlessly. The wave held up well every time, no closeouts. It just kind of crumbled along with that fat, slopey face out ahead. Finally, I got myself in the right spot and one of the old dudes, shirtless with a big potbelly and a ponytail, nodded me in. As I paddled in, I realized that he thought I was being polite, showing good surf etiquette by letting a bunch of waves go and letting the old guys get theirs. I was kind of laughing to myself about this as my board planed and I jumped to my feet. It was easy. The wave was so clean and well-shaped. I looked down the line ahead of me and watched it unfold to the right, my strong side. I made a couple of long turns from the top to the bottom and it was heavenly. I turned off the top and paddled back around to the lineup with a huge smile. Once again, I know it sounds ridiculous, but I was so proud of myself. It felt like a serious accomplishment.

We went on to have a nice session. I got another three or four big rights and then ended up surfing the inside for the rest of the session because I didn't have the energy to keep paddling all the way back out and around. On the boat ride back to the lodge I opened up the cooler to grab a water or a Gatorade, and saw that it was stocked with bottles of Tona, the local beer. "Sorry, bro," Kai said. "My bad. I forgot to stock the waters."

"No problem," I said. I sat on the cooler with the wind flying by, on a gorgeous morning in one of the prettiest places I've ever seen. It'd been an epic session. I had everything I could've wanted in that moment, but God knows I could have crushed a few of those cold beers.

After a breakfast they called "the greasy spoon," consisting of fried eggs, hashbrowns, and bacon from a pig that had probably lived down the road, we all crashed for a couple of hours and then piled into Mike's truck for the forty-minute drive to Popoyo. We drove north along 62, which is a pretty good road, not paved but well-maintained. That group meets Mondays at 1 p.m. at Popoyo Loco, a surf hostel and restaurant on Guasacate Beach. The hostel was about fifty meters from the parking lot for La Bocaina, one of the more popular surf spots in Popoyo. It's a point break that serves up five- to seven-foot perfect rights that could run for hundreds of yards when the swell hits from the southwest and the wind is right.

Paula and Freddy run that meeting. We met Paula for the first time when she greeted us outside as we climbed out of the truck. She's a really cool lady from nearby Honduras. She was in her mid-forties and talked openly in meetings about working in the sex trade for twenty years. It was impossible to imagine her that way, but her stories nearly curled my hair. When we met her, she reminded me of my seventh grade Spanish teacher, Mrs. Perez. She was cheerful, kooky and maternal, probably fifty pounds over her healthiest possible weight but carrying it proudly, as if it represented prosperity and abundance.

Paula introduced us to Freddy, who was super-friendly but anxious and honestly seemed a little shifty. Freddy had a red beard that was well-groomed and a crewcut of red and gray hair. His blue eyes never seemed to settle on anything for long. It looked to me like he was always scanning and checking everyone. He was from Cincinnati and had moved to the area shortly before we arrived. I have no proof whatsoever, but I'd bet that Freddy was running away from something . . . and that he wasn't really from Cincinnati.

The meeting started just after we arrived, so we took our seats. It was a step meeting and they were on step six ("Were entirely ready to have God remove all these defects of character"). We started by reading the chapter in the 12 & 12 (shorthand for *The 12 Steps and the 12 Traditions of AA*). We went around the meeting and each one of the ten or so people in attendance took turns reading a section. Then a speaker talked for about fifteen minutes about what the step meant for him and shared some of his experience with it. The guy who spoke was in town on a surf trip with some buddies. They were staying at a surf camp in Popoyo that was run by a group of born-again Christians. Different vibe than Dale Daggers, I guess.

I don't remember much about his remarks, except for one part when he said that there was no point in doing an inventory (step four) if you weren't going to do anything about it. "Sure, here are all of my harms and resentments, and here are the character defects that caused them," he said. "Good to know. Now what? I'll tell you now what. Now steps six and seven. Now I spend the rest of my life trying to change them. I replace them with character traits that serve me better, that make me happier, that make me a better person, a better father, husband and friend. If I don't change the person I was when I came in, that guy will fuck up my life again."

After the meeting we hung around and met some of the group members and tourists. There was Claude, a big guy with bright blue eyes and lots of neat white hair, parted to the side. He looked to be in his mid-sixties. He was from Montreal and had a pretty heavy French accent. When he found out I was from Florida, he asked me if I knew "Florida Man." I guess that was a joke.

Rita was middle-aged but had deep ruts in her eyes from smoking, and sun that made her look older. She was all different types of small . . . short and skinny, with fine features and tight curls in her hair. She put her tiny hand in mine and said, "Hey, I'm Rita. I'm from LA," with a pretty thick New York accent, either Brooklyn or Queens. I almost said, "By way of which borough?" But I caught myself and just said, "Cool. I'm Troy. Nice to meet you, Rita."

That was also the first time I met Andy. He was wearing a t-shirt that read *Faith Over Fear*. He introduced himself quickly before speed-walking out the door with body language that said *Gotta run, I'm going to be late for a meeting*. Before he left, he made a point of shaking all of our hands, asking our names and then repeating our names back to us and pointing at us as he did. I guess this was his trick for remembering. "Troy. Jose. Rob. Awesome. Looking forward to getting to know you guys."

6

My mother's brother lived in a big apartment in Yonkers, the first city in Westchester County, just north of The Bronx. He hosted Rosh Hashanah every year because his dining room opened up to the living room, so he could add folding tables that fit my mom's whole extended family. We had just finished dinner one year when my mom started to tell a story about something that had happened when they were all kids. I wasn't listening carefully, but when she was finished, I remember my uncle's reaction perfectly. He clapped his hands and laughed. When my aunt Sissy asked him why he was laughing, he said, "Because that was a great story. Unfortunately, none of it ever happened." That turned the light on for me and confirmed in my mind something I had felt in my gut. My mom lied. A lot. I thought about some of the stories that she had told me just within the prior few weeks. I had sensed that something was off—they sounded fantastical. She would look off into the middle distance, and her tone turned into one like someone reading a story from the pages of a book.

Aunt Sissy slapped my uncle's forearm as if he had said something naughty. Or, perhaps it was because he said out loud the thing everyone had been keeping quiet about. Then she adeptly changed the subject. *Those were all lies*, I thought, but even then, I understood that maybe that wasn't the right word. They were more like stories or fantasies.

The older I got, the more stories she told. They got longer and more detailed. By the time I was an adult, her stories had reached excruciating levels of detail. There was always a lot of dialogue: "And then he said. . . . And then I said. . . . And then he made this face and then I thought. . . . And then I said. . . . And can you believe what he said next. . . ." These scenes could go on for twenty minutes. It was painful to listen to. It was like streaming the worst podcast in the world.

When we were in Nicaragua, I told Jose and Rob about this at dinner one night, but they dismissed me and said I had to be exaggerating. The next day, she called after lunch, so I put her on speakerphone so they could experience the podcast. She did not disappoint. "I have very good news for you, Troy," she said.

"Lay it on me, Mom," I said, putting the phone down on the coffee table and sitting back on the sofa. Rob and Jose stood behind me, listening in.

"I got a job. My friend Suzie, who I know from my Mahjong game . . . I've told you about Suzie, right? She's the one whose son is a big-shot lawyer in Miami.

He lives an hour away but he never visits her. Honestly, she's nice, but she's not really my cup of tea. She's a little bit of a cold fish, if you know what I mean." She went on about Suzie for another couple of minutes, so I muted the phone and turned to interpret for Rob and Jose.

"When she says that someone is a 'cold fish,' that means they've stopped returning her calls because they've finally figured out she's nuts."

"*Aaaanyway*," she said, coming back around to her story, "Suzie turned me on to a nice rich couple who live at St. Andrews, Marty and Linda Rosenfeld. They're retired. Linda has one of those neurological diseases, like MS or something like that. The poor thing can hardly walk some days. She has her good days and her bad days, but mostly bad at this point."

She did another few minutes on Marty and Linda, and I sensed that Rob and Jose were losing interest. She hadn't really gotten to the lies yet and I didn't want them to miss that part, so I unmuted the phone and interrupted. "Skip to the job, Mom," I said. She didn't hear me. I could picture her laying on her bed with her eyes closed and her phone tucked between her ear and her shoulder. She was on a roll. "Mom!"

"Yes, honey?"

"Skip to the job. Tell me about the job."

"Well, they live in a very fancy neighborhood here. It's called St. Andrews. It's about a twenty-minute drive for me to get there from my place in Century Village. I walk their dog, Ralph. He's a nice little black Scottish terrier. I do one walk at 8 a.m. and one walk at 8 p.m., every day. They pay me twenty dollars per walk. Can you believe that? That's real money. And I'll tell you another thing, Troy. There's lots of old rich people in there with dogs. I could have a real business on my hands before long."

For a moment, I was actually a little bit impressed that she had pulled this together. It was pretty enterprising. "That's great, Mom," I said. I was happy she had done something productive and normal, but a little disappointed that she wasn't going to put on a crazy show for Rob and Jose. But then she continued.

"Now here's the thing, Troy," she said, lowering her voice to a whisper, even though there was nobody who could possibly overhear. "At night in St. Andrews, they have these frogs. They're everywhere. Thousands of them, all over the sidewalks. It's terrible. And let me tell you, these are no ordinary frogs. They're these little green ones that have purple stripes. These frogs, do you know what they do? They spray poison from their eyes!"

I sat back. Here we go. Showtime.

"It's terrible. I have to step very carefully or else I'll crush them under my feet. I have to weave my way along the paths, trying to avoid these damn things. They're disgusting. You know what I did? I started wearing my knee-high rubber rain boots when I walk Ralph, in case I step on one of these damn things, or they try to spray me in the leg with their venom. I told Linda and Marty about them. I told them how dangerous it could be for Ralph. I told them about the poison and he's a little dog. He could get killed out there at night. I told them the whole thing, and do you know what they said? This man, Marty, he says to me, 'I wouldn't worry too much about that.' So then I said, 'It's terrible out there. He's such a nice little dog. It would be terrible if something should happen to him. And I would be held responsible. And I'm far from home here. I don't have any medical training. I'm not capable of protecting him or resuscitating him from a poison venom attack.' And then he says, *'Don't worry,'* like in a really arrogant voice, you know. Like he knows all about frogs and venom and he's some kind of big-shot expert, right? 'We won't hold you responsible for any frog venom attacks.' He actually said that to me! 'We won't hold you responsible.' How can I work for people like this?"

By the end of the full dialogue scene with Linda and Marty, my friends were gone. They were believers. They patted my shoulder sympathetically and scattered to their own bedrooms, leaving me with the phone on mute, watching surf videos on the couch. I picked up my phone and decided to check for updates on my daughters' Instagram accounts.

"What if the dog gets poisoned while I'm walking him? I don't know how to rescue him. It's my responsibility. He's a small dog—he could die and I'll be up on charges. They'll sue me for everything I have. I didn't work my whole life to lose everything for twenty dollars per walk." It was starting to sound like her dog-walking business might not get off the ground.

7

Wednesday morning, we surfed Playgrounds and it was terrifying. Kai said it was going to be smaller, so I borrowed an old longboard from the lodge. The surf wasn't smaller. It was overhead and firing. The wave was the absolute wrong shape for a longboard. Everyone else was out there on high-performance short boards. I spent the whole session trying to scrape out some rides on the shoulders of these bombs. I was pretty annoyed by the time we got back to the boat. It had been a waste of a session. Rob took a beating and spent half the session trying to paddle back through the relentless inside break, and the other half sitting on the outside, trying to recover and build up enough courage to move back into the lineup. The boat ride back was quiet. We had been spoiled from our first few sessions and expected every outing to be better than the last.

Maria made blueberry pancakes with sausage for breakfast, which lifted our spirits. After the beating we took, we crashed pretty hard. Kai had to wake us up to get to the San Juan Del Sur meeting in time. In fact, by the time we got there the meeting had just started.

It was a small meeting; I think our group just about doubled the attendance when we walked in. Jacq was the Chair. She was introducing Barry as the speaker just as we walked in. Barry is a freaky-looking guy, so I didn't really know what to expect when he qualified. He waited for us to take our seats in the restaurant and then started his qualification. The details of his story were nothing like mine, but I related to him completely. Same feelings.

He broke the ice with a little self-deprecating joke. "Jacq only lets me speak at small meetings . . . *dama intelligente* . . . smaller blast radius . . . less damage. . . ." Barry went on to describe part of his early childhood. It was hard to listen to. I squirmed in my seat a little bit when he described it. "When I was a kid, I lived in a brothel near Mexico City for a couple of years. My mom and sister were both prostitutes there, and we all shared a dirty, dingy bedroom. I would have to leave the room when they had customers. They were heroin addicts. They were deep in the hole, you know?"

No, I thought. *I really don't know. I don't want to know.*

"Eventually, I got pulled out of there by my father's brother and I went to live with his family in San Diego, so things got a lot more normal. He would beat on my aunt when he got drunk, which was hard to be around and honestly, he wasn't a great guy or even a good person really, but my circumstances were definitely better. I went to school and had good food and stuff like that."

I didn't relate to any of that and my heart was kind of breaking for the guy, but then he went on to say something that was really interesting to me. He said, "But here's the thing . . . I'm not an alcoholic because of my upbringing."

It certainly didn't fucking help, I thought, but I also leaned in a bit, because I sensed I really should hear this part.

"One of the most important things I've learned over the past decade or so of being sober is that I'm an alcoholic *from the inside out* . . . meaning that my circumstances were never the problem. The cause of this disease was not my fucked-up childhood, it was the way I felt in my skin." I was skeptical, but he continued on to say, "Here's how I know: because my circumstances changed and improved many times during my life, but the way I felt in my skin stayed the same. *That* was what I had to change to get clean and stay clean. In my skin it felt uncomfortable on a good day and unbearable on a bad one. Drinking and drugging took that away. I would've given anything, and eventually I gave up everything, so I could numb that feeling." That part I related to.

He said that after a while he drank against his will. "For the last few years of my drinking, I drank when I didn't want to drink. I drank when I swore I wouldn't and sincerely meant it." *Check and check*, I thought. Barry went on to talk about giving up the resentment he had for his mother for raising him the way she did. "I had to learn to look at her with compassion, as a sick and suffering person. If I didn't learn how to do that, I would've kept hurting myself and the people around me. One of the great truths I've heard in these rooms is that hurt people *hurt people*." He paused for a moment to let that settle in. *Yes, absolutely*, I thought. This was turning out to be more than I had bargained for.

He continued, "Rather than continue the cycle of hurt, by being resentful and angry, I forgave her and worked on loving her for who she was." He described a project that took about a month to complete. "I made a list of all of the good things she did, or the positive or just normal stuff." He started to count them off on his fingers. "She loved fashion and she was super-talented at making her own clothes. She loved music and could play the piano pretty well. She was pretty. She never left me, even when life crumbled around us."

He put down the fingers that he had been counting on. "There were others, but I can't remember them off the top of my head anymore. Anyway, the list went on and on and these things were just as true about her as the bad things. I decided there was plenty on that list to focus on. Yeah, it took a lot more effort and energy to do it this way. I could've woken up every day and been justified in my anger and keep telling myself the same old sad story about the junkie whore who ruined my life. That was true, too. But which thought serves me better? You gotta choose your thoughts wisely. They form your life."

Finally, he described another trick that worked really well. "I prayed for her every day for months. I said the Buddhist lovingkindness prayer: *May she be filled with lovingkindness; may she be safe from inner and outer harm; may she be well in body and mind; may she be peaceful and truly happy.* Every time I thought of her, I said that prayer." It was all really heavy and it was a lot to absorb, but I understood on a fundamental level that I had just heard the truth.

Barry was covered in tattoos from his hairline to his toes. He would've looked like a convicted murderer biker gang badass except that he was around 5'7" and 120 pounds soaking wet. He wore tank tops that revealed the bones of his shoulders and arms. That day, he wore one that looked like it was straight out of a *Magnum PI* episode from 1981. Tom Selleck would've looked ripped in this flowery, whimsical piece, but Barry looked puny. He folded his arms in front of his chest as he talked, giving himself a hug, and I thought that both of his arms together weren't as big as one of Thomas Magnum's. He wore black oversized women's sunglasses, Jackie O-style. His hair was long, frizzy and pulled back in a ponytail that poofed into a ball behind his head.

It was odd to hear this strange-looking little guy basically tell a different version of my story from the other side of the hemisphere. I spent the first few years of my sobriety telling anyone who would listen that I was an alcoholic because of the shit that happened to me. My assumption was that anyone would be an alcoholic if they went through what I went through. I never usually do this, but as soon as Barry finished with his qualification, I raised my hand to be the first to share. Barry saw my hand shoot up, so he pointed at me and said, "Okay, big dude is first."

I thanked Barry for his share and his honesty. "Here's the thing," I said. "My dad walked out on me and turned out to be this huge drug-dealing, drug-smuggling, psycho criminal. I was raised by a crazy single mom who worked all the time and was totally absent. I gave up my future and handed back a college scholarship after my freshman year to become a dad at nineteen. I married my baby's mom, a white-trash nightmare who ended up fucking everyone in town. I worked as a corrections officer and then as a police officer, which are both insanely stressful jobs. I was surrounded every day with ignorant, racist, anti-Semitic assholes on one side and criminals on the other. I went to school at night while being a dad and working two jobs." I paused for a moment and then continued, "So I went around for a few years with an attitude like, *You try being that guy.* You'd pound vodka to change the channel in your head, too.

"But here's the thing." I paused and tried to bring it back to Barry. "Like you just said, maybe someone else wouldn't. Right? I've heard hundreds of people tell their stories in these rooms and they're all different, right? Some were raised in normal families. Some were raised in great families. Some were raised in brothels in Mexico. Some had everything go their way every step of the way, but they became drunks anyway. I guess this is something I've been thinking about for a while, but when I heard you say that it was an inside job for you ... I don't know, I guess I was just ready to hear that. Sure, my circumstances or your circumstances may have sped up the clock, but if I needed booze to survive the day living in my head, eventually I was going to lose the choice over whether or not to drink."

After the meeting we all stayed around and chatted for twenty minutes or so. In AA they say that there are no strangers, just friends you haven't met yet. We met some more of the locals and they were just as warm and welcoming as the people we had met a few days earlier. They each came over, shook hands, introduced themselves and made a bit of chit-chat with us. Barry was accompanied by Margherita and Bradley, a pretty-looking couple that looked to be in their mid-thirties. They were in tourist uniforms: board shorts, t-shirts, flip-flops and sunglasses. Margherita was kind of racially ambiguous; if I had to guess, I'd say she was half-white and half some kind of Latina but not Nica, probably more Dominican or Puerto Rican. She was tall and lean with a long-distance runner's body. Bradley was a fit *gringo* who gave out Boston vibes. His hair was very purposely styled in a not-styled way, and he had on an expensive surf watch, one of the ones that counted your paddle distance, waves caught, water temp, calories burned, etc.

Barry invited us to La Tostaderia with them for some coffee. We had the whole middle of the day free and they seemed cool enough, so our group seemed to nod in unison. We followed behind them on the short walk through the cobblestone streets to the coffee shop. There wasn't a cloud in the sky and the sun was intense. "How do you guys know each other?" I asked Barry, nodding at his friends.

"We're old friends," Barry said, jumping down from the high curb onto the street. We all followed him as he walked alongside a slow-moving car until it passed, and then crossed behind it to the other side.

"We met yesterday," Margherita corrected, as we followed Barry onto Paseo del Rey. "Bradley and I are guests at The Dreams Hotel."

"It's just up here to the left," Barry said, and then switched gears to pick up where Margherita left off. "I have a kiosk in the lobby over there for my tour business. We do surf tours, excursions, deep sea fishing, all that stuff. Whenever a guest at the hotel is a friend of Bill's and looking for a meeting, they send them over to this guy." Barry pointed to himself with both thumbs as he turned into the shop. "These two arrived yesterday and got stuck in my web. I left a group of surfers down at Playa Maderas with my guide this morning so I could take them up to the meeting."

La Tostaderia was the most popular coffee shop in town. There were three large sets of French doors that led through a sidewalk seating area into the restaurant. There were also half a dozen huge windows that were wide open, so it had an indoor/outdoor feel. We walked up to a beautiful counter along the far wall that looked like it was made of driftwood to order our drinks, and then took seats at one of two long beautiful communal tables made of Guanacaste wood and finished in a high gloss. The chairs were an eclectic mix. There were a few cheap plastic ones, some fabric swivel chairs, a few wickers and a few fancy dining room chairs. There were some comfy sofas over on the side.

"This place is so cool," Bradley said. "This little town is awesome." We all nodded. "I'm pretty new to the program," he continued. "I just passed seven months this week, so I'm stoked to be able to hit meetings while we're away."

"What's your deal?" Margherita asked. "Where are you guys from?" We gave them our basic stats.

The coffees came to the table and each one looked like a work of art. "This place is awesome," Bradley repeated. He asked if we had been to any other meetings in the area and we told them about the meeting we had attended in Popoyo the day before. We all sat for a little while watching people arrive and leave. We watched the town move by outside the doors and windows. The breeze was blowing through in the most delightful way, helped along by the big ceiling fans.

"Where is The Dreams Hotel?" I finally asked.

"Just over the border in Costa Rica," Barry said. He pointed down toward the sea. "If you head down the coast about forty-five minutes south of here, just past Manzanillo you hit Salinas Bay, which is pretty much the northern tip of Costa."

"How long have you been in Salinas?" Jose asked.

"About three years," said Barry. "I've been in Costa since 2001. I came down from San Diego in a school bus with my buddy Joe Walsh. We started up Witch's Rock surf school in Tamarindo. Joe ran the business and I ran the surf tours for a long time."

"Oh sure, Witch's Rock," I said. "That place is an institution. Robert August runs his board-shaping operation out of there, doesn't he?" I grew up watching *The Endless Summer* and was a big fan of August. I actually met him one time at the bar at Witch's Rock a bunch of years back. He was super-cool, friendly and nice as can be—took pictures and gladly answered all my stupid questions. That place is awesome.

"Yeah, man. Absolutely. It's a great place, but it turned into the IBM of surf schools. That's why I left. No hard feelings. I love those guys, but I just needed a change of pace. I didn't move to Costa Rica to build an empire. I want to live a simple, honest, sober life and be chill and healthy." He started to smile at that point but then seemed to think better of it. His teeth were messed up; they were discolored and broken, and a few of them wanted to point in other directions. He seemed to favor lip smiles when he could remember.

I was impressed that Barry was one of the founders of Witch's Rock. The place had been started back when Tamarindo was a sleepy little surf town. Since then, the entire area has blown up. The initial surf camp, which was not much bigger than Dale Daggers to start out, has grown into an eighteen-room hotel with a thriving school, two shops, and three restaurants. The popularity of Witch's Rock helped fuel the growth of the town, and the growth of the town enabled Witch's Rock to grow into a global brand and case study on surf entrepreneurship.

Barry didn't look like a successful entrepreneur, but his resume said otherwise. Apparently, he played a big role in getting Witch's Rock up to cruising altitude and he seemed to have a nice little business going in

Salinas as well. If you pointed him out to me on the street and asked me what I thought his occupation was, I would have said dishwasher or parking lot attendant. I was trying to figure out how old he was, although I guess it didn't really matter, but he was one of those guys who could've been anywhere from forty to sixty. He obviously had a lot of hard miles on him, but I was guessing he was more or less my age.

Barry talked with my friends and his guests about what it was like getting sober in Costa, the difference between Costa Rican and Nicaraguan AA groups, and some of his sponsees—people who came for vacations and ended up staying for longer periods of time. I was kind of listening, but my mind was more focused on how different my life had been from this guy's. This was basically Kai thirty years down the line. He was kind of ridiculous-looking with his Jackie O sunglasses and face piercings, but there was no doubt the guy had genuine chill. There was no way to fake that kind of serenity. It has its own vibration. He really had what I wanted. I could understand *gringos* coming down with their dicks tied in a knot, spending time with this dude and saying to themselves, "I think I'm going to hang out here for a while and let this guy take me through the steps. I want what he has, and maybe if I do what he does, I can get it too."

"How many guys have you sponsored?" I asked.

"I don't know, man. A lot." I nodded. *I bet.*

—

On the ride back to Gigante, Kai let us know that his band, Devil Dog, was playing that night at Ruamoko, the youth hostel at the south end of Playa Gigante. "If you guys want to come down and check it out, it should be pretty chill," he said.

"Three middle-aged sober dudes hanging out at a bar in a youth hostel isn't weird?" Rob asked.

"Nah, man," Kai said. "It's all good. It's all types of people from all over in that place. You can drink sodas or whatever."

We weren't super-stoked on the idea, but agreed it'd be better to make an appearance than to face Kai the next morning after blowing off his show.

It turned out to be fun. Despite Kai's protests to the contrary, we were decades older than the next oldest person in the bar, but it was fine. It was clear why we were there. In AA they tell us we can go into any bar if we have a reason to be there. We were there to support Kai. There was one guy there who looked older than us. He sat at the end of the bar, drinking beer and smoking cigarettes by himself. He had a long gray beard. His gray hair was pulled back in a ponytail and he wore a torn t-shirt and sandals. I didn't see him speak with a single person the whole time we were there. *There by the grace of God go I.*

There were lots of young girls. They seemed to outnumber the eligible guys two to one. The kids got hammered on Tona beer and Flor de Cana rum. Both were bottled locally, so they were super cheap. A hippie chick with blonde dreadlocks and ironic-looking horn-rimmed glasses was selling homemade weed muffins for two dollars. They were wrapped in purple cellophane and tied closed with jute. The empty wrappers and strings littered the tables and floor.

Kai cruised by our table and held up both hands as he passed. "Ten minutes till glory," he said. We gave him a table of thumbs-up.

"Yo," Rob said. "What's all this about your dad being a drug-smuggling psycho criminal? I never heard you share about that before."

Jose jumped in. "Yeah, what's up with that?"

I took a swig of my club soda and decided to not get into the whole thing. I understood it was an interesting story and would make for entertaining conversation while we waited for the band to play, but it was also emotionally draining. It was hard not to relive it a little bit in the retelling. "Yeah, man," I said. "My dad was a real piece of work."

"What was his deal?"

"It's hard to summarize, you know. It's a long fucking story. A whole life of drug addiction and crime.

A lot of damage done along the way." I thought about it for a moment and then added, "If my dad was here right now—or, if forty-year-old Joe Martin was here—you'd love him. He was charming and funny. He was a pro ball player, a war hero, an international criminal, a Wall Street millionaire ... I don't even know, something like three or four times over. He had amazing stories to tell, and he was one of the world's great storytellers. If you were introducing him to someone, you would say, 'Hey, you gotta meet Joe Martin. He's a great guy. You're gonna love him.' Everyone loved him. Women wanted to fuck him and men wanted to be his friend. But here's the thing." I leaned over the table and got close to them to make the point clearly. "He was a terrible human being. He was a *bad person.*"

They both looked at me without talking for a moment and I settled back into my seat. I know I can look like a psycho sometimes when I get worked up, and I suddenly got self-conscious about that. I was trying not to be that guy anymore. "I'm sorry," I said. "I know you wanted to know the details. You'd like me to read the back of his criminal baseball card for you, but that shit is irrelevant. You can Google him if you're interested."

Kai's band was competent. They played an utterly random mix of covers, from Creedence Clearwater Revival to Pearl Jam to The Police. Kai played drums. He was so high that his eyes were nearly shut the whole time, but he kept up and played well enough. We stuck around long enough to hear his set and one karaoke performance before pulling the plug on the operation. Kai thanked us profusely for coming. He had the excruciating sincerity of someone who was wasted and really needed you to know exactly how they felt, even though they couldn't seem to communicate. I've been on the other side of those exchanges a few times, and cringed as we tried to break away from him to walk back to Dale Daggers.

The hostel was a couple hundred yards down the dirt road from the lodge. We could've walked down the beach to get back, but were warned at some point that that wasn't a good idea at night. Other than the festivities at Ruamoko, the town was pretty much shut down for the night. A few stragglers remained on their porches, sitting in rocking chairs and enjoying the cool evening air. Halfway back, we spotted a figure stumbling along ahead of us, carrying a bottle. He passed under the one streetlight on the road and Jose and Rob both said in unison, "Is that Walter?"

He was a hundred feet ahead, but moving slowly. He moved along with no determination, as if he didn't really care which direction he went. It was a few steps down the street, a couple to the left, and then back down the street. At one point, he reached out to stabilize himself, but there was nothing there so he stumbled badly in that direction before catching himself.

We sped up to catch up with him. "Walter?" I said, "Is that you, buddy?"

He stopped and turned. It took him a moment for his eyes to adjust to the distance, and then another moment to register the face. "Troy," he said. He looked terrible. Sad . . . no, distraught. His eyes were red and puffy, as though he had been crying.

"Yeah, man. Are you okay?" Rob and Jose came around the other side of him. Rob put his arm around Walter's shoulder to stabilize him because he was swaying. He collapsed onto him and wept. We all traded *holy shit* glances. "Hey, hey, hey," Jose said. "*Que paso?*"

Walter stopped crying but held onto Rob. He dropped the bottle of rum on the road, but kept his face buried in Rob's shoulder. It was scary to see him so shattered. He was usually such a sturdy and lighthearted guy. I couldn't imagine what could've made him so miserable.

I picked up the bottle and asked, "Walter, what happened? Is there anything we can do to help?"

"*Dulce,*" he said, but we could barely understand him because he had a face full of Rob's shirt.

"What's that, buddy? Did you say *dulce?*"

"Sweet," Jose said. "*Dulce* means 'sweet.'"

Walter righted himself a little bit and reached into his shorts pocket. He pulled out his phone and clicked and swiped a few times. He held it up for us to see a picture of the ugliest dog I've ever seen in my life.

She was small and skinny with scruffy black hair on her back and a brown and white mask around her eyes. I don't think a team of veterinarians and geneticists could have solved the mystery of her breed. "Dulce," he said again. "My sweet. She's dead. She's gone," and then he convulsed in grief, folding onto himself in the road. He rolled into a fetal position and cried like a child.

"Wow," Jose said. "What the fuck do we do?"

"Let's take him back to the lodge," I answered. "We can't leave him here."

"I got him," Rob said. He reached down to pick him up by his armpits, but Walter was heavier than he looked. He was a solid little guy and Rob couldn't get him halfway up. I grabbed his legs and we carried him together, Rob moving backward the rest of the way. He was passed out by the time we walked in the door, which made the rest of our job easier. We put him on the couch, covered him with a blanket, and stuck a pillow under his head.

The next morning Kai explained, "Yeah, he really loved that dog. Him and Maria never had kids. That crazy-looking mutt was his baby." Apparently, she had run out in the street yesterday and got run over by a car. Kai showed us pictures of the three of them out on the boat. "He used to take her fishing. She would eat her weight in fresh tuna."

—

We got a late start while Walter nursed himself. We insisted that we skip the session and take the morning off. It seemed morbid to ask him to work after the episode the night before, but he wouldn't hear of it. Around 10 a.m. he paddled the kayak out to the boat and came back to pick us up.

We went to Playa Amarillo because the swell was very powerful and the wind was stiff offshore, which would make the other breaks too hairy for our group. Kai had seen us struggle the day before, and figured out that he needed to dial it down to get back into our comfort zone. Amarillo is the beach just to the north of Gigante. You can actually walk there if you walk to the end of the cove and hike over the cliff. It's a protected cove, but not quite as protected as Gigante, so you get some great stomach-to-chest-high sets on the bigger days. On the smaller days it could be a mellow longboard spot not that different from a good day back home. We loved it. After a couple of scary and frustrating sessions, clean chest-high waves were just what the doctor ordered.

Kai's friend Dave came with us that day and took pictures and videos from the shore. Dave would join us every third or fourth session, I guess whenever he was available. He got some great action shots. At the end of a tourist's trip, he would offer to sell them on a per-picture basis, or you could buy all your videos and pictures for a flat hundred bucks. He was another young vagabond surfer-type. He had an interesting look. His face was unusually handsome, with perfect bone structure and a neatly trimmed beard, but his body was small and scrawny. It looked like it belonged to someone else. He kept all of his camera gear in a dry bag inside of a backpack. He paddled in, rode a wave to shore, and then set up shop on the beach. At times, he would actually get in the water with us and use his waterproof camera to get shots of us coming down the line. He was a nice, quiet kid and a talented photographer.

We were all super-stoked from the session during the short ride back and then we wolfed down Maria's bacon and cheese omelets, with the same great hashbrowns on the side. The woman was a genius on that griddle. The meeting at San Juan Del Sur that afternoon was kind of interesting. The speaker was a middle-aged guy named Keith. I didn't catch where he was from, but he was there with Barry; another guest from The Dreams who had fallen into his web, I presumed.

Keith seemed like he was there to entertain everyone and impress us with what a huge ol' alcoholic he was. He talked in ridiculous exaggerations about the quantities of liquor he drank. At one point he said, "I used to drink five bottles of Kettle One a day." A few minutes later he claimed, "One night I ran out of whiskey and the liquor stores were all closed, so I drank a case of champagne I found in the basement." The logistics of these statements didn't make sense, never mind the physical and medical impossibilities. He did tell some entertaining stories, though. I remember one of them distinctly, because I had heard the exact story told by another drunk once before.

Standing in front of the group, he said, "Last year, I got pulled over for a DWI. It was my third one that month. So, the cop has me over on the side of the road trying to prove my sobriety by performing circus tricks on command. . . ." He comically walked heel to toe in rapid succession with his hands out, badly balancing himself. "So, as I'm doing this another car crashes into a light pole, BAM, full speed, just up the road. Debris goes flying, the car catches fire. It's crazy. Right, so the cop goes to me, 'You wait right here. Don't you go anywhere,' and he runs down the road to see if he can help save the crash victim."

Keith made a funny face at this point and put his palms up in the air, as if to say, *What should I do?* "So, I decide it's about time for me to get going. I stroll over to the car and drive my ass home. A couple hours later, the doorbell rings at my house. It wakes me up. I'm passed out on the couch. I open the door and it's the same cop. I'm like, 'Hey, what's up, bro?' Long story short, it turns out I accidentally drove the police car home. I was so wasted I didn't even notice. I looked over and it was parked in my driveway. The cop still had my driver's license from when he pulled me over. Dude walked all the way to my house because he didn't want to get in trouble for getting his squad car stolen. He asks me if I feel like trading my driver's license for his car keys."

Funny story, but not only did I know he was lying because I had heard the story before, but I could also just tell that he was bullshitting. I have an excellent ear for bullshit. From growing up with my mom, I know the tone and cadence of a bullshit story when I hear one. On the one hand, it didn't really matter. He was entertaining and a good change of pace. On the other hand, sobriety is a life-or-death matter for a lot of people, and honesty is one of the few absolute requirements. Coming into a room full of bullshitters and laying out a bunch of bullshit stories is not just insulting, it's also dangerous. Someone more impressionable than me might think, *These guys are all just full of shit*, and never come back.

After the meeting, Andy came over. He recited our names—"Troy. Jose. Rob"—pointing at each of us in turn, which was kind of impressive. For a million dollars I could not have remembered his name. "Andy," he said, putting his open palm on his own chest. "We met in Popoyo last week." He was wearing a t-shirt that said *GOD: Group of Drunks*. The number of beaded bracelets on his wrist seemed to have increased and spread to his neck.

Outside Josephine's, Andy kept us engaged in conversation by asking question after question. Kai was parked across the street in the Hilux, waiting for us, and

Barry had already taken off. Andy asked where we were from, where we were staying, what kind of work we do back home, and what we thought of the two groups. He asked if we had ever been to Nica before, what we thought of the place, and how long we were staying. It was turning into a pretty thorough interview. I was sure he was just being friendly, and I realized that some people like to be asked questions and talk about themselves, but after a while I was starting to get annoyed. There seemed to be a bottomless pit of questions. I think he might have sensed this, so he switched gears to tell us about him.

"My business takes me all over the area. I do electrical work and general contracting, so we build houses, remodels, extensions, all that stuff. I have connections up and down the coast and I know the way around like the back of my hand. If you guys want to know about the area, or you want to tour around, just let me know. I'd love to be a resource. I can be a set of wheels or whatever you need, you know?" We all thanked him and he kept going. "Yeah, I know you're all away from home. If you need a sober ear to bend, I'm around. I do cookouts at my house all the time, too. It'd be great to have you guys out to Rancho Santana."

Kai got out of the truck and started to mosey across the road. He looked like he wanted to move things along and collect his fare. I cut in, "Hey we gotta jet, Andy. Our ride is here."

"Let me give you my number," Andy was saying as Kai came up and stood beside me with his hands in his shorts' pockets.

I punched it into my phone and said "Thanks." I smacked Kai on the back. "You ready to roll?"

He smiled. "Born ready." He and Andy smiled at each other.

"Hey man," Kai said.

"How's it going Kai?" Andy answered.

As we all walked back to the truck, I asked Kai how he knew Andy. He seemed to take an extra moment to choose his words carefully. "I don't know," he said. "Just from around, you know? I see him in the water now and then, and he built a guest house for Mike's neighbor up in Santana." He fired up Spotify, linked it to the truck's Bluetooth, and turned the volume up.

The conversation in the backseat turned to the subject of lunch and a possible afternoon session. The guys were pretty sore and beat-up from our two-a-days. They were debating the merits of downtime vs. a "take it easy" type of afternoon session and whether or not that's even a thing. "He owes people money," Kai suddenly said.

"Who?" I answered, because I had stopped thinking about Andy a few minutes ago.

"Your friend back there," he continued. "I think he has to pay off like the government people to do his work or something like that. I heard he owes them a lot of money. He doesn't like to pay up on time."

I nodded, pretty much disregarding the tale. Kai was high, and a story like that about Andy didn't really make sense to me at the time. It sounded like small-town gossip that had been exaggerated through an extended game of Telephone. Who knows how much of it was true? I didn't, and I didn't really care anyway.

—

Later that day, the boat pulled up to the beach for the afternoon session. Kai called out, "Saddle up!" and we collected our gear. As I was walking to the back door, I heard the Facetime ring from my phone. I turned around and saw it on the coffee table. Ceci's picture popped up. I jogged back over and swiped to answer. "Hey honey," I said. "What's up?"

Ceci was sitting at her desk in her dorm room with her laptop open in front of her. She had on her white pajamas with pink piglets. Her hair was pulled back in a messy bun and I would've bet she had woken up no more than thirty minutes earlier. "I need your help," she said. "I have to do a paper for my criminology class. We're supposed to write about someone we know who's broken the law. I figured I'd use Grandpa Joe, since he's a big ol' criminal, isn't he?"

I took a deep breath. "Yeah, that's right," I said, "But the boat just pulled up, honey, and the guys are paddling out. . . ."

"Troy, let's go!" Rob called from the beach.

"Can we do this later, when I get back?" I asked.

Ceci stared off to the side and seemed to be contemplating. *Was she stoned?* I wondered. There was something in her posture and expression. I was getting ready to ask her about it when she said, "It's due tonight and I have to get to the Alpha Delta Pi softball game in like two hours. I'm the starting right fielder." She did a little dance with her fingers and said something like, "Woot, woot."

"Of course you are," I said. "So, you're telling me this is due today? And you waited until now to start working on it?"

"Troy!" Jose yelled. "What the fuck, bro?"

"Hold on," I said to her. I muted my phone, jogged outside and yelled down to the beach, "Sorry, guys, I have to bail. I have to help Ceci with a school project!" They all booed and a couple of middle fingers were held up high.

Ceci had been talking pretty much continuously, giving a long series of excuses for why she had left her work to the last minute. I only heard a couple of them and decided that it didn't matter. I couldn't control her. She was on her own. I would help when I could, and at that moment I could. I unmuted my phone and said, "Okay, what do you need to know?"

"Well, tell me about his *drug empire*," she said. I could practically hear the air quotes in her voice. "He was like a big-deal smuggler, right? And hey, by the way, if he was like Pablo Escobar, why were you and Grandma always broke? I mean, why did you grow up poor?"

I rubbed my forehead with my hand, closed my eyes and then rubbed them too. There were so many things wrong with that question, I didn't know where to begin. I had also already thought way more about my dad in the prior twenty-four hours than I cared to. "Okay, well, first of all, we weren't poor. We were fine. Second, when Grandma found out how Joe made his money, she cut him off. We moved and she never took another cent that came from drugs."

"That was stupid," she interrupted.

I sighed. "No, it was incredibly brave, and it might be the most honorable thing I've ever seen anyone do in my life, but I don't want to argue with you." I held up my hands in a stop gesture. "Listen, I don't think you should write about that part of Grandpa. He was actually never convicted for any of that. There were some other crimes he was convicted of that would make a better essay. White-collar stuff."

"Like what?" she asked. She had unwrapped a lollipop and had it stuck in the side of her mouth so that she had to talk around it.

The irritation that I had pushed down a moment earlier nudged its way to the forefront. "Wait, let's go back a minute," I said. "Are you telling me that my mother working two jobs for twenty years, moving to an apartment she could afford by herself, and doing without any luxuries on my behalf was stupid? She chose to live that life and raise me as an honest person, rather than sitting in the lap of luxury on drug money. Is 'stupid' really the best word you can think of for those choices?"

"Whoa," she said, pausing to suck and swallow a mouthful of dissolved lollipop. "Chill, Dad. Don't get ragey with me, please."

I walked out the back door to finish this call on the patio. Maybe I would draw some chill, as she suggested, from the ocean and the beach. "Okay, honey. Here's the deal. Grandpa worked at a series of low-end stock brokerage firms throughout his career."

"This is after his drug stuff?"

"Yes. He had a trial in Miami. You can Google this. There are a bunch of articles from *The Miami Herald* and some national papers. They threw the book at him. Racketeering, smuggling, dealing, tax fraud, you name it. But they didn't convict him on anything. A couple of key witnesses recanted their grand jury testimony and the whole case was dismissed after two or three weeks in the courtroom."

I started putting away my surf stuff. I put my wax on the shelf by the back door, fished the wax comb out of my bag, and placed it on top so I wouldn't lose it.

"Oh shit," she said. "They recanted, huh? I wonder why." She made a little finger gun and shot it at me on the screen.

"Not funny," I said as I folded up my rash guards and went back inside to put them away in my drawer. "Anyway, he decided then to get a real job for the first time. And since he was a world-class bullshit artist and had no problem with lying and stealing, he became a stockbroker. He joined a firm in Boca and learned the business. He convinced some smart kid in the office to commit fraud by taking his series seven and sixty-three license exams for him, so they handed him a license to steal and set him loose on the rest of the nation. By the time Black Monday came in 1987, he was making almost as much as a stockbroker as he used to in the drug business. He thought he had completed his transformation to a respectable businessman.

"Anyway, he went broke after the market crashed. He lost all his cash, both legally gained and illegally. He built his money back up during the Dot Com boom, and then lost everything again in 2002 when that blew up. And then he did it again during the subprime mortgage craze, and lost everything *again* when *that* market crashed in 2008."

"Wow," Ceci said. "Grandpa Joe doesn't learn lessons very easily, huh?"

"Yeah," I said. "That's a family trait. Important for you to know."

"So, what happened?"

I went back outside and opened the gate down to the beach. I started walking down to the water, but the WiFi got weak so I had to come back up to the patio. I pulled out a chair and turned it around to face the ocean. "He got clean. Went to rehab for the first time. He lost his securities license, so he knocked around for a while. He tried out some twelve-step meetings, but decided it wasn't for him. I think he was doing the old marijuana maintenance program for a long time, probably eight or nine years. One day, I got a call at work that he had been arrested again, and was asking for me by name."

"Oh shit. What did he do?"

"I don't know exactly. I think someone cut him off on the road and he freaked out. Pulled the guy out of his car and smacked the shit out of him in the middle of the street."

"Did you go down and get him out?"

"Nope. I hung up the phone and pretended it never happened."

"Ooooo, that's cold."

"Here's the thing, Ceci, and you should remember this. Hurt people *hurt people*. You can put that in your essay. My dad's a damaged guy. Vietnam fucked him up, he had terrible learning disabilities, he was a drug addict. He had lots of what they call 'isms.' So, he hurt me, he hurt my mom, and he pulled that guy out of his car and hurt him, too."

"And you hurt him back by not helping him," she said.

She was clever. I had never thought of it that way before. "Sure," I said with a sigh. "Yeah."

"So, what were the details about the crime part?"

I was all over the place and I realized she was going to have a hard time turning any of this into a usable essay in the next hour before she had to be at the softball game. "Tell you what," I said, glancing at my watch. "Why don't you text me the essay prompt as it exactly reads, and I'll crank it out for you?"

Ceci closed her eyes and put her hands together in prayer position. "Oh my God, you are the best. Thank you so much, Dad. And I promise, I won't wait until the last minute anymore."

"One more question before you go," I said.

"Shoot."

"Are you high right now?"

Her eyebrows shot up and she let out something halfway between a cough and a laugh. "No, Dad. I just haven't been taking my ADD meds."

That sounded like bullshit, but I was on record now for at least asking the question. I didn't want her to think that I couldn't tell. That other people couldn't tell. "Well, take your meds. They'll improve your softball skills."

Doing my kid's homework for her was not my finest piece of parenting, but the conversation had sparked my interest. After talking about him during the meeting and then at the bar the day before, he was lurking in the back of my mind. It seemed like a good way to visit with him that afternoon. Besides, the guys wouldn't be back for a couple of hours, and I had nothing else to do.

8

Days passed in a blur. We surfed, ate, slept and went to meetings. It was awesome, but I missed my girls. One morning during our second week, we went out and surfed a break called Lance's Left. Lance's is an unusual wave. It's a point break that can get really big, but it's a soft wave so it's easy to paddle in. When the swell and the wind are right, like they were that morning, the wave can jack up to ten feet and run for hundreds of yards. It breaks in pretty much the same spot every time, so the lineup is very orderly. You wait your turn, paddle hard, and drop in. It's the biggest wave I've ever surfed, but it's just a big ramp that goes on for what feels like forever. In reality it's probably a minute or so by the time you get to the end, kick off the top, and begin the long paddle back to the lineup.

Surfing that wave was a once-in-a-lifetime experience for me, but for some reason I kept thinking about my girls while I was out there, and I felt like crying most of the time. I had an awful pit in my stomach and actually shed some tears while coming down the line on my third or fourth wave. It was a great wave and I realized, as the tears flowed down my cheeks, that Dave was taking pictures of this ludicrous moment from the beach. I just missed them so much. My girls both FaceTimed me almost every day, so I didn't feel panicked and disconnected from them. I just felt sad. The reality of the situation was that I wouldn't have been able to be with them even if I was home, so there was nothing to do but to sit with the sadness and wait for it to pass.

During the long paddle back to the point, I had some time to think about what the next phase of my life was going to be. Whatever it looked like, it was going to be a big adjustment. My girls had been the center of my world for the past couple of decades. It had been twenty years since I had made a plan without thinking about where they were going to be and what they were going to need. Raising those girls was the most important thing I would ever do. I got more enjoyment out of it than anything else. It was incredibly hard and I was absolutely committed to it. And then suddenly it was over. They would never come home in the same way again. They would always be just visiting. It was emotionally devastating. It was over. I had a deep sense of loss and grief that I can only describe as traumatic.

That afternoon I shared about it at the meeting in Popoyo, which is near Lance's. We asked Walter to drop us at the beach after the session and we had lunch up at Popoyo Loco before the meeting. When something is weighing on you, you're supposed to share about it in meetings. My old sponsor said that when you share a burden in a meeting you cut it in half. My home group in Florida was definitely sick of hearing about it. I had cut it in so many halves that they each now owned a piece of this trauma. I raised my hand at Popoyo Loco and said that this escape to Nicaragua was exactly what I needed in many ways, but that I was still struggling with a deep sense of loss from my last girl going off to school. I could feel Rob's eyes start to roll back in his head and imagined him thinking, *Here we go again*.

"You know," I said, "when they were little, I would tell you that they were the most important things in the world to me, and it wasn't even close. That was the God's honest truth. I would've passed a lie detector test. But it was also true that I couldn't handle it. I didn't have the skillset. I really wanted to. With all my heart. But I usually stayed away. I ran away. To the bar, where it was safe and I could get my head to feel the way I needed it to feel. When I walked in the door and they jumped on me it was suffocating. I felt like I was being buried alive. That's what it means to be a selfish, self-centered alcoholic. I didn't think much of myself, but I was all I ever thought about.

"I justified it in those days by saying *I have to do whatever I have to do to get through the day*. My wife and my kids were depending on me. I had to stay employed, stay sane and alive . . . so my attitude was, whatever's good for Daddy is good for the family. Let me tell you something—when this is your guiding philosophy, it leads to some bad behavior." I stopped and rubbed my face to try to shake it off a little bit. I thought maybe I was done, but then I realized something I thought was important. "And the irony is, it doesn't even work. In fact, the opposite happens. The more I focused on making myself happy, the more guaranteed I was to be miserable. If I had been focused on my girls and my wife, I would have been happier, and they would've had the father and husband they deserved."

I put my hands behind my head and arched my back, stretching in the chair. I was stiff and sore from the session. I felt like I had to wrap up my share. "So, I have to accept that I'm not going to get back any opportunities to sit on the floor in their room and play with their dolls or have any more tea parties." That last part did me in. The idea of my girls in their pajamas and pigtails with their tea set laid out on the floor of their bedroom made me blubber on the spot. *Shit*, I thought. *Here we go.*

Everyone just let me cry for a minute. I expected them to move on to whoever was next to share, but nobody raised their hand. *Fuck*, I thought. *I have to stop.* I finally pulled it together. "I'm sorry," I said. "I don't think I cried five times between the ages of ten and forty-five, but since I got sober it's been a waterfall. Michelle, my ex-girlfriend, started calling me Dick Vermeil." A few of the people who understood the joke were kind enough to chuckle. I explained, "He was the old coach of the Rams. He was known for bursting into tears in the middle of press conferences. That's me now. These days, when sadness or grief hits, it feels really heavy and overwhelming because it's a new thing, you know? I'm like an exposed nerve. Anyway, thanks for letting me share."

"Thanks, Troy," the group said. Cut it in half again.

That happened to be the day of my four-year anniversary. At the end of the meeting, they asked if anyone was celebrating an anniversary. I raised my hand and said, "Hi, I'm Troy, and today I have four years sober."

While the group was clapping, Paula was fishing around in their plastic coin holder. "Sorry, Troy," she said in her gravelly Marge Simpson-esque voice. "We don't have any four-year coins. But on behalf of the Popoyo group, congratulations on such an important milestone. Tell us, Troy, how did you do it?"

"One day at a time," I said, and everyone clapped again.

After the meeting I had my first substantial conversation with Andy. The group did the Serenity Prayer to close the meeting and then everyone folded up their chairs and started putting them back in the rack on the side of the room. He came up to me in a t-shirt that read *Life on Life's Terms* and put his chair in the rack on top of mine. "Hey, man, I'm Andy," he said. By then, I had actually managed to remember his name. We shook hands. "I was just thinking about what you shared before and wanted to tell you that you kind of made me jealous." I nodded, although I had no idea what he was talking about. "Yeah," he continued, "I never had kids and honestly never loved anyone that much." Huh. "Yeah, you should be grateful you have all that love in your life and that you're able to feel it so deeply. That sounds like the real deal. That's the stuff they write songs about. I understand what it is, but I've never felt it. You're lucky you have that."

I was a little frozen. We were blocking the chair rack and people were waiting. He put his hand on my arm and guided me out of the way. "I was just going to head over to this little Buddhist temple in Nacascolo for a sit. Why don't you come along? I think it'd do you some good to hit the cushion today."

Rob and Jose wanted to get back to the lodge for Maria's fried fish tacos. We had all gone nuts for them the week prior. Plus, they wanted to nap and hydrate and get ready for the afternoon session. To be honest, that all sounded pretty good to me too, but this seemed more important. Since I was an open wound, I figured I could use some spiritual healing if someone was offering. Besides, Andy said he would drop me off at Gigante afterwards, that it was more or less on his way back to his house in Rancho Santana.

We jumped in Andy's Jeep, which was an old bright red CJ7 with big wheels and no roof. "Sweet ride," I said. We climbed in and he fired up the engine, and the old Blaupunkt blared Radio Zinica, the local Spanish-language pop station, right that moment playing The Doors' "People Are Strange."

"Thanks," he replied. "It's a '77. One of my buddies owns a repair shop in Rivas. He's helping me rebuild it. It was a real piece of junk when I bought it a couple of years ago."

When the song ended Andy synced up his Spotify account to the radio and played a mix that included Nirvana, Stone Temple Pilots, Jane's Addiction and Iggy Pop. I asked him how long he'd been living on the Emerald Coast, and he pretty much told me his origin story for the rest of the drive. He stopped at one point, in the middle of his story, and held up his finger for a moment like he was trying to remember something. "Yeah," he said. "There was something else I wanted to say to you about your share today." It was kind of a weird non-sequitur. One minute he was telling me about his first year in Rivas and how he had built up his business there, and the next minute he was trying to grab a thought out of the air about a conversation from half an hour ago. "Yeah, that was it," he said. "You were talking about why and when the pain of your girls leaving your house was going to go away. Right?"

"Yeah," I said. "I'm fucking done with it already. I don't want to walk around crying about it anymore."

He pulled the Jeep up a dirt driveway that looked like it wound around the side of the hill. There was a fancy sign alongside the drive that said *Eden on the Chocolata*. "That's not up to you," he said. "The pain will go away when it's done teaching you what you need to learn."

That was a sentence I was going to have to file away and deconstruct another time. It sounded like there might be something to it, but it also sounded like it might be a fortune cookie. In the meantime, we were driving up into the property and I started to realize that we weren't at a Buddhist temple. It was a pretty high-end yoga retreat, up in the hills overlooking Nacascolo Bay, the kind of place upper-middle-class housewives go for their fortieth birthdays after reading *Eat, Pray, Love*. But just as I started to feel judgmental, I realized I was pretty much on the middle-aged-man version of the same trip.

We parked the Jeep and walked past some freshly painted casitas and canopied yoga decks made of beautiful balsa wood. The decks overlooked a nice garden and the ocean beyond. "Fancy," I remarked.

"Yeah, yeah, I know, it's a soccer mom retreat, but the meditation center is legit.

It's run by a guy named Scott Tusa. He was an actual monk. He lived in a monastery in Colorado for like eight years. He's the real deal. Trust me."

It didn't take that much trust to meditate with a sober guy for a little while, so I followed along on the gravel path and then down a couple dozen stone steps until we got to a simple concrete building with a thatched roof and a hand-carved Arts & Crafts-looking sign above the door that said *Meditation Center*. Scott wasn't there, which was vaguely annoying, but Andy pulled out a couple of cushions and fired up a pre-recorded concentration meditation on an iPad. "This is Scott. I like this one—it's super simple but it does the job for me."

We sat side by side on our cushions for twenty-five minutes, following along to the instructions on the recording, which played through a pair of Bose Bluetooth speakers behind us. Like Andy said, it was pretty standard stuff—a body scan followed by some box breathing, and then an interesting practice on the awareness of mind states.

Andy dropped me at Dale Daggers afterwards. When we pulled in front he asked me, "How long are you planning to stay?"

"I'm scheduled for another ten days or so," I said, closing the door behind me. "I have to admit, though, I've been thinking about staying around for a while longer."

Andy's eyebrows lifted above his sunglasses. "Cool," he said. "This place gets even better with time."

For the last few days, I had been thinking about extending my trip. I didn't really have any reason to be home. My surfing was improving the way I hoped it would, and I wouldn't mind continuing that progression. I checked the University of Florida calendar. The next time my girls would be home was the third week of May. That gave me two more months, and even then they'd only be home for a week. I could visit with them and then come back, or I could call it quits at that point and just stay home. That seemed like the next logical decision-making point. Plus, the job I was starting a few weeks later was purely remote, so there was no reason I couldn't do it from here. The WiFi was reliable and we were in the Central time zone. "Yeah," I added. "I think I might hang out for a while. I really like it here."

Andy's face lit up. "Sweet," he said and put his hand out for a fist bump.

—

The next day we surfed at Playa Colorado again. It was a totally different experience this time, so much so that it was actually surprising it was the same break. When we paddled in from the boat, we found mellow, rolling, chest-high waves. It was delightful. All fun, no fear, no consequences. Each of us caught our share of long rides—lefts and rights, depending on where you were in the lineup. This might have been the most memorable session overall for the whole trip, because we just had so much fun. We were laughing and cheering for each other. After a few sessions where we had been paddling for survival, it was a relief to feel entirely competent and safe in the water.

Even by the time we got to the meeting in San Juan Del Sur, the buzz from our session still hadn't worn off. We were laughing and chatting it up as we walked in. By then, we felt quite comfortable in the meetings. We knew a number of the people in the room and were glad to be able to say hello to them by name. We felt like regulars. There were two guys visiting from New York at the meeting, Daniel and Matthew. Not Dan and Matt. They were pretty formal for drunks on a surf trip to Nicaragua. They were a bit uptight too, and seemed to take themselves quite seriously. Daniel, a "former investment banker" (he didn't say what his current profession was), qualified during the meeting. He had played soccer for the University of Pennsylvania, then got recruited to Goldman Sachs. I understood and respected the type of effort and focus that took. After a two-year rotation at Goldman in which he averaged ninety hours per week, he went into private equity. Every aspect of his life plan was being ticked off, one at a time. He took on a well-bred spouse and they inhabited an expensive apartment in Tribeca. Cocaine took all of that away.

He was a tall, thin guy in his late twenties. He wore the man bun/beard combination that had become standard for men his age. His story didn't include the

triumphant conclusion customary in qualifications—
"I got sober and my life improved beyond my wildest
dreams," etc. He ended his story post-rehab and living
a simpler, more modest life, in the suburb where he
grew up. *Living with his parents?* The farthest extent of
positivity in his message was that he at least no longer
had to do cocaine all day just to get out of bed. My heart
kind of broke for the guy, and I felt bad for judging him
as stuck-up and arrogant at first. He might have been
those things, but it was probably because he was an
unhappy person. He hadn't found peace and happiness
in sobriety. Not yet, anyway. Maybe that's what he
was looking for in Nicaragua. I honestly couldn't even
picture the guy surfing, he seemed so stiff.

I went over to shake his hand at the end of the
meeting. "Thanks for your qualification," I said to him.
"It was important for me to hear your message."

"Sure, no problem," Daniel said.

Barry came over and high-fived Rob and me, like
we had just won a game. "Come on, motherfuckers,"
he said. "Let me buy you guys a round of cappuccinos."

I laughed. "One sec," I said. "I just want to finish
talking to Daniel."

"Go ahead," Daniel said. "Don't let me keep you."

He didn't seem to want to hear the rest of whatever
I had to say, but that was fine. I wasn't necessarily saying
it for him. If it happened to help him, all the better. "I just

wanted to tell you that I was an athlete and a top student in college also. I was planning on living a life like the one you lived. I've always been resentful that I didn't get to do those things. Investment banking, private equity, working with the best and brightest, making big money. That resentment has done a lot of damage, but listening to you today, I understand now that I would've ended up in the same place, either way. I am who I am, and I would've ended up here no matter what."

Daniel was kind enough to nod meaningfully. "Well, I'm glad you got something out of it," he said. "It was nice meeting you, Troy. I hope you enjoy the rest of your vacation."

We headed out together and yelled across the road to Kai, who was parked and waiting for us. We told him he could join us for coffee or jet, and that Barry would drive us back in that case. He chose to jet, so we all joked and chatted our way up the uneven sidewalks and across the cobblestone streets to La Tostaderia. The sun was strong outside, so it felt great to walk into the cafe, into the shade with the big ceiling fans throwing around breezes. I noticed for the first time that the lights were off. There was no need with all of the big open windows and French doors.

Rob and Jose loved Barry. He was such a freak show. Once he started gabbing, he just talked nonstop. It was nothing of consequence, but it was always funny and insightful and always, always positive. He gave silly, wordy, eclectic, optimistic observations on everything. He ordered us four cappuccinos at the counter, and we sat down at one of the big communal tables in the middle of the room. This one was a long, narrow piece of sanded and polished driftwood, with a wavy shape and grain. It was too narrow to be a proper dining table, maybe thirty inches at its widest, but it was perfect for people to sit across from one another and have coffee. It was a good conversation distance. Barry was waxing poetically on the perfection of the width of the table— "An inspired design decision or a wonderful mistake?"— then jumped to the next subject before anyone could try answering.

Our coffees came about ten minutes later and, just as the waitress put them on the table, we heard music outside and we all looked through the big open French doors. Andy had pulled up to the only traffic light in town, at the corner outside the cafe. He was in his red jeep with the big tires. Daniel and Matthew were with him.

"In the spider's web," Rob joked. He had heard the stories about Andy recruiting customers out of the AA rooms and had started referring to him as "The Spider." I didn't love the joke, but I wasn't the humor police and so never said anything about it.

"He's probably taking them to meditate at the soccer mom retreat," I said.

"You mean the 'Buddhist temple?'" Rob said, laughing into his hand.

The light changed and Andy pulled away. Barry, who had been an absolute jabbermouth until then, was suddenly quiet. "Hey, Barry," Jose said, "You know Andy, right?" It seemed almost rhetorical, because Jose understood very well that Barry had to have known Andy. He seemed to be trying to get him to say something about him.

The guy who gives his opinion about every light fixture and piece of furniture suddenly had very little to say. "Yeah, I know him. He's been down here for a while now." He then just left it at that.

We all sipped our coffees. "He seems like a great guy, if you ask me," Jose said.

"Very spiritual. He was super nice to Troy."

Barry wouldn't be baited. He just drank his coffee and looked quietly out his oversized sunglasses. There was no expression to be read on his face. He looked like he was reading the *Wall Street Journal*.

After a few moments, we moved onto other subjects and Barry became reanimated. We asked him about the surf near Salinas and he gave us a thorough rundown of the best three spots, but as he was talking, I was getting a little bit annoyed that he had refused to say anything, good or bad, about Andy. I started thinking about it and decided that could only mean that he didn't like him. Otherwise, he would spout off rainbows and positivity like he always does. He must really not want to talk shit about another group member. This is the etiquette in AA. In fact, it's more of a rule. Gossip is rigorously avoided, or at least it's supposed to be.

"So, what's the deal with Andy?" I finally asked him. "What's your view of him? I've heard some of the guys say he's done them dirty in business deals, but he's been nothing but kind to me. What's your opinion?" No more beating about the bush.

"Look, man," Barry started, and then stopped and seemed to reconsider. Finally, he restarted, "I don't talk shit about people. I won't. Especially about people from the rooms. None of us in there are saints. None of us should be put on pedestals. We're all a bunch of drunks."

"But . . ." I said, trying to get him to elaborate.

"No buts, dude. I'd just be careful not to fall for *anyone's* games in the rooms, no matter who they are. A lot of addicts are very manipulative, dishonest people. Just because someone stops using and drinking doesn't mean they've turned into a saint. You dig? Just because Mel Gibson knows all the lines doesn't make him Hamlet. You'd do well to remember that in all AA rooms. They're not bastions of mental health."

It was hard to argue with that. Rob chimed in, "My first sponsor," then corrected himself. "Actually, *our* first sponsor," he added, pointing to me and then to himself to clarify, "used to tell us all the time that he's not the one getting us sober. That it was between us and God. He said not to rely too much on any person in AA for our sobriety."

"My man," Barry said, nodding. I guessed that meant that he agreed.

9

The next morning was crazy. Walter took us to Playa Santana. It was interesting because Playa Santana was the beach break behind Rancho Santana, which is the fancy expat community that had a four-star hotel and hundreds of expensive private homes. Andy lived there; Mike lived there. It was *gringo* central, so you'd think the lineup would be mostly white dudes like us. You would be wrong. At the south end of the beach there was one of the most convenient public access points of any beach on the Gold Coast. This made it a popular beach for locals. It also made the lineup the most crowded one we saw during our trip.

Santana is a weird wave. It breaks in a horseshoe, so that you could take off going left and then the wave would literally turn right, or vice versa. The local guys *shred* on it. The talent level is unbelievable. Some of them look like they could be professionals. They grew up at that beach, they knew the wave intimately, and they had no interest in making room for tired old *gringos* paddling in. It was more competitive than I had bargained for. I only got two waves and one of them nearly ended in a collision, when I got to the turn in the horseshoe and a Nica ripper was pumping down the line right at me. I turned down the face and thankfully he went high. The wave closed on me and drove me down into the reef, which wasn't fun, but I just ended up with a few scrapes and a bruised ego.

Just as I was recovering from my encounter with the reef, I heard a deep voice bellow, "Yo, man, you don't throw your lumber around here!" About fifty feet down the line was a thick, bare-chested Nica with long hair pulled back tightly in a ponytail. He was holding the side of his head, where a surfboard had apparently just smashed him. Still floating next to him was Rob's sky-blue longboard. *Shit.*

Kai cruised up next to me. "Yo, your boy's fucked," he said. "That's the wrong group to mess with out here."

The big guy with the ponytail examined his fingers to see if there was any blood. He didn't like what he saw and paddled over to Rob, who had his hands up and was apologizing profusely. I later found out what happened. Rob was paddling back out to the lineup when a big wave broke in front of him. He tried to do a turtle roll, which is when you spin underwater and pull the board down to let the whitewater pass by, but the board got away from him and was launched backward ... right into the face of the guy who was paddling out behind him.

It only took the Nica four or five paddles to reach Rob, who was climbing back onto his board and trying to escape. The guy grabbed Rob's ankle and pulled him into the water, then grabbed his rash guard and started punching him in the head. "Don't do it, man!" Kai yelled out behind me as I paddled over as fast as I could. "These are not the guys to fuck with!" By the time I got there, a circle of surfers surrounded them. Rob was taking a beating. He was trying to fight back, but kept getting dunked under and then punched when he got back up for air. These guys had been fighting in the ocean since they were kids. They knew how to do it. I did a hard push-up on my board and thrusted with my legs so that I could launch myself at the closest guy in the circle. It was a muscled smaller guy who wore a black baseball hat and a thick silver chain. I had seen him in the lineup several times that morning. He had a bunch of really bad tattoos that ran from the middle of his back and chest up his neck.

I caught him around the shoulders and tackled him into the water. After a few seconds, he squirmed out of my grasp and swam back up to grab his board, but I caught him by his long hair and pulled him under. I came up myself, but was able to keep him under. I probably outweighed him by fifty pounds. "Let him go or I'll drown this little bastard!" I yelled out. My guy was splashing around and fighting to get to the surface.

The big guy with the ponytail let go of Rob, who instinctively swam away, gasping for air. I let go of the little guy's hair and he lurched up, choking and coughing, with seawater flowing out of his mouth and nose. One of the guys in the circle, a tall skinny kid who wore a red rash guard, chimed in. "None of you are going to make it out of here."

Jose saw what was going on and got through the breakers onto the other side of the circle. "Are you okay?" he said to Rob, and then promptly got punched in the face. Jose grew up surfing in Venezuela. He knew how to fight on a surfboard. He positioned himself quickly and started pounding the guy who hit him. Then we all got attacked. We were trying to stay on our boards, trying to protect ourselves and trying to fight back. It was really hard. Really awkward. Underwater, I was kicking like mad to keep myself stable and close enough to land shots. None of my punches had much on them because I had no leverage, so I was just trying to throw as many fast, short jabs as I could.

After a little while I got clocked in the side of the head and fell off my board. Underwater, the little fucker with the bad tattoos grabbed my balls. As soon as I came up, I caught some elbows and punches to the head. They weren't hard enough to injure me, but they hurt. Finally, I had enough of playing around with those guys. *This is hilarious*, I thought to myself. *These motherfuckers think they're tough.* I reached for my ankle and grabbed my leash. I pulled the loop to remove it from my ankle and grabbed a length of it with my other hand. Throwing it around the neck of the little bastard who grabbed my balls, I twisted it closed, choking him. His face went red immediately and his eyes bulged. He was tearing at his neck to try to create space, but I pulled it tight. "You like that, ya little fuck?" I spit out. I held it tight with my right hand and started swimming backwards, away from the circle, with my free hand and my legs. When he started to get some slack in the leash I pulled it tight with both hands, kicking with my legs to create more distance from the circle of thugs.

Across the other side of the circle, Jose was still trading punches and Rob was being held in a chokehold from behind. I yelled out, "*Hasta luego*! I'm going to go kill this little motherfucker!" My idea was to get them all to back away until we could get back to the boat. I was getting ready to tell them that if they wanted to go home with their long-haired, ball-grabbing, bad-tattoo-sporting piece-of-shit friend, they would paddle down the beach right now. Otherwise I was going to choke him to death right here. What I didn't know was that one of their guys was paddling furiously around the back of me. He had a sheathed fishing knife between his teeth. He pulled up behind me, sat up on his board, pulled the knife out of the sheath and was getting ready to stab me in the back of the neck when I heard a loud *thwack* a few feet from my ear. I spun around to see what that noise was and saw Walter standing up on a paddleboard, holding the oar like a club. My would-be attacker was laying on his board, holding the side of his head.

"Back to the boat!" Walter yelled at us. He looked at me. "Troy, let him go!" He looked at the guy holding Rob and yelled, "You let him go or I'll find your uncle when I get back to Gigante and cut his fucking balls off!" He went on to yell a bunch of similarly graphic and disgusting threats to the other guys, followed by a lecture and admonishment. "These are nice people. This is no way to behave. This makes us all look bad. I'm ashamed to be from the same community as you boys."

"This one threw his lumber!" one of the boys yelled, pointing at Rob.

"He made a mistake!" Walter yelled. "Now he knows. You have to teach people. You don't attack them. This is no way to behave. Like a pack of wolves!" His face was red and his eyes bulged. He poked the paddle as he spoke for emphasis.

When we got back to the boat, Kai was waiting there with ice packs and Band-Aids.

—

After the session I was chilling on the hammock, running that morning's scenario through my mind a dozen times and trying out alternative endings, when someone tapped my shoulder and I nearly jumped out of my skin. "Sorry, dude," Andy said. "I just wanted to swing by on my way to work to give you this." He was holding a purple coin.

It took me a few seconds to process what was happening. I took the coin and looked at it. One side had the Serenity Prayer inscribed in cursive. The other side had the familiar triangle with "Unity, Service, Recovery" written on the three sides and "4" in the circle in the middle. Andy stood there in a t-shirt that said *Read Banned Books*, along with his usual cargo shorts and work boots. He wore a Cargill baseball hat and Oakley wraparound sunglasses, looking like he was heading to a jobsite. "I couldn't let you leave Nicaragua without a four-year coin, so I wanted to give you mine," he said.

"What? No. I can't take your coin."

Andy waved at me dismissively. "Sure you can," he said. "This is what we do, right? Pass it along to the next guy."

Overcome with emotion, I thought it'd be better not to try to talk, because I was definitely going to start crying. "Wow" was all I could croak out of my tightened throat. I studied the coin for long enough to recover from the surprise and let the emotion settle down. When I was confident I could talk, I invited Andy to stay for breakfast. He patted my shoulder and started walking off. "I'd love to, pal, but I gotta get to the job. We're building a guest house for some Bitcoin millionaire from Seattle. I gotta lay the cable before they close the walls."

I climbed out of the hammock. "Hey, before you go, let's exchange numbers. I'm leaving soon and I'd like to keep in touch."

"You already have my number," he said, walking away. "Just call me and then I'll have yours."

During our last few days, I had debated whether or not to leave with Rob and Jose. We discussed it together. They had to get home; three weeks away was already pushing the limits of their domestic and professional relationships. I had nothing to go back to. My surfing was improving, and I was making friends. I envisioned myself staying for a couple of months, establishing some roots in the area, and then splitting my time going forward. I could buy a condo or a small house here eventually, and live this life six months every year. I imagined my girls coming to visit me during school breaks. When they got married and had kids, I imagined their families vacationing with Hippie Grandpa in Central America. I loved this idea. The sober community here was strong. It was nice to have a steady stream of tourists coming through the meetings. I liked the idea of being on the other side of that equation and greeting those people, making them feel welcome and even showing them around.

The morning we were due to leave, Mike came by to see us off. We all stood in the gravel driveway in front of the lodge while the driver loaded the bags and boards into a van bound for Sandino Airport. After we shook hands, I said, "Hey, I'm thinking about staying for a while longer."

Mike laughed. "You got the bug, huh? Sure, bro, we'd love to have you. How long you thinking about staying?"

"Probably another month or two," I said. "I'm starting a new job in a few weeks, but it's completely remote, so I figure I can do it from here."

I'm pretty sure Kai had already told him I was thinking of staying longer, but Mike acted surprised and glad for the good news. "Yeah, cool, man. We definitely have room for you."

"Cool. How much would you charge me if I wanted to stay another couple of months?"

"I don't know..." he said, rubbing his beard. "We're not real booked for the next couple of months, to be honest. How about four hundred a week, and you can join any surf tours other guests are taking? But no solo runs if you're the only one in the house. Sound okay?"

That sounded perfect. Sure, I could rent a room down the beach for less, but I loved the lodge, I loved Maria's cooking, and I had become hopelessly spoiled by the surf tours. I could supplement that by running out and catching sessions on my own when there were no boats scheduled. We shook hands.

I hugged it out with Jose and Rob. I was sorry to see them go, but I was also excited. As long as those guys were around, I was on vacation but once they left, I was living my actual life in this place. I sat down on my bed later and called Roxy to tell her the news. "Okaaaay," she replied. "Three weeks wasn't enough?" This seemed to be rhetorical, because she followed it quickly by asking, "How much longer are you planning to stay?"

"I was thinking of coming back the third week of May, before you and Ceci get home for break."

"Two more months." It was a statement, not a question, so I didn't answer. "Where are you going to stay?"

"Same place," I said. "It's comfortable here."

"Sounds expensive," she commented. "Another two months at a tourist surf camp?"

"Not really," I explained. "I worked out a deal with the owner. It's actually going to be about fifty bucks a night, including my meals."

"What about travel visas and stuff like that?"

"Tourists can stay for three months. But it's pretty easy to get an extension if you apply."

I heard the clicking of a keyboard. *Was she verifying my answer?* Finally, she added, "And you think this is a good idea?"

I took a breath. It was starting to feel like I was explaining this to a mother, not a daughter. That was annoying, but I could see she was concerned, maybe even upset, about the idea. Roxy has always been a worrier. The conversation gave me a snapshot of what our relationship might look like in the future. She was going to want to take care of me once I became an old man, but she was also going to need me to make her feel that everyone and everything was safe. "Rox, listen," I said. "This is a once-in-a-lifetime chance for me. I'm having fun here. I have nothing and nobody to go home to, so why not? I'm going to hang out down here, work on my surfing, go to AA meetings, and next month I'll start my new gig. It's okay. It's totally safe here. I'm fine. It's going to be fine. I promise."

"Switch to FaceTime," she responded, suddenly hanging up on the voice call. Seconds later she called me back on FaceTime, so I answered and watched her study my face. *Jesus Christ*, I thought.

"You see?" I said, grinning like an idiot. "All in one piece. Happy, healthy, and sober."

She was standing in the kitchen of her apartment with the window behind her. She looked good. She looked skeptical as hell, but she looked healthy and put together, in a small white polo shirt and a matching headband. She walked over to her kitchen table and sat down as she scanned the screen on her phone for evidence. "Did you call Michelle?" she asked.

"No, honey."

"Maybe you should."

Jesus Christ, not this again. I was over the hurdle of making the decision to stay, and now wanted to get off the call while I was ahead. "You don't have to worry, Roxy. Michelle's not going to disappear from your life. She loves you."

Roxy laughed out loud. "Oh God, Dad, you're so fucking clueless."

"Hey, c'mon," I said with a frown.

"I'm not worried about her disappearing from my life. I talk to her almost every day. I talk to her more than I talk to you. You should call her because she loves *you*, and she's disappearing from *your* life."

"She. Left. *Me*, honey," I argued. "She's a grown woman. I have to respect her wishes. If she wanted to be with—"

"Why didn't you propose?"

"What? Where is this coming from? Did she say something to you about that?"

"Never mind."

The next call with Ceci was much easier. She laughed when I told her I was staying. "Sounds like a midlife crisis to me, dad," she said. "How do you even get around down there?" was her only question.

"I'm staying at the lodge, so they take us surfing by boat and I'm renting a dirt bike from the guy who runs the youth hostel in Popoyo," I explained.

That gave her a good laugh also. "Of course," she said. "That makes total sense."

"I'll be home in time for your spring break," I explained, although I was pretty sure she wasn't worried about it.

"Well, it sounds like you have it all figured out," she said, cracking herself up again. "Have fun at summer camp!"

I will *have fun*, I thought to myself after we hung up. I was glad that was over with, and I was glad that they both seemed okay with the plan.

—

That afternoon I ran into Andy at the Popoyo meeting and told him I was going to stay for a while. We agreed to meet up for dinner that night and I headed back to the lodge. Later that afternoon, as I was watching Netflix on my laptop, I started to feel cold. I got up and adjusted the air conditioning in my bedroom and as I walked back to my bed I felt dizzy. *Just tired*, I told myself. I closed the laptop and took a nap. When I woke up, my sheets were soaked with sweat and my head was throbbing. I had a hard time getting up to walk over to the bathroom. My joints were sore. My whole body was sore. *What the fuck?* I texted Andy and told him I wasn't feeling well and would have to bail on dinner. I ate a quick bowl of cereal out of the kitchen and went back to bed for the rest of the night.

The next day I felt even worse. Kai and Dave came over in the morning to run the surf tour. We had a young gay couple from Los Angeles in the house, Keith and Harry. They reminded me of twentysomething versions of *The Odd Couple*. I nicknamed them Oscar and Felix in my mind because one was fastidious and the other was kind of a dirty hippy. Kai knocked on my door to see if I was coming for the session. "Come in," I moaned from the bed.

"Yo, man," Kai said. "You look like shit."

I told him what was happening and he called Dave over. They agreed that I probably had a case of chikungunya, a very common virus in those parts, spread by mosquito. "It's basically like a bad flu," Dave said. They assured me that they had both had it in the past themselves and had recovered fine, and that it'd probably last another four to five days. I wasn't totally confident about getting a medical diagnosis from these two, but they sounded pretty sure; and although they were both stoned at 6 a.m. on a Monday, at least they were speaking from experience.

Andy came by that afternoon with a case of Gatorade and a bottle of Tylenol. "The good news is that you can't get it again," he informed me. "It's like chickenpox. Rest, fluids, and Tylenol." He shook the pill bottle. "I had it a few years ago. I was miserable for three or four days and then weak for another few after that. Most people get it around here. It sucks, but it's not dangerous if you're healthy." He stayed for a couple of hours and kept me company.

The following afternoon he came over with a plate of *arroz con pollo* he said his girlfriend had made. I had hung out with him several times by then and he'd never mentioned having a girlfriend before. "She's a Nica and cooks this shit like a pro," he said. The plate was covered in aluminum foil and he put it in the refrigerator for me as I sat on the sofa. "Just pop it in the microwave for two minutes when you get hungry," he instructed. He also brought me a book, which he came over and handed to me. It was a dharma book written by his guru from the soccer mom retreat center. "*Bringing the Teachings Alive*," I read aloud.

"Great shit," Andy assured me. "Scott wrote this while he was living in the monastery." That seemed industrious for a monk in a monastery, but I thanked him and promised to give it a read. He sat and gave me a breakdown of the meeting from that afternoon in Popoyo and then talked about some of the projects he was working on. After an hour or so he said he had to leave, because he was about to go broker a deal between two friends. One guy wanted to sell off a piece of his land and the other wanted to build a little vacation home. He was going to help them come to terms and navigate the local bureaucracy to make it official.

On day three he brought a big plate of empanadas and a bunch of real estate brochures. He sat down with me to point out the new developments being built in the area. "Because you seemed to be interested," he explained. I didn't remember expressing interest, but was happy for the company. He sat down at the kitchen table and fanned out the pamphlets. "This one's just north of Colorado's. The community that sits on the beach over there is called Hacienda Iguana. There's a couple of condo buildings, and lots that go anywhere from a hundred grand to five hundred, depending on how close you are to the water. This place is right next door. It's going to be a little gated community with just eight houses. You can literally walk to Iguana in ten minutes. You're surfing at Colorado in another five. Here you can buy the property and the house for two hundred grand. Check it out—look at the pictures. Nice little brand new two- and three-bedroom houses." He pulled the next pamphlet out of the stack and opened it up. "This is interesting. For my money, this is where I would buy if I were going to be here part of the year and I wanted to rent it the rest of the time. It's a new division in Santana."

"Fuck that place," I said.

Andy laughed. "I heard about your problem there."

"It was a war there, not a problem," I said. "I'm never going back there again."

He kept laughing. "Okay, fair enough," he said. "Great rental potential, but it's a warzone in the water. Non-starter."

He pulled up the last brochure. "This is the best bang for the buck," he explained. "They're building this townhouse community right down here in Amarillo." He pointed to the north. "Great mellow little surf spot there. It's going to be two clusters of eight townhouses. Each cluster has its own pool. Gated community, nice new construction, five-minute walk to the beach. They start at a hundred twenty grand. You can get an end unit loaded with every upgrade and fully furnished for a hundred sixty." He looked up to see my reaction.

It was interesting. He seemed to know his stuff. I had the sense that he was letting me know that he could and would broker a transaction for me. "Okay, cool," I said. "When I'm ready to buy something, I'll definitely let you know."

"Yeah, cool," he said. "No pressure. I just wanted to give you the lay of the land, since you have nothing but time here. I'll leave these with you so you have something to flip through."

Maybe a couple of months or a year from now, I could see buying something here, but in my mind that was still so far off as to be theoretical. I was more interested in the fact that I had made a good friend on the other side of the world who was now going out of his way to take care of me. Other than my mom, nobody in my life had ever taken care of me before.

A couple of hours later, Kai came in. He asked how I was feeling as he searched through the refrigerator. "Stoke," he said. "Where'd these empanadas come from?"

I told him to help himself. "Andy brought them over a little while ago," I explained.

Kai bit into a cold empanada and moaned. "So good," he said. "I'm starving. So, Andy keeps bringing food over here? Dude is like the wolf in 'Hansel & Gretel.' Trying to fatten you up to put you in his stew."

I looked up from my laptop. I had been busy returning emails and only half-listening. "The witch," I said.

"Huh?" Kai said, stuffing the rest of the chicken empanada into his mouth.

"In 'Hansel & Gretel,' it's a witch who fattens up Hansel, not a wolf. I think you're combining two fairy tales." *That kind of thing probably happens a lot when you smoke the amount of weed this kid does,* I thought.

Kai chuckled. "Right—the witch. My bad." He plucked another one off the plate and then covered it up with foil and put it back in the refrigerator, holding the empanada in his mouth to free up his hands. "Yo, it's probably none of my business," he said as he chewed the second empanada. I looked up from my laptop again, starting to get annoyed. I guess he saw the look on my face and said, "Never mind."

"No, go ahead," I said. "Please. What were you going to say?"

"I don't know."

Now I was getting really annoyed. "Just say it," I said.

"Dude is coming over here like every day to bring you food and books and magazines and shit. Didn't you just meet this dude like a few weeks ago? My dad wouldn't even take care of me like that."

I looked back at my computer so that I didn't have to look at Kai. I didn't answer. I didn't think I owed him an answer. It wasn't really a question anyway. Nobody ever took care of me. I took care of myself and I took care of other people. That was my dynamic to other humans in the world. It was nice to have someone give a shit. Calling him a wolf or a witch for being a good friend sounded weirdly hostile to me. Why do people have to question other peoples' motives when they do nice things? When people do terrible things, we assume they're terrible people. Why isn't the reverse true?

In any case, Andy and I ended up getting pretty close by the end of the week. I felt close, anyway. Aside from the daily visits, we had an ongoing text dialogue. "Are you reading about this Covid shit?" he asked one day. "Be glad you have chikungunya and not that shit." I was sitting around in bed all day long, so yeah, I was reading a lot about it. There had been just a couple cases in all of Nicaragua so far, nothing like what had already happened in the US, and there still hadn't been a single case in our area of the country.

On day five I went for a surf. I was feeling better, but still pretty exhausted. I was just really bored by then. The surf was small that day, so I figured I'd just go paddle around and take it easy. Twenty minutes into the session I realized that I'd made a mistake. In my condition, I was a danger to myself and the people around me. I paddled back to the boat and hung out with Walter until the other two guests—a husband and wife from Germany—were finished, then we headed back to the camp.

I slept for a few hours after I got back and then rode the dirt bike down to the San Juan Del Sur meeting. I ran into Barry there and told him about my morning. "Yeah, dude, you gotta chill a little while longer," was his advice.

I agreed. "It's just hard to sit around and do nothing for days and days on end."

"Yeah, I get that," Barry said. He rubbed the stubble on his cheek for a moment and then said, "Hey, why don't you . . . I have some fishing charters scheduled this week. I could use some company and a little help, if you feel like coming along."

"Guests from the hotel?" I asked.

"Yeah, man. That's my gig."

So for the next three days, Barry picked me up at the dock in San Juan Del Sur at 8 a.m. for a four-hour deep-sea fishing tour. He ran a super-chill tour. It was relaxing and fun and he was good company. The guests were all pretty cool for the most part. Barry played a great mix of music on the boat. The guests pounded beers, smoked a copious amount of weed, and had a blast.

Barry and I didn't really talk much, but along the way I turned into his de facto assistant. I know my way around boats, from my years in the Fort Lauderdale PD marine unit. I would captain while he was baiting lines.

I iced the fish, prepared bait, whatever needed to be done.

On the second day, while we were heading back—it's about an hour ride—he told me about a guy he was sponsoring. He had just done a fourth and fifth step with him. "It was pretty emotional," Barry said. "Heavy stuff. A lot of trauma. Stuff my guy did to cause trauma to others." He dunked his cigarette into a half-empty seltzer bottle. "Trauma inflicted on him, too." He was quiet for a minute. "I think it's kind of an honor when someone unburdens themselves to me." I nodded. "Have you done all your work?" he asked.

"Yeah," I said. "I did it a few years ago. I would call it a solid onceover. Did the job, you know?" Then, paraphrasing the Big Book, I added, "Had a spiritual experience sufficient to remove the obsession." I looked at him. He was stone-faced. The wind blew his long frizzy hair straight back as the boat zipped across glassy water. I couldn't see his eyes through the dark Jackie O sunglasses, but I got the sense he wasn't convinced.

"I guess maybe I left some pretty significant harms off my fourth step." I looked for some kind of reaction, but didn't get one. "I think I just wasn't ready to look at that stuff yet," I finally concluded.

"What kind of stuff?"

"I've done a lot of violence to people."

Barry guffawed and then giggled in a silly, embarrassed way. "I'm sorry," he said. "I didn't mean to laugh at you." He shook his head. "It's just . . . how the fuck did that not make it onto your harms list?"

I shrugged. "I don't know. To be honest, I kind of justified it by saying that these were shitty people and they all deserved it. Some of it was on the job. I was a police officer, so it was more or less in the line of duty. I beat the shit out of some real scumbags. Terrible people." I stopped and thought about it for a minute. I watched the water spray up off the side of the boat and then added, "My general attitude was that the world was better off for what I did. God wouldn't mind too much."

Barry looked at me and then looked back to the water ahead. "You know that's bullshit, right?" he said. "It ain't about what these *bad people* did. That's got nothing to do with you. The fourth step is about what *you* did. You gotta clean up *your* side of the street." We rode along in silence for a while and watched some seagulls that were flying alongside the boat, floating effortlessly in the wind. Then he added, "You gotta clean that shit up or it could fuck up your life."

"Yeah," I said. "I guess so."

He didn't let it go there. I never knew him to preach or lecture, and I'd never heard him do either before or since, but that morning Barry went into a pretty long monologue about how dangerous it can be for an alcoholic to go through life without processing their harms and resentments correctly. Yes, he explained, those things could "take you out," make you relapse. But ending your sober time is far from the worst-case scenario. "There's worse things than relapse, bro," he said. "Walking around with that shit in your head can ruin your life, ruin the lives of the people you love, or get you killed." He told me about friends he had had in the program back home who didn't do this part of the work thoroughly. They never picked up another drink but they fucked up their lives in other ways by staying dishonest, resentful or fearful. The bottom line seemed to be that you don't need alcohol to make huge mistakes. You just have to be the same person who fucked up his life the last time around. "Trust me," he said, "your addictions will spread sideways and you'll find a new tool for your destruction."

—

We pulled the boat into the San Juan Del Sur marina at 12:00, so we made it to the meeting a little late that day. Andy was there. We chatted for a while after the meeting and I asked him to sponsor me. "Listen, I need to do a new fourth and fifth step," I told him. "I did it a few years ago and left a bunch of stuff out. Would you mind being like a temporary sponsor and taking me through it?"

"Yeah, man," Andy said. "No problem. I'd be happy to. It'll be good for me, too. It's been a little while since

I've done serious step work. Let's do it. Why don't you get to work on writing it out and then we can meet up whenever you're ready to talk about it."

I went back to the house that afternoon and downloaded the templates for step four inventory. I spent the rest of the night writing out the harms I had left off the first time. Andy texted me that night and asked me when I wanted to meet up to start step five ("Admitted to God, to ourselves, and to another human being the exact nature of our wrongs"). I was flying through the worksheet, so I replied, "Tomorrow?"

"Love it! Strike while the iron's hot," Andy texted back. "I'll come by after breakfast. We can do some work and then hit the Popoyo meeting."

My harms list contained the following:

Jeffrey Bencoa was a meth addict who crashed a car into a streetlight during my second year on the job. That was suicide attempt number one. Suicide attempt number two was when he crawled out of the car and walked toward my partner Rick and me with a meat cleaver in his hand. Rick wanted to shoot him, but I tased him instead. A German tourist recorded the rest. Apparently, I kicked and punched him twenty-one times once he was down. I don't remember any of that.

Travis Parker was my first sergeant. He was a big, thick redneck who tormented me after he found out I was Jewish. When the department got a new shipment of tasers, he waved one at me and said, "Maybe it'll smell like Auschwitz when we start zapping everyone with these." When I saw him in the bathroom at Dicey Riley's later, we had a vicious fight. Eventually, I smashed his forehead on the porcelain sink with all of my body weight and strength. That split him open so that blood gushed down his face. Once on his hands and knees, I stomped down on the back of his neck. He hit the ground hard and went unconscious. I turned him over onto his side and propped him up against the wall. I stepped back to stomp on his face, wanting to destroy his jaw, when the door to the bathroom opened and a few guys from my squad walked in and saved us both.

James Smith was a run-of-the-mill neo-Nazi who cooked and sold meth, until he suddenly became a political figure because he was violent at the infamous "Unite the Right" rally in Charlottesville. During one of his white nationalist meetups, he tried to rape his fourteen-year-old stepdaughter. Her mother wouldn't press charges because she couldn't stand to lose the love of her life (and live-in meth dealer). On my day off, I followed his truck around until he went somewhere where there wouldn't be any cameras. As he walked up a trail to a cookout in Greenacres Freedom Park, I beat him to within an inch of his life.

Roy Petrov ran over a nine-year-old girl on a jet ski while I was working for the marine unit. The girl barely survived. He never stopped. When we got to his seventy-two-foot Azimut yacht, we saw a dent in the front of the jet ski the size of a nine-year-old girl's head. While my partners questioned the crew of the boat in the cabin, I smashed his face on the jet ski and broke his nose. Then I grabbed him, kicked his leg back, and took him down face-first onto the deck so hard, I broke the orbital bone in his eye and dislocated his shoulder. While he was down there, I got the idea that I would like to hold his head under water, so I dragged him to the edge of the swim platform and pushed his head under. I held him down there long enough for him to think he was going to die. Eventually I pulled him up and pumped the water out of his lungs. When my partners came back to check on us, I told them that a struggle had occurred when the suspect tried to escape on his jet ski, so that's what they wrote in the police report.

There were also lots of fights I had had while drunk. I had a pretty low tolerance for ignorant racist bullshit toward the end of my drinking career, and a lot of the bars I went to were frequented by Florida cops. You do the math. When I was drunk, I had a harder and harder time letting the latest Tucker Carlson discussion points slide. I had to argue, and arguments escalate quickly among arrogant, drunk cops. I can remember four that got violent, but there were probably more. There was Dominic Russo, Eric Evans, a buzzcut guy with thick glasses who had been there with a fat blonde girl, and a blonde guy in a hooded sweatshirt.

On my resentments list I included:

- Cops—lazy, entitled, insecure, racist, babies, bureaucrats. I don't know three guys who became cops to help people. They're mostly power-hungry, small-minded, angry, simple, petty, ignorant motherfuckers who have civil service work ethics. Everything is someone else's fault. They refuse all attempts at accountability. The combination of ignorance, arrogance and power is infuriating.
- Rednecks. Ignorant, angry motherfuckers.
- My father.
- Michelle, for leaving me.

Having finished my homework for step four, I went to sleep that night feeling accomplished. I said my prayers and ran through a gratitude list in my head. I was grateful for Barry and his influence. I was grateful my babies were healthy, happy and doing well in college. I was grateful my sobriety now enabled me to be the father I always wanted to be. I was grateful for being in this beautiful place with new friends. I thought about doing step five with Andy the next day and my stomach churned a little and my skin got hot. It'd be embarrassing, maybe humiliating, but growth comes from pain. Grateful for the opportunity.

Andy came by at 9:30. There were no other guests staying at Dale Daggers at the moment. We went outside to the big table on the patio. He sat down at the head of the table in the wooden armchair. He opened up his *Big Book* and read pages 72 to 75, the first three pages of the chapter entitled "Into Action." He closed the book and said, "Okay, let's hear it."

I sat on the bench, my back against the house, looking out at the Pacific. I put the pages on the table and took a big breath. "I'll start with my harms list. There's a lot of them, and a lot of violence, so . . ." I wasn't sure how to finish that sentence. "So, listen," I continued. "These harms weren't on my original step four because I really thought I was right and I was justified and they had it coming, you know . . ."

"Whoa, whoa, stop," Andy said, holding both hands up. "It doesn't matter what they did to you. It doesn't matter if they had it coming. Even if you were a hundred percent justified . . . it doesn't matter. You did harm. Right?"

For the next forty-five minutes I walked him through my harms, giving him enough detail about each story to make clear the extent of the harm I did. Several times I had to stop myself in the middle of a big explanation of why this guy had it coming and why I was in the right. Andy just kind of closed his eyes and nodded his head when I got into these explanations, as if to say, "Yeah yeah yeah, come on, get to your part."

When I finished, he said that he understood why I would leave these out of my initial steps four and five.

He said it was clear that in my mind I was justified in these actions. He didn't seem overly impressed one way or another with my stories. I didn't know if I was relieved by this or annoyed . . . or how to feel, really. I guess I expected more of a reaction. I had just told him some pretty heinous shit and he was totally poker-faced about it. He opened up his book. "This is from step ten." He searched down the page with his finger and said, "Here it is. I love this." He read:

> *It is a spiritual axiom that every time we are disturbed, no matter what the cause, there is something wrong with us. If somebody hurts us and we are sore, we are in the wrong also. But are there no exceptions to this rule? What about justifiable anger? If somebody cheats us, aren't we entitled to be mad? For us of A.A. these are dangerous exceptions. We have found that justified anger ought to be left to those better qualified to handle it.*

"In other words," Andy said, "What other people do is none of our business. You need to keep your side of the street clean. You are responsible for your actions, not theirs. That's the only thing you can control. You need to do the next right thing. Ask yourself, what would God have you do in this situation? His will be done, not yours. God doesn't need hitmen. He needs people acting as He would. With compassion and forgiveness."

I had read this section several times before and always liked it. I wasn't entirely sure about Andy's interpretation, but his point was generally valid and correct. I nodded.

"These people who you hated were sick and suffering. You should treat them like sick people. If they had cancer, you wouldn't want to beat the shit out of them, right?" He closed his step book and opened up his *Big Book*. He flipped through until he found what he was looking for. "Here, page sixty-six. This is from 'How it Works,' which is the chapter that deals with step four." He read:

> *This was our course: We realized that the people who wronged us were perhaps spiritually sick. Though we did not like their symptoms and the way these disturbed us, they, like ourselves, were sick too. . . .*

> *We avoid retaliation or argument. We wouldn't treat sick people that way. If we do, we destroy our chance of being helpful. We cannot be helpful to all people, but at least God will show us how to take a kindly and tolerant view of each and every one.*

He closed the book. "It doesn't say, 'God give me the strength to split their heads open,'" and he laughed. "Right?"

Again, I smiled and nodded. "Sure," I said, "I get the point."

We never got to my resentments that morning. In the back of my mind, I knew they were on the next page, but we had covered a lot of ground already and I figured that was enough for one day. We could cover those next time. Andy handed me a sheet of paper he had been jotting notes on while I talked. "This is a list of character defects I heard when you were telling your stories," he said. As I was reading through it, he told me I did a great job, and mentioned how impressed he was with my honesty and willingness.

The list said:

- Wrath/Anger (fear), selfishness, violence
- Judgmental, Wrath/Anger (fear), Pride, self-centeredness, violence
- Judgmental, Wrath/Anger (fear), Pride + dishonesty, selfishness, self-centeredness, violence
- Judgmental, Wrath/Anger (fear), Pride + dishonesty, selfishness, self-centeredness, violence
- Judgmental, Wrath/Anger (fear), Pride, violence

These looked pretty serious to me, but his tone and his compliments undercut the weight. He saw that I was still focused on the page and added, "Yeah, so when you go on to do your step six and seven work, you can focus on these character defects," he explained. That was it? Focus on them and I would be a new man?

I looked at him and then back down at the page of character defects. "This looks pretty serious," I said. I was glad to be done with the step five confession, but these notes looked like the character defects of a really fucked-up person. It was unsettling. I was holding the sheet of paper with both hands and looking at Andy for guidance.

"Hey, listen," he said. "This was you in the past. This was years ago, right?" He didn't wait for me to answer. "You're sober now. You're a different person." He was nodding and making a face that said *trust me, I know what I'm talking about.* "We were all fucked up before we came into the program. Four years of sobriety. That's amazing. It's a miracle. You've changed."

It seemed like he was letting me off the hook pretty easily, but then again that was the whole point of this, and he seemed sure. That's why you tell your harms to another person, because you're likely to either let yourself off the hook too easily or swing the opposite direction and beat yourself up too badly. "You don't have to behave like that anymore," he said.

In hindsight, it probably would've been more appropriate for him to at least put these statements in the form of questions, i.e., *Do you think you've changed since then? Do you feel like the same person who did these*

things? How do you feel about these harms? None of
that. He acted as if the confession was the only point.
That was not my understanding of how it works. I'm
supposed to work on the character defects that caused
me to do these harms in steps six and seven, and then
make amends for them in eight and nine. Andy was
absolving me from the next four steps, but I wasn't
looking for absolution and he didn't have that power.

Plus, when I told Andy about these harms, they
sounded very different in my head than when I had written
them out the night before. The night before I was still
the good guy in these stories. Sure, my behavior might
have been bad, but my intentions were good and I was just
expressing them in a negative way. When I heard them out
loud in front of another person and then read his reaction
to them, I saw myself as a dangerously sanctimonious
motherfucker. I didn't know how much of this behavior
had changed in the years since these things happened,
and how much I had changed since getting sober, but
these were terrible harms. Not just for the violence, but
for the hate and anger I was bringing into the world.
People who didn't measure up to my value system were
not deserving of basic humanity. They were to be struck
down by my righteous hand. I was really fucked up.

I folded his list in fours and put it in my pocket,
resolving to address this more thoroughly in the near
future.

10

New York
1988

When I was a teenager and my mom was acting crazy and annoying me, I nurtured a fantasy that my dad would come and rescue me. He would realize he had made a mistake. He would show up and apologize and we would get to know each other for a while and then he would ask me if I would like to come and live with him. He would sweep me up and get me out of that shitty apartment and take me to a beautiful house like the one we used to live in together. We would have a swimming pool and a refrigerator stocked with name-brand food. I went to sleep hundreds of nights thinking through the details of how this could happen.

During my dad's first run in the brokerage business in the '80s, I didn't know what he did exactly, but I knew that it made him rich. This meant that the handful of times I saw him, he was driving a convertible Mercedes, and that he put hundred-dollar bills in my birthday cards every year instead of tens or twenties. It seemed to also mean that my mom got her child support payments on time and in full, because we had a car during this period and she didn't work at restaurants on the weekends.

After the Black Monday stock market crash in 1987, he was missing in action for a while, and my mom let me know that he had gone broke because of something called "margin calls." I was in ninth grade. The following Monday I asked my econ teacher what a margin call was and how it could make someone go broke. I got an earful.

Lacrosse was the official religion of Manhasset. I had started playing in fourth grade, which was already considered a lost cause there, way too late. The other kids were playing year-round starting in kindergarten. But I was bigger, faster, stronger and more athletic than anyone else in town, so I caught up quickly and was stomping the shit out of them by middle school. Lacrosse and school were 99% of my life. I worked as hard as I could at both. In hindsight I think these were my first addictions, meaning that they were things outside of me that I was able to lose myself in. I focused all my energy, time, thinking and planning into academics and lacrosse. It distracted me from what was going on in my head. I was pretty much a robot.

Even though I outperformed 95% of my classmates in school, and all of them on the field, I always felt *less than*. We were Jews living in an almost entirely

Christian town. We were broke and living among millionaires. My friends' dads were captains of finance, while my dad was a disappearing act and a criminal. My friends' parents employed drivers to take them around town. I rode my bike. My friends wore Ralph Lauren. My clothes were from Walmart. My friends' moms went to exercise classes, lunched at the club and drove Range Rovers. My mom was a secretary and a bartender and crazy as a loon.

The truth is that I was not deprived. We had everything I ever needed. I never skipped a meal in my life. I slept in a comfortable and safe bed every night, and I never doubted for a second that my mom loved me. As a teenager it was impossible to keep that in perspective. On the lacrosse field I was a machine. I developed the ability to shut off my brain and let my body do what it was trained for: brutality. I hurt people all the time. Once I shut off my mind I had zero empathy. During games I would go so deeply into this zone, I often couldn't remember the details of the game afterward. I would watch it on film as if it was the first time.

My dad was still broke by the time I finished high school, but it didn't really matter because I was heavily recruited. I was at the top of my class academically and I was one of the top twenty-five lacrosse prospects in the country. I visited Yale and Princeton but decided to attend UVA because Jim Adams, the head coach, told me that I would start as a freshman, plus I was more than a little bit intimidated by the Ivy League blue blood types at the other places. I didn't need four more years of feeling less than. I got a full scholarship and enrolled as a biomedical engineering major.

My freshman year I carried on with extreme focus. The academics were brutal in my major. During my first semester I studied as much as I could, considering the demanding training and practice schedule, but at the end of the semester I could only pull out a 3.5 GPA. I got the first two Bs of my life and it was a huge shock to my system. It would be hard to overstate how upsetting it was to not be at the top of my class. It shook me. I didn't realize how much being academically elite was part of my identity until I finished a semester in the middle of the pack. It was disorienting and depressing.

I lost sleep and I had no appetite, both of which were big problems for an athlete. Coach Adams asked me to see him in his office one day after practice to ask me what was going on. He could see that I had lost a step. Coach was a retired marine. He played lacrosse for the Naval Academy and then did a bunch of combat tours around the globe. He still wore a flat top haircut and his sweatsuit was ironed, tucked and fitted like a uniform. He was fifty pounds over his service weight, but his arms and his chest were stacked. He was pushing sixty at the time, and I would have hated to have to fight him.

Coach was not a warm and fuzzy man, but I knew that he loved his players. He pushed us hard and honestly past our limits at times, but I could tell that he loved us.

You can't fake that. Plus, I always thought that he liked me.

Coach had been at the helm at Virginia for twelve-years when I got there, but his office looked like he had just moved in. There were no decorations, no pictures on the white painted cinder block walls, no curtains on the windows. He didn't even have any photos. He had a legal pad and a pen neatly placed in the middle of his desk. A few binders were lined up symmetrically beside them. The jacket from his sweatsuit was neatly folded on the back of his chair when he sat down and pointed to the chair across from him. "Have a seat, Troy," he said.

I sat down and searched his face for a moment, trying to find some clues about what was coming. I couldn't tell if I was in trouble or if I was there for some kind of pep talk.

"Tell me what's going on with you," he said. "You're dragging your ass around the field lately and you don't look like the guy I know. Your body language sucks."

I felt ridiculous, but he asked, so I told him. "I got a couple of Bs," I said. "One in Differential Equations and one in Engineering Mechanics. They wrecked my GPA. I finished the semester with a 3.5."

He waited to see if I was done and then nodded his head and closed his eyes for a moment to absorb what I had said. "Listen here, Troy," he said. "You're a competitor. There's nothing wrong with that. There's nothing wrong with being upset about getting those B's. You've been an A student your whole life, haven't you?"

"Yes, sir," I said, and at this point I was trying extremely hard not to cry.

"Let me ask you one question, son," he said. "Did you try your hardest in those classes?"

I drew in a deep breath through my nose and held it for a second or two before answering. *I am not fucking crying in my coach's office about my grades.* "Yes, sir. I did."

"Good," he said. "That's good. Then you did your job. You are responsible for the effort in this world, son. God is responsible for the outcome." He sat and looked at me as though a response was called for.

I nodded.

"Are you telling me that you gave it 100%?"

I nodded and sucked more air in through my nose, holding my breath.

"Then let it hurt for as long as it wants to hurt and then get back to work," he concluded. "You understand?"

"Yes, sir," I said. "Thank you, sir." I made it all the way back to my dorm room and closed the door behind me before I bawled my eyes out.

I didn't realize it at the time, but I had been starving for fatherhood back then. Yes, I was genuinely twisted about the grades, but the attention and guidance that

I got from Coach Adams that afternoon was like a meal for a starving man. That came out in the tears also.

Our team finished sixth in the nation, losing in the first round of the NCAA tournament to Towson that year. We entered the tournament as the three seed. Towson was ranked tenth. They beat us in triple overtime 14-13 in the Carrier Dome in Syracuse. I have never in my life been more physically exhausted than I was after that game. I ran my lungs out, scored four goals and probably played the best overall game of my life.

On the other side of the field was a midfielder for Towson named Rob Steck. I was selected as second team All American as a midfielder. I was the first All American freshman in UVA history. Rob was also an All-American midfielder and he was voted Midfielder of the Year. He was a junior from Westchester, NY, and I had played against him in some tournaments in high school. There was no way in the world that I was going to let him outplay me. I always gave it my all, but that day I went insane. Thankfully, it was televised and recorded so that I could rewatch it later because I had almost no recollection of what happened. It was purely action, reaction and blind fury.

Towson went on to lose to North Carolina in the finals. They had a magical season. We were disappointed to go home after the first round, but it was my freshman campaign. I assumed that this was a speed bump on the way to greater glory.

As it turned out, that was the last lacrosse game that I would ever play. In hindsight, it was the last game of any kind that I would ever play as a kid. Life was about to kick me down the stairs into adulthood.

11

Nicaragua
2020

The next day, Barry and I had a charter with a father and son from New York. The father was a small bald corporate lawyer who was dressed in designer golf wear. The kid was ten years old and wore a Knicks jersey and a Mets cap. I liked them immediately. They were genuine and friendly, but we didn't talk much. They were in their own orbit.

"It's nice," Barry said to me, out of nowhere, following an extended period of quiet. We were on the stern while they fished on the bow. He smiled as he watched them interact. They moved in sync. They laughed at each other's jokes. "Real love," he added.

I agreed. It was wonderful to watch, but I was more interested in Barry at that point. I had known him for over a month, but for whatever reason, at that moment it occurred to me that I wasn't sure whether I knew him at all. I had been in his company dozens of times, we had many conversations, I knew the story of his life more or less, so I knew all *about* him. In terms of who he was as a person, or what makes him click, as people say, all I knew was that he seemed to spend his whole life helping other people. It was all I ever saw him do. It's all I ever really heard him talk about. I guess I realized that I must be missing something, because I was missing everything else.

"What's your story?" I suddenly asked him.

He turned to me. "Hmmm?" He was wearing one of his floral tank tops and a green baseball cap that probably should have been thrown out five years back. He looked at me through his oversized women's sunglasses. "What's up?"

I wasn't even sure what I meant, but I continued. "You're like the fucking Buddha," I said. "What is that? I don't understand."

He laughed. "I'm not sure I understand either," he said. "What are you asking me?"

We sat in silence for a while, watching the father and son, the sea, each other. I flipped through the Spotify playlist on Barry's phone to change the music a couple of times. Finally, the words came to me. "It just seems like maybe you're not real." Barry nodded. He waited for me to continue. "Tell me something bad about you. Tell me something you do that doesn't involve helping other people or *practicing the principles in all your affairs.*" I said this last part like it was an annoying character flaw.

He nodded some more and seemed to be thinking it over. "I used to be a bad dude," he said. "You wouldn't want to know me when I was on the streets. All I did was lie, cheat and steal."

I interrupted. "Yeah, but what about now?"

He held up a hand, as if to say *Chill bro, I was just getting to that.* "Now I just annoy people." I sat down in the passenger seat and waited for him to continue. He asked me, "Do you know how many long-term friendships I have in my life? Shit, relationships of any kind, for that matter?" I shook my head. "Zero." He climbed into the captain's chair and sat down. "People use me. They either dismiss me because of how I look or they get tired of being around me pretty fast."

"Why?" I asked. That didn't make sense to me. I thought he was awesome. I hoped we would be friends for life.

"I think I'm what's called an empath," he explained. "Do you know what that is?"

"Yeah, kind of," I answered.

He nodded. "Yeah, so, since I got clean and spiritual and shit, I feel other people's emotions all the time. I can't help it. It's kind of a curse, you know? I feel their pain and my gut says I have to help. I have to pass along my gifts. *I have to.* You hear me? The serenity.

It's a compulsion." He grabbed his cigarettes, popped one out and lit it. He took a drag and let a long stream out from his nose. "They usually take a little bit of it, and they're sometimes grateful, but then they're like, alright bro, that's about enough of that. Get out of my head. Go fuck off. Leave me alone already."

He went on to describe his life to me in painful detail. It was a solitary life. He was friendly with lots of people, he had helped hundreds, but he had nobody who was close. "After a little while, people are just like, come on Barry, enough of the spiritual shit. Just act normal for a minute so we can hang out and relax and have fun. Nobody wants to hang out with Saint Fuckin' Barry. Ain't no fun."

He told me about two instances when people wanted to be close with him or wanted to be his friend. "They were both nuts," he said. "Psycho or narcissists or whatever. I'm not trained in that shit so I don't know what to call it, but they just needed someone to babysit them for life. That ain't friendship."

I suddenly felt real compassion for him. "I'm sorry to hear that," I said. "That sounds really hard."

He shrugged. "Yeah, dude. Everybody got somethin' wrong with their life. Normal people—like, sane people—befriend me and then they move on when I've served their purpose. For whatever reason, I'm a friend you make but not a friend you keep."

I imagined that if Barry had lived in India a thousand years ago, people would travel hundreds of miles to visit his cave and get advice or spiritual cures. Then they would say thanks and leave him alone in his cave. Maybe they would leave a gift or an offering behind. Nobody ever wondered if the monk in the cave was lonely. They just ditched him and went back to their lives. Nobody wanted to hang out with the swami from the cave. He smelled bad and it was embarrassing to introduce him to your friends back home in the village.

12

Virginia
1991

After the loss to Towson, I was at a party in Charlottesville with my teammates. Kirk Lawson was my best friend at the time. He was a stocky sophomore defenseman from the Baltimore area. He came over to me and said, "Hey, bro. There's somebody I want you to meet." He turned and extended his hand to a pretty blonde girl who was about a foot shorter than me. "This is Lisa White. She's Alison's sister at *Alpha Chi*."

Lisa looked up at me and smiled. "Nice to meet you, Troy." She had a heavy rural Virginia accent and it made her short blonde hair, bright blue eyes and full lips seem exotic. We didn't have girls like that in Long Island. "I heard you played an amazing game in Syracuse. The guys over there were going on and on about it."

"Thank you," I said. "I really tried."

"Where are you from?" she asked.

"New York," I said. I never told people that I was from Long Island. New York sounded much better. Before she could reload with the usual follow-up question, I asked, "What about you?"

"I'm from Westham," she said. "About an hour from here." Kirk later told me that she was lying. She actually grew up in Crestview, another suburb. Apparently, Westham was a better known, more affluent town.

I went over to get some punch and she followed, so I got one for each of us. Then I went to talk to some guys from the team. She followed me there, also. She never left my side and she laughed at almost everything I said. After a couple of hours, I looked at my watch and told her, "I'm going to head back to the dorms."

She smiled and said, "I'm coming with you," and then she practically lived in my room until we went home for winter break.

I returned every third or fourth call after we went home in May. When she didn't take the hint, I told her that we were done. Three weeks later, she called me. I didn't answer, so she left a message on my answering machine. "Now listen, Troy," she said. "I know you don't want to be with me and that's fine. I'm just calling to let you know I'm pregnant and I haven't been with no one but you in quite a while. Don't get all upset and don't think you have to *do* anything. I don't want anything from you and I don't need anything. I'm going to take a break from school and move in with my sister Eleanor in Florida. She'll help me with the baby and she says she can get me a job as a bank teller at the same branch as her. I just thought you should know, is all. I really liked you, Troy, and I hope you have a nice, happy life. I mean it. No hard feelings, okay? Okay, bye now."

I called her right back. "Lisa, please," I said. "I'm begging you. Please consider having an abortion."

"We don't do that in my family, Troy. And besides, I really want this baby. With your genes and mine I think she'll be real pretty and smart. I don't really like college that much and I'd just as soon get my life started in Florida with Eleanor. I'm excited about it." She told me again about the bank teller job. I couldn't imagine anyone being excited about a bank teller job.

"I'm begging you, Lisa. Please. I'll do anything.'

"Oh boy," she said, and I could hear that she had walked outside. "This doesn't have to have anything to do with you, Troy. Go live your life. I want to start my family and my career," she insisted. "I want to live my life."

I slammed down the phone and tore the cable out of the wall. I stood in the kitchen of our apartment, squeezing it with all my might, strangling it. "This can't be happening," I said. It calmed me a bit, so I kept repeating it.

When my mom got home, I sat down on the sofa in our den and told her what was happening. "It's just so far outside my plan," I said. "I've worked tirelessly all my life to try to follow a certain path to success. To a great career and . . . and a life. How can I go on to have that life with this? With a child out in the world that's mine that I have nothing to do with? I'd be . . ." I could barely get the words past my teeth it was so disgusting. "I'd be just like Dad."

"Troy," my mother said. She was standing with her hands on her hips. Her face was getting redder by the minute. She was waiting for me to finish so she could get out what she was dying to say.

"There's nothing worse than that. There's no life that I want less than his life . . ."

"Troy," she tried to interrupt.

"But I don't love her, Mom," I said. I thought about it for a moment. "I don't even like her very much."

"Troy!" She couldn't hold it in anymore. She tore into me like I had never heard before. "If that dumb bitch wants to fuck up her life, that has nothing to do with you," she said, pointing at me with a finger that trembled with fury. Now she stabbed the air with the finger, emphasizing each word with its own stab. "She. Doesn't. Have. Your. Upside!" She spit when she yelled it. She paced back and forth in front of our coffee table. I'd never seen her so irate. "She isn't giving up anything to go do this! She's going to go live her white-trash life the same way she always was going to. This changes *nothing* for her. Don't you even think about fucking up your life, swooping down there and 'making an honest woman' of this fool."

But that's exactly what I did. After a month of painful soul-searching, I decided my first impulse was correct. The worst thing I could possibly turn into in this world would be my father. I researched careers I could start without a degree and discovered I could get hired as a corrections officer with the Broward County Sheriff's Office at the age of nineteen. Since all I wanted was to be the opposite of my dad, working in law enforcement seemed nicely antithetical.

We got married at the city clerk's office and moved into a two-bedroom rental in Coconut Creek. We lived on a street called Cocoplum Circle. I was immediately embarrassed by the name. It seemed idiotic and effeminate. Coconut Creek was halfway between Fort Lauderdale and Boca Raton. The community we lived in was called Advenir at Cocoplum. It was a mix of low-rise condominium buildings and attached townhouses. The townhouses were built in a loop around a man-made lake while the condo buildings were set up in a cluster at the rear of the property. We started in a condo and moved a couple of years later into a townhouse.

All of the buildings were freshly painted taupe and tan. The condo buildings were taupe with tan accents. The townhouses were painted tan with taupe accents. They had a small clubhouse that was mostly used by retirees to play cards, a fitness room that had the dimensions and equipment of a hotel gym, and a big lagoon-style community swimming pool. When the realtor drove us through for the first time, the phrases that repeated in my mind were: cookie cutter, sterile, clean, and standard issue.

Lisa had a different experience. Through a big smile, she said it was perfect. "When I daydream about what life with you and the baby will look like, it's in a place just like this." She described it as safe, clean, new and fresh. "I can just picture myself pushing the stroller along the sidewalk, down to the pool, and then sitting out with some other moms for a Saturday morning coffee chat."

Our ground floor unit had white linoleum floors, white particleboard cabinets, and beige Formica countertops. There was an open floor plan so that the kitchen flowed into the dining room and then down one step into the den. At the rear of the unit was a sliding glass door that opened onto a concrete patio and looked out across the man-made lagoon and more taupe and tan units across the way.

The townhouse had the same setup, except it was a couple hundred square feet larger and the two bedrooms were upstairs. I assembled all the IKEA furniture myself and we hung framed prints of black-and-white Ansel Adams photos on the walls. The girls' bedroom was elaborately decorated with a Disney princess theme. It was painted pink and turquoise. There were bookshelves filled with toys, trinkets, baskets full of dolls, doll clothes and accessories, a row of picture books, and a row of nighttime reading books. The curtains were Disney princess-themed.

The rest of Coconut Creek was mostly strip malls and other gated communities like ours. All the shopping centers followed the same formula: one or two big-box retailers, one or two chain restaurants, and the rest a mixture of franchises and local stores. There were more than twenty churches in Coconut Creek's twelve square miles. It felt like a middle-class suburban hellhole.

—

I transferred my credits to Florida Atlantic University and started a part-time bachelor's degree program in Electrical Engineering as I attended the academy. On February 12, 1992, Roxanne was born. I would love for this to be the point in the story where I grew up quickly to be the best dad I could be, but that didn't happen. I was young, selfish, angry, but mostly scared. I was scared of not getting all the things I ever wanted, and I was scared of what was going to happen to my little family. Those were my dominant feelings each day.

I badly wanted to be a good father. Not just because I had had a bad one, but because I loved Roxy. I have never loved anyone more. But I traded my life and my future for her, and as much as I wanted it to, that idea never went away. I know that nobody asked me to do it, least of all her. I didn't resent her. I adored her. I had deep resentment for my situation.

She was sweet and pretty. She smiled easily and often. She was an easy baby and a wonderful kid. She did everything well from the time she was in diapers, sleeping, eating and pooping like clockwork. In school she was conscientious about her work, thoughtful and kind with her friends, forgiving and understanding toward her crazy parents. She was beautiful to look at and easy to be with.

My worst nightmare turned out to be my greatest blessing.

13

Nicaragua
2020

I was about fifteen minutes into the movie *City Slickers* on Netflix one night when there was a knock at the door. In the movie, the three middle-aged friends from New York had just arrived at the cattle ranch and were getting ready for their big adventure. It was hard not to project Rob, Jose and me into these roles, and I was looking forward to watching the film. We didn't get many unannounced visitors at the surf camp, so I was kind of surprised and a little annoyed. There weren't any other guests at the house, so the knock was probably for me. As I walked over to the door, I remembered that Mike paid a security guard to walk around the property all night, so the guest was probably someone known to the house. *Unless they managed somehow to miraculously slip past the two-dollar-an-hour guard*, I thought.

"Hey, bro," Andy said when I opened the door.

"Hey," I said, a little taken aback. It was kind of weird of him to just pop in. *No text? No call?*

"Mind if I come in for a minute?" he asked.

"Yeah, of course," I said. "Come on in."

We went over to the sofas in the living room and sat across from each other. I closed my laptop. "What's up?" I asked.

Andy sat on the edge of the sofa across from me. His t-shirt, which read *Pray, Believe, Repeat*, was soiled and ripped. His green cargo shorts were dirty also. It looked like he'd been rolling on the ground. *Fighting?* I wondered. We exchanged pleasantries quickly, but he looked like a man who had something on his mind. He sat with his palms pressed together in a prayer pose and his eyes closed for a moment, as though he was trying to find the right words. "What's up, man?" I repeated.

"Okay," he said, opening his eyes. "Here's the situation." We sat, looking at each other silently for another moment as he continued to put it together in his mind. "I'm going to grab some water," he said, and got up to walk over to the cooler in the kitchen. I watched him walk away, and spotted some dried blood on the back of his neck. *Did that drip down from his head?* It was hard to tell because his hair was dry, but what else could it be?

"Dude," I said. "Out with it."

"Yeah," he said as he filled his glass. "Okay. You know my business, right?" It was kind of a nonsensical question, but I nodded to try to move things along. He took a drink of water. "Well, in my business, as I'm sure you know, I have to spread around some cash from time to time for the authorities." He walked back over and stood behind the sofa. "Sometimes they're cool and they're happy with a couple of bucks here and there, and sometimes they think they're entitled to more. They want to be partners with me in certain situations when we're developing . . . selling and developing properties."

"Okay," I said. "I get the concept. Fast-forward to the end, please."

He nodded. "Well, today, two of Nicaragua's finest walked onto my jobsite and informed me that my payments were past due. I figured I would give them a hundred bucks and they would fuck off, but no." He came around and sat down again on the sofa. "They wanted ten grand."

"For what?" I asked. "That seems . . . extreme."

Andy took a drink of water and nodded. He closed his eyes. "I know this is going to sound fucked up," he said. "But I'm not even sure what it's for."

I sat back and crossed my arms, turning on the sofa to face him squarely. "Yes, that does sound strange."

"I know. I know. But here's the thing," he said. He held his water in one hand and seemed to orchestrate a small symphony with his other as he explained. "I have so many of these fucking jobs going on at once, and

I have so many of these projects I'm trying to get into development, that I honestly can't keep track of who owes what. So, for example, I have three parcels I'm trying to sell right now. I have this Australian dude who paid for one of them and wants to build. So after I sell the land . . . I'm an intermediary, mind you. I don't own the land. I'm just taking a commission on the deal and will help build the house. Right? So after I sell the land, these motherfuckers tell me they want half the proceeds. How am I going to give them half the proceeds when I'm taking a ten-percent commission? They're fucking retarded. So we go back and forth and they smack the shit out of me in the street one day and I give them half my commission. Done deal, right?

"A month later they come around asking for the rest of the money. Like they have amnesia. Then these guys today tell me that if I want to build this extension, it's going to cost me ten grand. The whole fucking job is forty grand. I'll be lucky to make ten out of it myself. We argue. They fucking pistol-whip me and kick me once I'm on the ground. They tell me they'll kill me if I don't get them ten grand by midnight tonight."

I listened to all of this almost without blinking. It was a mesmerizing performance. It sounded to me like a web of purposely confusing half-truths. "So you need ten thousand dollars?" I asked.

"Yes."

"Or else they'll kill you. Tonight."

"Probably not," he said. "They always say stuff like that." He sat back and ran both hands through his hair. "But they'll definitely kick the shit out of me again."

"These are police officers?"

Andy laughed. "Yeah. Listen. All the cops down here take bribes, right? A few bucks on traffic stops or if you're walking around drunk in town. That's normal. These two work for the team that runs this area. They're the muscle for the biggest local politicians. The local politicians roll up to the big guys who run the country. These two are fucking animals."

"Don't you have any money?" I asked. "It seems like you have a very successful business."

"Yeah," he said. "Of course. And Monday, when the bank opens, I can get more. I have twenty-eight hundred bucks in my Jeep right now. I just need some help to buy me a day or two to scrounge up the rest."

"Wow," I answered. "I don't know what to say."

"Look, Troy," he said. "We haven't known each other for that long, but I've been straight with you, right? I've done right by you. I've helped you in every way I know how whenever you've needed something. Right?"

"Yeah, but it seems like you're leveraging that to manipulate me into giving you ten thousand dollars … which I don't have, by the way. Why the fuck would I? Who travels with ten grand in cash?"

Andy sat up straight and held his chest as if I had wounded him. "I'm not *leveraging* you," he said. "I'm not *conning* you." He held his arms out and his palms up. "I'm asking you for help. As a friend. As a fellow sober man who no doubt has been in tight spots himself."

Wow, I thought. It seemed pretty low to throw my sobriety into the mix. I wanted to get to the end of this conversation as fast as possible. "Okay, look," I said. "I have about three grand in the safe in my room. I took it out to pay Mike the rent in cash each week. I can give you that, but you have to give it back to me before my rent is due next Saturday."

"Yes, of course," he said. "Thanks, man. I really appreciate the help."

I went into my bedroom and came back with the money. I handed it to him and said, "You're living dirty, Andy. You may not be drinking, you may be going to meetings, but all of this dishonesty is going to catch up with you."

He nodded and slapped the small stack of cash into his hand. "You're right," he said. "I need to work on that."

I walked him to the door. On the way, I added, "This is the last time, okay?"

"Yeah, of course," he said.

I grabbed him by the shoulder and spun him around so that we were face to face at close range. "No," I said. "Seriously. Don't bring me into your shit again. I don't want any trouble down here."

He nodded and said, "Got it." He opened the door and stepped out to the front of the house. I stepped out behind him to watch him walk through the outer gate. When he opened the gate, I saw two Nicaraguan police officers in their neat blue uniforms. We made eye contact for a moment and I thought I saw the taller one smile at me before Andy closed the gate behind him.

14

Florida
1993

Jon Adelson was the only one I could really connect with at work. He was a skinny little Jewish guy from Staten Island who moved down to Florida at the age of nineteen, just like me. We worked together in the prison for two years. Jon was the one who gave me the nickname that stuck throughout my law enforcement career. It started when our sergeant ordered us to search a cell one night. The two inmates decided they'd rather fight. One of them grabbed Jon and smashed him into the concrete wall, knocking him unconscious. I didn't have time to call for backup. They swarmed on Jon, who was folded on himself against the wall. Jon was my only friend at work. He was actually my only friend in Florida. When I saw him go down and get stomped, I lost it. My mind switched off and I have no memory of what happened for the next few minutes. By the time backup arrived, one of the convicts was lying unconscious with blood flowing from an open gash on his forehead. The other was doubled over with a bunch of broken ribs and a busted jaw.

Jon had a concussion, cracked ribs and a black eye. He got a bunch of stitches in the back of his head, but he healed up fine. When I went to visit him in the prison infirmary he yelled out, "There he is! The Big Hurt!" The name stuck. For the rest of my tenure, I was known as Hurt Martin. After each of my violent outbursts on the job, the name gained new life. For months after each incident, guys at work, when they passed me in the hallways or when they saw me at the gym, would say, "What's up, Hurt?" It was used so widely, I think some of the guys actually thought my name was Hurt Martin.

A year later, we were sitting at the bar at Dicey Riley's. It was our first week on the job as cops for the city of Fort Lauderdale. The move was a big pay raise and it got us onto the day shift. Jon held his palm up to my face. "Hurt, do me a favor and take a breath," he said. "Drink your fucking beer." An hour after our shift had ended, Dicey Riley's was in full swing. There was still a bit of sunlight coming through the glass door and front windows, but the place was mostly lit with the strings of Christmas lights that never came down. It was a creepy vibe until you had a few drinks. Then it became cozy. It was the same with the smell. After a while, you kind of accepted it and then it was comforting.

I did as I was told and took a big swig. "Fucking Christ," he said. "You've done nothing but complain since we walked in here."

"I have not," I argued. "All I'm saying is that in both jobs, we've worked with animals on all sides. The other hacks and cops are stupid, small-minded, angry motherfuckers, and then we have the inmates and violent felons on the other side. It's a very unhealthy environment."

"Dude," Jon argued, "you are not one of the inmates. You signed up for it. You're there voluntarily. They pay you to do this work. If you hate it so much, go do something else." It was a stupid thing to say. He knew that wasn't an option for me. At least not at the moment. I needed the job. I needed the benefits. He was just sick of listening to me bitch.

"Think about the guys we're friends with," I persisted. I started counting them on my fingers. "Pete. Good guy. Right? But he's a huge fucking racist." I peeled back finger number two. "Steve. Great guy. We all love him. But he's a violent fucking psycho." Jon raised his eyebrows and nodded. He had to give me those two. "Roger. Good dude. Mostly, you know. If you're his friend. If not, he's an ignorant, arrogant prick."

Jon shrugged and nodded. "Yeah, so what?"

"And that's the guys we're *friends* with! The other guys have no redeeming qualities at all."

Jon drained the rest of his Budweiser and started waving two fingers at the bartender to get another round. "How does Lisa like staying home?" he asked, trying to change the subject.

I finished my beer. "I don't know, dude. I think maybe it was a mistake for her to quit her job and stay home with the baby."

He was still waving the two fingers. "This prick," he muttered. The bartender was flirting with a woman at the other end of the bar.

"Get two rounds from him this time," I said. "So we don't have to wait again."

"Look at the big brain on Hurt," he replied. "Good idea."

I started thinking about Lisa again. She quit her job because the cost of decent daycare was about the same as she made at the bank. "You know, her sister works at the same branch and they had a whole crew over there that hung out together," I said as the bartender arrived.

"Four beers," Jon said.

"And two shots of tequila," I added.

Jon nodded. "Full of good ideas."

He lit a cigarette from his pack on the bar. I didn't think he was really listening, but I continued anyway. "I think she got some self-esteem from earning a paycheck and being a mom at the same time, you know? Her mother never did that."

"Yeah, I can see that," he agreed. He blew out a stream of smoke and started scanning the bar for single women.

"I thought I was doing her a big favor by letting her stay home with Roxy," I said as the bartender popped the tops off the Budweiser bottles.

"Don't forget the shots," Jon said. The bartender ignored him.

"But I think her world got cut in half."

"What's that?" he asked.

"Nothing," I answered. "Here's the shots. *Salud*."

My new partner, Rick Syndergaard, and a couple of other guys from our shift came over to hang out with us for a while. "Let me get a round of shots for these Yankees," Rick called out to the bartender.

We drank with Rick, did some shots with Roger and Steve and then I had to call it quits. "I gotta go," I announced.

"Where you going?" Jon asked. "It's Friday night." One of his eyes had started to close. He had a cigarette hanging out of the corner of his mouth.

I patted him on the shoulder and got up from my barstool. "It's 7:30," I said.

"Two hours past wine o'clock. I gotta get home before Lisa is shitfaced."

Half an hour later, as soon as I walked in the door of our condo, Lisa was walking out of the kitchen with a glass of wine in one hand and Roxy in the other. She handed me the baby and said, "There you go, Hurt. You're on duty."

—

The next morning, I was coming out of the shower when Lisa said, "Hey, Troy, don't forget, we have dinner with Connie and Bill tonight."

I stopped in my tracks. "What?"

"Yes, that's tonight," she said. "We're meeting them at Chili's at seven."

I knew perfectly well that she had never told me this before. She had used this trick in the past with mixed success. "No way," I said as I continued on to my closet to get dressed. "I'm not using up my Saturday night hanging out with those fucking people."

Lisa came over to the door of the closet. "Why not, honey?" she said. "They're nice people. Connie is real good to me. She watches Roxy when I'm in a pinch. The girls get along nice. She's a good friend. Can we please?" She looked good. She had on a pair of ripped jeans shorts and a tight tank top. Her hair was pulled straight back into a tight ponytail. She was leaning against the door jam and pouting her lips.

I pulled a shirt over my head and said, "I don't like them. He's trash."

This seemed to hurt her. She gasped a little bit and then looked at the floor. "Why is he trash?" she asked. She wasn't angry, which would have been easier to deal with. If she was angry I could have escalated things and stormed out. That would have gotten me out of dinner.

I pulled on my jeans and tried to come up with a good answer as to why her friend's husband was trash. I ran through the list in my head quickly: his profession, his truck, his bumper stickers, his clothes, his sunglasses, his political views, his accent, his haircut. All white trash, but I couldn't say any of them out loud because I would sound like a judgmental asshole. "He just is," I finally said. "Excuse me." I was trying to get out of the closet and she was still standing in the doorway. I went over to my dresser to get socks and then sat on the edge of our bed to put them on.

Lisa stayed near the closet. She watched me and seemed to be weighing whether or not to say something. "Am I trash?" she finally said, and then covered her face and gasped. She gasped for breath a couple of times and then the tears flowed. "Is that what you think of me? You think you're better than me. You don't like my friends. You don't even like me. Your wife, who loves you and gave you a beautiful, perfect baby!" She made herself hysterical with this little speech and then she walked into the bathroom to close the door and cry in private.

—

During this time, my dad was busy making his next fortune. He was working for a brokerage firm called Stratton Oakmont at the beginning of the Dot Com boom. He made it sound like he was working for Morgan Stanley, but it was a pump-and-dump shop from hell. It was a great fit for him. There were no rules. Everyone was doing cocaine in the office and selling and stealing as fast as they could.

He lived twenty minutes away from us, but we rarely saw him. When I did see him, he was back in the convertible Mercedes and the hundred-dollar bills were back in our birthday cards. I even had some moments when I started up the rescue fantasy again. Lisa and I were broke. We got by, but life was paycheck to paycheck. Roxy wore Walmart clothes and played with hand-me-down toys from Lisa's nieces and nephews. It was fine, but it was one big blow to my ego after another. When my dad pulled up every so often in his hundred-thousand-dollar car, I hoped that he would hand me a fat envelope full of cash to take some of the pressure off. That never happened and I was incapable of asking.

By the time the FBI raided Stratton Oakmont's office, he was one of the top guys there. He was also a full-blown drug addict and alcoholic. The following nine months were a nightmare for him. Legal bills, drug addiction and the bursting of the Dot Com bubble broke him quickly and brutally. There were two positives that came out of this latest rags-to-riches-to-rags cycle: he checked himself into his first rehab center; and he still owned his two-million-dollar house on the intercoastal. In Florida they can't take your house when you go bankrupt, and the SEC can't touch it either. It's called the Homestead Law and is largely the reason why Florida is the white-collar crime capital of the USA. He lost his brokerage license, blew through his cash, and lived without income for two years, but he had a little bit of sober time for the first time in a long time.

He started calling me more often and trying to get more involved in our lives, but I was extremely busy, deeply resentful, and well along the way to becoming an alcoholic myself. My dad being sober gave me the creeps. All my life he had been a degenerate. When I needed him, he was a bum. I wasn't feeling charitable when he finally felt like making amends.

Ceci was born right before Roxy's third birthday, and she turned into a major handful. While her sister was working her way toward sainthood, Ceci had other ideas. She was a serious and demanding baby. She was in charge. Lisa used to complain to me that she thought Ceci was "staring her down" while she was in her stroller or in her crib. I would laugh and tell her that was crazy, but I kind of understood what she meant. She was calm, calculating and strangely intimidating.

Ceci was less than two years old when we went to have family pictures taken at the beach. The photographer was making all kinds of funny noises and faces to get her to laugh. Nothing worked. "How do you make her smile?" he finally asked.

Lisa and I looked at each other and shrugged. "She smiles when she feels like it," I answered.

The best picture from that session sat on our fireplace mantel. Three of us were grinning like idiots and Ceci was looking skeptical about the situation. As a toddler and a little girl, she spent half her life in timeout because she was biologically incapable of not having the last word in an argument. If you yelled at her, she had to yell back louder and angrier. If you told her she did something bad, she would have to do something worse. She went through four or five bedroom doors over the years because she would lay on the floor and kick the door with all her might while she was in timeout.

Roxy would sit in the laundry room on a stool when we put her in timeout. The laundry room didn't even have a door. She would look at the ground and seem to shrink to half her normal size when she was in trouble. She would need hugs and reassurance when her timeout was over. Ceci would come out of timeout like a mafiosa sprung from prison. Her attitude was, *Fuck you. I'll let you know when I feel like being a good girl. Go get your shine box.* It was hard to believe they were from the same gene pool.

15

Nicaragua
2020

A few nights later, I was back on the sofa watching Netflix. This time I had an open box of Cocoa Puffs in my lap and a big glass of ice water on the coffee table, and I was watching *The Godfather, Part II*. My laptop was open on the coffee table and I had the whole lodge to myself. I had just gotten through the opening scenes: The funeral of Vito Corleone's father, who was murdered for insulting the local mafia lord. In the next scene Vito's mother tries to kill the mafia lord because she knows he'll kill Vito to prevent him from seeking revenge later in life. She dies trying.

Five-year-old Vito was running away down a long dirt road when there was a knock at the door. "Damnit," I whispered. I was just starting to get into the movie, and there was only one person who came by unannounced. A couple of minutes later, Andy was back on the sofa across from me. I closed my laptop. This time he came in with a spring in his step. I guessed that was because he hadn't had his ass kicked in a few days.

"Dude!" he yelled as he sat down. "I have great news for you." I was still pretty annoyed about our last conversation, and was hoping that his great news was that he had my money and was going to pay me back. He rubbed his hands together in anticipation. "You know the house down at the corner of Isla Verde, across from the mini-grocery? The one right across the street from the beach over here in Gigante?"

I had no idea what he was talking about. "No," I said. "The only mini-grocery that I know is Juan's shop right next door."

He pointed toward the south end of the beach. "Isla Verde," he said. "Down at that end."

I shook my head and shrugged. I started to hope that he was going to tell me he had just sold the place, or made a lucrative deal to renovate it. *Please don't tell me that you're here to sell me a house,* I thought.

"Whatever," he said, waving his hand at me. "It's a great property. Sick location. Anyway, Luis Lopez, the owner for the past fifty-something years, just got into some serious financial trouble and he needs cash . . . fast." I guess I twisted up my face at that point because he stopped and said, "What?"

"You're going to suggest that I buy it?"

"I can arrange a quick sale, if you're interested."

"I'm not interested," I responded immediately.

"But you haven't even asked me the price," he said. "It's too good to be true."

I got up and started walking toward the door and said, "Dude, that's probably the first honest thing you've said since you walked in here."

"Troy!" he yelled, from the sofa. "It's fifty grand. The property goes back two hundred meters from the road. Across from the beach. You love Gigante!"

I stood in the hallway watching him and started to feel conflicted. There was zero chance of me wiring funds to some Nicaraguan bank for a quick sale of a property. That was not the conflict. I was more conflicted about how to feel about the situation. I was getting angry. I could feel my heart in my chest and my ears were starting to ring. It felt like I was getting ready to fight. But I wasn't. *I'm not going to get nasty here and turn myself into the asshole in this situation,* I decided. *I'm going to be civil and get him out of here and get on with my evening of Netflix and eating cereal out of the box.*

He went over to the kitchen and filled up a glass of water from the cooler. Along the way, he went on about Juan Lopez's financial troubles. I was barely listening, but it was something about a divorce, a sudden death and cross-border tax liabilities. Experienced liars are great at details. I remembered Barry's comments about Andy. Then I thought about the lady in the white sundress who had been trying to punch him in the face.

"So," he finally said. "What do you think? Do you want to go check out the property?"

The feeling that eventually settled in was disappointment. Maybe a little bit of disgust was mixed in. "What? Like, right now? No thanks, dude," I said. "I'm not interested in buying anything right now."

For an instant he looked like he had been punched in the gut, but he recovered quickly. He put the glass of water in the sink and clapped his hands loudly. "Yeah, no problem. Your loss." He spun around and walked toward the door. "If I had the cash free, I'd buy it myself," he said. "I could flip it in a few months for twice the price." He left without saying goodbye.

I stood, looking at the door for a minute after he walked out. *I'm done with that guy,* I thought. I guess some part of me had been waiting for something like this. I had wanted to put Andy on a pedestal. I really would've liked him to be the friend in need, the spiritual seeker, the role model he sold himself as. But I was a grown man. I had 46 years of experience in getting kicked in the balls. By the time he sat across from me and finally revealed his magic beans for sale, I guess I was half-ready for it. Especially after he had hit me up for cash just a few days earlier. I felt like I was midway through the phases of a con man's playbook.

My goal was to step out as gracefully as possible. I would act like a sober man. If I had to write off the three thousand dollars, then so be it. It was a valuable experience. I've paid more for less. Before long, I settled back into the sofa and got back into the movie. A couple of hours later, I was engrossed. There was a flashback scene where Vito visited Sicily for a family vacation for the first time in over twenty years. He was introduced to the ninety-year-old mafia lord who killed his mother and father. He had been importing the man's olive oil to New York. When the old man asked him who his father was, Vito got right up next to him and said, "My father's name is Antonio Andolini, and this is for you!" He cut the old man's stomach open with a knife.

Just then, my phone rang. I looked down and saw it was Andy. I debated whether or not to answer, but on the third ring decided to pause the movie again. He started right in. "Hey! I know, this is going to sound crazy, but you have to hear me out. This could literally be a once in a lifetime opportunity." He sounded manic. I don't know why, but I pictured him sitting in his Jeep with sweat pouring down his face. *Was he using?* He rolled out a long story about how Mike, the owner of Dale Daggers, had become desperate to sell the lodge. "I don't know the specifics," he said, "but I heard he ran into some kind of political trouble in Mombocho, where he owns his other lodge. Dude needs fifty thousand dollars to stay out of jail."

He then went into an unnecessarily detailed explanation of land ownership laws in Nicaragua. I don't remember it all, but essentially nobody can own property closer than a hundred meters from the shoreline. All of that technically belongs to the government . . . so the owner of Dale Daggers can't sell the land because he doesn't own it . . . but he can sell the lodge and the business and the assets. "Bottom line, if we can wire fifty thousand dollars by the end of the day tomorrow, you can literally own Dale Daggers Surf Lodge. You can own the lodge you're renting a bedroom in right now! Is that crazy or what?"

I was frozen in place as I listened to this. My eyes and mouth were wide open in disbelief. I wished there was someone else there, so I could put the call on speakerphone for their ears, because I couldn't believe my own. I was sitting on the couch with the ceiling fan blowing cool air on me. Surf videos were playing on the big screen in front of me with the sound off. Netflix was paused on my laptop. I waited for him to finish. "So, you think I should buy Dale Daggers today. Right this second. That's what you're telling me."

Andy paused for a moment. "No, man, I'm just doing you a favor and telling you what's going on. Honestly, if you don't want to buy it, I think I'm going to do it. It just seems like too sick of a deal to pass on. I just know you love the place, so I thought you might be interested."

Wow. This was so much worse than anything Barry or any of the other guys could have warned me about. My head spun. For a moment, while I held the phone in silence, I started to get really worried about him. I was done with the guy, but he had been a friend and he was obviously in trouble. This was real distress I was feeling from the other end of the phone. I was about to ask him if he was okay. For a moment, I wanted to say, "Hey, why don't you tell me what's really going on? Maybe I can help. None of this makes any sense. Your behavior today has been insane and I'm hoping there's some good reason for you to be selling me not one, but two loads of bullshit in the same evening. Why don't you let me help you?"

Instead, I was pretty quickly filled with disgust again. Some kind of response was apparently required, so I said, "I'm good, dude. I'm not in the market for any Nicaraguan surf lodges today."

Andy laughed. "Yeah, I get it. No problem. I think I'm going to do it, then."

Long silence. "Cool. Sounds good. Then I'll pay *you* rent next week."

He jumped right back. "Maybe we can be partners. 50/50? I'm not sure I can get my hands on the full fifty grand by tomorrow, you know."

"No thanks, Andy," I said. "I gotta go." I ended the call and thought about calling Barry, or calling Jose and Rob to run the situation by them. There were no other guests in the lodge, so I sat there all by myself, staring at the frozen screen of my laptop. "Jesus Christ," I muttered to myself. I wondered again if I should call him back and try to have an honest conversation about what was happening. Maybe there was some other way I could help, but every bone in my body said to put down the phone and walk away from the situation, and from this relationship altogether. "Guy still owes me three grand," I muttered to myself. I pressed the spacebar on my laptop to wake it up and then pressed it again to restart my movie. "Fuck him," I muttered as I settled back into the couch.

An hour later, after a montage of assassinations and death where Michael Corleone settles all of his scores with his enemies, he is sitting by himself in silent contemplation overlooking Lake Tahoe. Right then there was a flurry of knocks on the door that startled me. I hit pause again and jumped up from the couch. Next was a series of bangs on the door. "What the fuck," I muttered as I closed the laptop and jogged barefoot across the tile floor to answer the door.

Andy was there with the same two Nicaraguan police officers. This time his shirt was ripped to shreds and his face was battered. His bottom lip was split down the middle with dried blood coagulated, and he had a huge swollen welt over his left eye. His hands were tied behind his back. They took him by the arms and shoved him inside, forcing me back. One had a handgun drawn and pointed down at the floor with his free hand. The other had a machine gun in a sling over his shoulder.

The one with the handgun was tall by Nica standards, pushing six feet. He was thin. His uniform was neatly pressed and tucked. He had a neat mustache and a scar that ran from the corner of his left eye to the bottom of his cheekbone. He had a few military-style medals on his chest and his black boots were polished to a bright shine. I started referring to him in my mind as "Flacco," because he reminded me of the caricature of a skinny man in my Spanish textbook from high school.

The one with the machine gun held Andy's other arm with both hands. The gun was slung over his shoulder with a strap. He was normal height for a Nica, around five-six. He was thick and powerful-looking. His legs bulged in his pants and his arms were squeezed into the short-sleeved uniform top. His features were all thick and broad and his large eyes appeared to be slightly too far apart, making him look cross-eyed.

He wasn't fat, but I started to refer to him in my mind as "Gordo" anyway.

They were both poker-faced but flashed with anger when they shook him. "Talk," Flacco instructed him.

Andy was slouched over and looking at the floor. They shook him violently one more time and he looked up at me through his one good eye. His expression was pitiful. He was begging before he even opened his mouth. "I'm sorry," he said and he started to shake with whimpering. They shook him hard and the thick one smacked him in the back of the head.

"What the fuck, Andy?" I said. "What are you doing here? What's going on?"

"Listen to me," he said. "Please. You have to listen."

"I'm listening. Say something. What's happening?"

For the next couple of minutes, he begged me to save his life. He offered no explanation and no details. Instead, in ten different ways he reiterated the same few ideas over and over: I had a chance to save him. It was only money. It was not a big deal. He would pay me back. He spoke in English, and I assumed the policemen couldn't totally understand what he was saying. The repetition of these ideas was infuriating. I gathered from his broken thoughts that he had told them to take him to me as a last-ditch effort to save his life. He probably told them I would pay. That was why they were there. "It's just money. All you have to do is wire some cash and I can live and pay you back and everything will be fine." I thought of Kai in the kitchen a couple of weeks earlier—the wolf, the witch. I thought of my dad pulling out of my driveway in his hundred-thousand-dollar Mercedes while I stood there, holding Roxy.

I was about to ask him again why he owed them money and what this was all about, but I decided that I didn't care. Andy had known me for about a month and I was the only person he could think of who might shell out some money to save his life. I fell for it once. Why get involved any more than I had to? He was a phony and a loser and a liar. The latest such man in my life. In the middle of his fourth or fifth repetition I said, "Stop, stop, stop. Enough." I waved my hands, then turned to the short, thick officer with the machine gun and said, "Sir, I would not pay a dollar for this man's life. Please take him away and do whatever you want with him."

Andy yelled, "No! Troy!" He started convulsing with sobs and whimpers. "You don't understand! Please! They're gonna kill me!" The tall skinny cop stepped back and cracked him on the back of his neck with the handgun. This sent him to the floor and shut him up. He lay there on his side, with his hands zipped behind his back like a calf in a rodeo. The tall cop took out his phone and stepped into the kitchen to make a call as Andy whispered, "Please, Troy, please," over and over again.

I was face-to-face with the small, powerful cop. "Sir, please leave now and take him with you," I said in my broken Spanish. "His business has nothing to do with me. I only met him a month ago. I made a mistake. I never should have become his friend." I stepped back and pointed at him. "Whatever he told you about me is probably a lie. That is what he does. He is a liar. He will say anything to get what he wants."

Flacco finished his call and said to his partner, "We're supposed to take them both to Chipote." He turned to me and pointed his gun. "Outside," he ordered. When we got out to the driveway, he pushed me toward the truck. It was pouring rain. "In the truck," he said. "In the back."

I turned around with my hands up. "No way," I said. "I am *not* getting in there. I have nothing to do with this."

They both pointed their guns at me. "In," Gordo said.

"Just wait a second," I insisted, waving my hands. "This has literally nothing to do with me. You are making a big mistake. I am an American citizen. You cannot do this. Take him and leave me out of this."

Gordo stepped up and pushed the AK-47 sharply into my back. "In," he said.

As I climbed into the back of the truck, I protested again, "He was my AA sponsor. I swear. That's it."

Gordo chuckled. "That's not what we heard, *jefe*."

"What did you hear?" I called as he climbed in the front. The tall one with the mustache got in the back with us. He kept the handgun pointed at me the whole time. As we pulled out of Dale Daggers, all the fear drained out of me. We drove down to the end of town and turned onto Guacalito de la Isla and I sat in total acceptance. This is how relationships go for me. This is my story. I know from experience the danger in hoping for others to rescue me. I know what happens when I become dependent on them. Of course Andy would turn out to be a liar and a criminal. Of course he'd violate my trust. How else could that possibly have gone?

After a while, the water had started to puddle in the truck bed. My t-shirt and gym shorts were soaked through, and my bare feet were in half an inch of water. Andy whimpered on and off. He kept his eyes closed as if he couldn't bear to watch.

A few minutes further down the road, Flacco got a phone call. While he listened, I thought about trying to disarm him and jumping out of the moving truck, but there were too many things that could go wrong. I could mess up and get shot; I could get injured jumping out of the moving truck and then get shot after they doubled back. The margin for error was too big. I looked at Andy again to see if I might be able to get some help from him, but he was still propped up on the cab, whimpering like a sleeping dog that was having a nightmare. "Why did you have to bring me into your shit?" I whispered to Andy.

"I'm sorry, man. I really am. I didn't have any choice. You could have just paid some money and bought me some time until my next payment comes due."

Next payment? What the fuck? This guy was in so deep. There were multiple layers to his lies. God knows what his deal was with these people. "Who was on the phone?" I asked him.

"I don't know," Andy said. "Probably Heredia, the governor. Maybe Harfuch, the chief of police."

"Hey," Flaco said. "Quiet."

We bumped along in the back of the truck for what seemed like an hour. The rain stopped. "Andy," I whispered. "What's Chipote?"

Andy groaned. "Torture prison," he whispered. "Somoza built it in the '30s to hold political prisoners. They keep you there until you confess."

"Confess to what?"

"Whatever they tell you."

"Hey!" Flacco warned.

It was another hour from there, and my general sense of direction told me we were heading toward Managua. The building was lit up with floodlights when we arrived. From the outside it didn't look like a prison at all. It looked like a rundown old government administration building. We walked into a large and dimly lit waiting room with crumbling plaster walls. The room was lit by broken and rusted light fixtures that must have dated back to the '50s. It was partitioned by stained and torn fabric cubicle panels that were probably earth tones at some point but now were ashen and moldy. Our police escorts sat us down in two swivel chairs that both had one broken arm. We were inside one of the many eight-foot-square cubicles. The only other furniture in the cube was a worn leather executive chair. The floor was old asbestos tile that was dangerously crumbling and probably infecting the workers there with lung cancer.

A few minutes later I heard the front door burst open, and the clip-clop of hard-heeled shoes on that nightmare floor was audible above the murmuring voices all around. I saw the man's head above the cubicle walls before he came around the corner and into my cubicle. He was another police officer in the neat baby blue button-down uniform shirt. This guy was closer to my age, maybe a little older. He wore some brass doodad on his shoulders that suggested a high rank. He was dark, with a neatly styled handlebar mustache. His clothes were pressed and neat, but his hair was a mess. He went through the motions of tucking in his shirt and straightening himself out, as though by routine, although it wasn't necessary. His uniform was already immaculate. Then he pushed his hair down, or tried to. It stood up stubbornly in the back and looked ridiculous. He looked like he had just been woken from a nap.

He walked directly over and stood looking down at us. He licked his hand and tried pasting down his hair again. We looked at each other for what seemed like a full minute before he grimaced and gestured for a guard to take me away. I thought seriously about making a stand right there and fighting my way out, but the odds seemed overwhelmingly against me. I'd be dead by the time I got to the door. "Wait!" I yelled. "Wait a minute! I don't have anything to do with this man. I just met him a month ago." The two guards were pulling me by the arms to the degree that I let them. I was moving slowly so that the officer who seemed to be in charge would hear me. "Sir, please, you have to believe me. I am an American tourist. I am here to surf and go to AA meetings. This man does not speak for me. I barely know him!"

Gordo had heard enough of my yelling and he was getting frustrated that he couldn't move me faster, so he stuck his machine gun in my ribs. "Go," he said.

They led me through the maze of cubicles, down a labyrinth of hallways and into a stairwell. We went down two levels below ground and then exited to hell. We walked down a dark hall puddled with water and God knows what else. He stopped in front of a solid steel door marked #7, but the hallway went as far as I could see, disappearing into the darkness ahead. It was dead quiet except for the sound of dripping water. It was hot and smelled like bodily waste. There was a box outside the door containing a roll of toilet paper and a toothbrush. He pointed to it and I picked it up.

The cell was a tiny concrete box with a low ceiling. I had to duck my head a bit to get through the doorway and it was impossible for me to stand fully upright once inside. The room was about eight by twelve feet. A dim light bulb next to the door lit the upper parts of the walls. The guard closed the door behind me and I heard the bolt slide closed. The floor was so dark that it took me a few minutes of staring down for my eyes to adjust enough to see anything. The air was damp and I guessed it was around eighty degrees. That ended up being one of the worst parts; I never stopped sweating the whole time I was there. A sawed-off piece of PVC pipe hung down from the ceiling. The guards would pump water through it once a day so I could shower and wash my shit and piss down the hole in the middle of the floor. Since there was no way for air to circulate, the room stunk of my own waste most of the day.

On my first day there I tried to make the place more livable. I broke up some of the wooden planks on the bed to try to level it out a bit. I used one of the planks to clear the spiderwebs and pushed the rat shit down the drain. *Okay*, I thought, *there are rats in here. What else is living in here?* Not long after this thought a couple of giant spiders the size of my hand came out to meet the new guy. They scurried across the floor and dove down the waste hole. After that I stayed on the bed as much as possible.

I don't know how many days I spent curled up on that bed. The walls around me were smeared with shit, which prisoners before me used to write charming and uplifting messages like: *Kill. Murder. Death.* There was no way to measure the passage of time, so I soon lost track of night and day. I slept often, but I never knew for how long. The food and water delivery were infrequent and irregular, which was even more disorienting. I started to feel weak and had bouts of extreme anxiety.

I prayed a lot and I tried to meditate as much as possible. I thought back to the dharma talks I had attended in early sobriety that had given me so much relief. The Three Noble Truths were key to my survival:

1. Life contains pain and suffering. Pain is unavoidable, but suffering is not.
2. The causes of suffering are grasping, aversion and delusion.

3. Freedom from suffering can be achieved if we let
    go of our grasping, aversion and delusion.

In my cell I experienced huge quantities of pain. My
job was to accept that these things were happening, to
say, "Right now, it's like this." Once I accepted the way
it was, I removed the suffering that came from extreme
aversion to my circumstances.

Understanding that it was "right now" also meant
that the conditions were temporary. I thought about
the Tibetan monks who had been imprisoned in
terrible conditions and tortured by the Chinese when
they invaded. They had had many years of practice
when they needed these principles. I had had a couple
of weekend meditation retreats in Orlando.

I spent hours reviewing what happened with Andy.
How did that go so bad so fast? I lay there and reviewed
what happened over and over. I kept asking myself,
*What was my part? What character defects of mine led
to this?* Laying on that bed in the brutal, damp heat,
I eventually lapsed into a kind of dream state, lingering
on the edge of consciousness. At times, I wanted to sleep
but was kept awake by the onslaught of mosquitoes and
flies that thrived in the damp, hot conditions.

Memories, fantasies and hallucinations ran through
my head until I couldn't decipher which was which.
I thought about my girls constantly. What would
happen to them if I didn't make it out of here? They'd

have Lisa, but she was such a flake. Michelle would always be good to them, but I desperately wanted to get back to them and protect them.

I lapsed into a fantasy about spring break. I'm driving up to Gainesville in my Jeep. The windows are open and a warm breeze is flowing through. I have to raise the volume on the radio because of the wind. It's the Beatles. "Get Back." I turn it still louder. Roxy is standing on the sidewalk in front of her apartment building with a suitcase. She is always on time. Ahead of schedule. I'm so happy to see her, I have to fight back tears. I pick her up when I'm hugging her. She feels light. I worry she isn't eating enough. *Don't say it.*

We park in front of Ceci's dorm. She's not ready and she's not answering her phone, so we go upstairs. She's sleeping. It's funny, but it's also scary. *Please God, protect her.*

On the car ride home they're talking and laughing. I can't hear anything they're saying, but it doesn't matter. They're happy and we're together. The tone and the vibe are like a cool breeze. *Oh, my God, the cool breeze feels so good.*

Roxy lowers the radio and looks at me. "What time are we picking up Michelle?" "She doesn't want me anymore," I say.

"You fucked it up, Dad," Ceci says from the back seat. "You fuck up everything that's good. You're so selfish."

The car gets hot. It smells. The air is thick. There are bugs flying around in there. *What did I do wrong? How do I get back to the coolness?* And then suddenly I was awake again.

The Nicas were feeding me and keeping me alive, so what was the point of this? Were they trying to scare me? That hardly seemed necessary—I had been terrified at "Hello." All they had to do was to tell me what they wanted, and I would do it. I thought back to a conversation I had had with Barry a couple of weeks earlier. We walked into La Tostaderia and everyone was watching a newscast intently. We sat down and watched. The newscaster said that Cristiana Chamorro was being held under house arrest by the Nicaraguan national police force. Chamorro was a journalist and the daughter of former president Violetta Chamorro. She's seen as a potential challenger to President Daniel Ortega, who was about to run for his fourth term in office. The day before, prosecutors filed charges against Cristiana Chamorro for money laundering and asked that she be disqualified from running for office.

The newscast showed an image of the Twitter profile of US Secretary of State Antony Blinken, with a tweet that said:

"Arbitrarily banning opposition leader @ chamorrocris reflects Ortega's fear of free and fair elections. Nicaraguans deserve real democracy."

I turned to Barry. "Do you understood what's going on?"

Barry stuffed his hands deep into his pockets and nodded. "Yeah, man. This is par for the course down here."

"You mean the corruption?" I clarified.

"*El pais de maravillas,*" he said.

"The country of marvels," I interpreted.

"My man," he said, taking out his hands and rubbing his face. "That's what the locals call it. And they're not talking about the great waves or the beautiful mountains. We're getting ready to drink coffee in the fifth most corrupt country in the whole world. You feel me?"

"That's the marvel?" I asked. "The level of corruption?"

Barry shook his head side to side. "Yes and no," he answered. "It's more the unbelievable *audacity* of the corruption. That's what's mind-blowing."

"Wow," I said. "That's heavy."

He laughed. "The authorities around here regularly pull off shit that leave these people stunned and speechless. That's the regular." He nodded and pulled his hair back tight to fix his ponytail. "So, what happens? What's the result?" He paused for a moment and then answered his own question. "They're left with the paranoid suspicion that anything can happen at any time. You understand what it is to walk around like that? Innocent people get dragged into trouble all the time."

It seemed sad and unfortunate for them. In a million years, I never imagined it could happen to me.

Trays of food would be pushed through the opening in the bottom of the door once or twice a day. I wasn't good at marking time, but they seemed to come at irregular intervals. For the first few days I would only eat the food that was wrapped in plastic or sealed in its original container. I didn't trust the plate of rice and beans or the stews or fish patties. I thought they might be poisoned. After a few days, I was too hungry. If they wanted to kill me, they could just open the door, shoot me in the head and dump me on the side of the road, so I finally decided to eat it. It was disgusting, but it wasn't poisoned. The rice was half-cooked and crunchy. The stew had unidentifiable pieces of meat.

I lay back down in the bed and waited for excruciating pain to hit my stomach. It never came. I went in and out of dreams again.

The night I got promoted to sergeant, I skipped the bar and went straight home for the first time in a while. I wanted to show the girls the new chevrons on my uniform sleeve. The girls weren't home, but Lisa was there. I heard her in the den as I walked down the hallway, past our kitchen. It sounded like she was scrambling around.

As I cleared the kitchen, I watched as she pulled her t-shirt over her head. The guy on the couch jumped up and was buttoning his pants. He looked older. Maybe fifty. Short grey hair and a little overweight. My first thought was to wonder where she could have found a guy like this.

Lisa took a few steps forward with her hands out, as if she was going to try to stop me from doing something. "Troy, please!" she yelled out. "Don't!"

The guy started side stepping his way to the other side of the room. He put his hands up in surrender.

It took me a moment to identify the emotion in my chest. It wasn't my old friend anger. It was sadness. "Fuck," I whispered. I shook my head. "Fuck."

The old guy started side-stepping his way along the wall. He held his shoes in his hand. He had to pass me to get to the hallway that led to the door. When he got next to me, we made eye contact. I punched him in the face. My fist landed on his forehead and he bounced off the wall, and then scurried down the hallway. It wasn't much of a punch.

I didn't even set my feet. It just seemed like the right thing to do.

"Troy, please!" Lisa wailed again. Her hands went back up. *Does she think I'm going to beat on her?* I wondered. She seemed to expect it, and on some level, I thought that maybe she even wanted it. It would show some kind of violent love for her.

"I never really loved you," I said and then turned around and went to the bar.

The feeling of sadness stayed with me through the night. What I told her was true. I was never in love with her. I wasn't heartbroken. We shared a life together and we had children together, so I was insulted. I was hurt and embarrassed.

I was sitting with Rick at the bar. Neither of us had spoken in a while, when I finally said, "Lisa and I can probably put this behind us. It's not that big a deal."

Rick put down his beer and looked at me. "Don't do that, Hurt." Rick had never given me a single word of advice in the years we worked together, nothing personal or professional, so I was surprised. I sat on the barstool, looking at him with one eyebrow raised and waiting for the rest of it. I waited for a while. "Are you going to elaborate on that at all?" I asked.

"I don't want to," he said. "But I guess I have to." He took a swig from his beer and rocked his head from side to side like he was loosening his neck up. He held up one hand, a couple of inches from my chest, as if to hold me back. "Here goes . . . I personally know of two other guys that she's fucked. Hurt, I'm sorry to be the one to tell you, but Lisa is a fucking whore."

—

My time in Chipote, which turned out to be eight days, was a real challenge to my sanity. It was as close to hell on earth as I can imagine. I thought about the convicts I had guarded as a nineteen-year-old. I hadn't thought about those men in decades. They were mostly kids, not much older than my daughters were now. Whatever happened to this guy? Or that one? I prayed they were okay. I think the compassion came from my own suffering.

My AA practices were key to my survival. I repeatedly said the handful of prayers I had committed to memory. I made mental gratitude lists. No matter how grim my situation was, I was always able to come up with a big list of things that I was grateful for. AA made me understand that my circumstances were almost irrelevant in terms of how I felt on any given day. It was all in my head. I might not be able to control a situation, but I could control my response to it. This situation was a serious test of that principle.

I didn't have access to my full recovery toolkit because I was on my own. Some of my most useful tools involve contact with other people. Calling other alcoholics and listening to what was happening in their day was always a quick and easy way to get out of my own head. When I was at home, I would call a few drunks every day. It kept me from the most dangerous conversation of all: Troy talking to Troy about Troy.

When I couldn't get my mind into a good place, I would move my attention to my body. I would spend an hour or so sitting in bed and going over every sensation in my body, one area at a time. Every time my mind moved back to fear, I would just say to myself, "That is fear. Hello, fear. Welcome to my meditation." The thoughts that crept in most often were: *How much longer am I going to be here? Am I ever getting out?* And, *Are they deciding whether or not to kill me?* It was dangerous for me to sit with any of these pinless grenades for very long.

At times, when my body was terribly uncomfortable, I would shift into fantasy.

With the heat, the bugs, the lack of food and water, the smell, and the lack of physical activity, my body ached quite a bit, so I spent a lot of time in a fantasy world. I made up stories and adventures repeatedly—surfing, traveling to Europe with my girls, reconciling with my dad, reconciling with Michelle. The fantasies were drawn out in extreme detail. I would stop and savor moments of them as if they were happening right in front of me.

This made me think of my mom. Escape fantasies were her stock and trade. It gave me new compassion for her. How bad was the world in her mind that she had to live in her stories? When I started to believe my fantasies, my heart broke for her. I was always on the receiving end of the stories. I never considered what might be going on in the mind that needed to create them.

My face was soaked. Laying on the mattress, it was the same combination: tears and sweat. It was the first night in our new apartment in Manhasset. My mom is chasing me down the hallway and I run into my bedroom and slam the door. Why was she chasing me? She looks really angry.

I remember. We were eating dinner at the counter in the kitchen. I threw my plate of food at her. I was so angry. I think this really happened. I remember the plate shattering when it hit the linoleum floor.

She banged on the door with both fists. Wow, it was really loud. My back was against the door, holding her back. "Go away! I hate you!" I yelled. I held the doorknob in my hand.

She forced it open and pushed me back into the room. No, it was more than a push. I went flying into the room, tumbling across the floor. She barged through the door with fury. It was violent. This was the most violent thing she ever did. It was shocking.

I jumped into my bed and yelled again, "I hate you!" because it was the most violent thing I knew how to say, and I yelled it at the top of my lungs. I rolled up and pulled my comforter around myself, like a cocoon to protect me against her. "Go away!

I hate you!" I yelled again.

"Troy!" she yelled back. "Do you want me to leave you, too? You want me to walk out of here and leave the way your father left?" Her voice was anguished now, not yelling so much as pleading. I can't see her face, but I imagine the pain in her eyes. My heart sinks down to the bottom of my gut and I wail.

"Well, too bad!" She recovered and found her yell again. She is standing next to my bed. She is leaning over me, just above the blanket over my head. She yelled, "You're stuck with me and I'm not going anywhere, and there's nothing you can do about it!"

"Just go away," I cried, over and over again.

"No," she said. "I will not go away." And she sat on the edge of my bed for a long time. She sat there until I cried myself to sleep. Just before I fell asleep, I heard her whisper, "I'm your mother, Troy, and there's nothing you can ever do to make me leave you. I'm here and I'm staying."

16

Florida
2016

I met Michelle at the gym at work. She worked out there in the morning because it was next door to the State Attorney's Office where she was an assistant district attorney. After I talked to her a couple of times, I rearranged my schedule so I could be there every day at the same time. I liked to look at her. She was pretty in a conventional way. She had nice features, glossy skin and things like that, but somehow the whole was greater than the sum of her parts. It all worked really well together. When she ran on the treadmill, wearing tights and a sports bra, no matter what else my workout schedule called for I had to run on the treadmill also. We were gym friends. We chatted for a couple of minutes when we crossed paths. A few times, I thought our smiles and glances were flirtatious, but I'm so bad at that stuff that I wouldn't have bet on it.

After a couple of months of this, she was running on the treadmill next to mine one day when she suddenly stopped running, took her earphones out and glared at me. I stepped off onto the sides of the treadmill, letting the track roll underneath me. I took off my earphones and looked back at her. She had a bead of sweat running down the side of her face. She looked annoyed and she looked like she was going to say something. "What?" I said, "What did I do?"

"Are you ever going to ask me out?"

Immediately I responded, "Will you go out with me, please?"

"Give me your phone," she said. She was still acting annoyed. She put her number into my phone while she said, "Honestly, what does a girl have to do?"

I laughed and took it back. "Thanks. I'll call you later. Or is this one of those wait two days situations?"

She smiled and said, "Call me later."

I did some research online to find the best places for a first date, and booked a bistro with outdoor seating on Atlantic Avenue in Delray Beach. It was nice, but not so nice that it looked like I was trying hard to impress her. I knew bits and pieces about her from dozens of two-minute gym conversations, but I wanted to know more. "So, catch me up on your life," I said. "Give me the two-minute tour."

"Oookay," she said. "Let's see ... I grew up in the Bay area. I have one brother. Older. I went to Smith. I played field hockey ..."

"I knew it," I interrupted. "Sorry. I knew you were an athlete. Please go on."

"I went to law school at NYU. I work in the hate crimes unit at the moment, but trying to move out of there."

"What about your parents?"

She laughed and took a sip of wine. "Thorough interview," she said. "My mom is a thoracic surgeon and my dad practices corporate law."

I was getting more and more excited as she went. She seemed like an absolute jackpot, at least from a resume standpoint. She was the opposite of Lisa in nearly every way. She wasn't trying to impress me. She was just answering my questions, but before our appetizers arrived, I was bewitched.

"What else do you want to know?" she asked.

"I'd like to know all the details about all of that," I said.

"That's going to take a while," she said. "Your turn. Read me the back of your baseball card."

I finished my vodka and was looking around for the waiter. The restaurant was nice, but they poured small drinks. "Lacrosse card," I corrected.

"Hmmm," she said, twisting up her lips. "Lacrosse player, huh?"

I laughed. "Yeah, sorry. All American. Full scholarship to UVA. I was the number four-ranked middie coming out of high school, number twelve overall in the country. Plus, I was number six in my class and got a 1560 on the SAT."

She nearly choked on her wine. She had to cover her mouth with her hand to keep from spitting any out. I caught the waiter's eye with a death stare across the room and pointed to my glass. "Holy shit," she said. "That was incredible. Thank you for the stats. What was your forty-yard dash speed?"

I had been half-joking, but it was still embarrassing to be laughed at. I took a deep breath. "Sorry," I said. "I'm trying to impress you and that came out ridiculous. Now I'm embarrassed."

She was still laughing. "No, that was awesome," she said. "I'm going to Google you when I get home to find your actual stats."

The waiter came over with my vodka. "You should," I said. "They're fucking elite." And then we both got to laugh and I got to recover. Eventually, I think the redness subsided from my face. "I didn't want you to think I'm just a dumb cop."

We went on to have a nice meal and I tried to act normal, but it was hard because I had a gnawing insecurity about my resume. I was supposed to be in her league but I wasn't. What the hell does "in her league" mean, anyway? She more or less asked *me* out. She was putting out all the flirty signals. At least I thought that's what they were. When she wasn't laughing *at* me she did actually laugh at all my jokes. There was a lot of kind, meaningful eye contact. She touched my arm and my hand a bunch of times. There was even a good amount of hair-flipping. Even for someone as bad at this game as me, these seemed like good signs.

It turned out they were good signs. We slept together that night and most nights for the next few weeks. Plus, several mornings and a couple of afternoons. But that night, and every day after that, I couldn't shake the feeling of being *less than*. I knew this feeling from high school, but at this stage of life I couldn't take refuge in academics and lacrosse. Thankfully, I had alcohol to change the channel in my head.

I really liked her. She was funny and smart. More importantly, she was kind to me. I needed that. Most importantly, she was amazing with my girls. They fell for her immediately and the feeling seemed to be mutual. I came home from work one night and found Roxy on the phone with Michelle, who was helping her with her statistics homework. Ceci started calling her to ask advice on clothes and makeup. It was incredible. So, what was the problem? As usual, the problem was me. I cringe when I look back on it, but the truth is that I needed constant reassurance that I was good enough.

Michelle and I talked a lot about my struggles with my colleagues. One night, when we were in bed together, I brought up my partner, Rick Syndergaard. Rick seemed to embody the conflict. He was a six-foot-tall Scandinavian blonde who carried a badge and a gun, and all he ever complained about was how white men no longer have any power in society. "I just want to scream at him, 'Rick, how much more power do you need?'" I yelled out to her. "This motherfucker has *all* the power a society can possibly give a person, and he's totally convinced he's being victimized. It drives me insane!"

Michelle laid on her side with her head on her arm. "Let me guess. He listens to all that right-wing media stuff every night?"

"He quotes it line for line," I said. "They have him convinced that the country is out to get him. They repeat the same shit every night until he knows, in his heart, that there'll be no place in America's future for his blonde, heterosexual sons. They will be downtrodden outcasts. He accepts this ridiculous fantasy as plain fact." I slapped my hands on my lap in frustration. "Now here's the thing. Rick is a great guy and a great friend. Shit, he might even be my best friend, if men in their forties have besties. We've trained together at the MMA gym for years. He's had my back in every gnarly situation we've ever come across on the street. He's never hesitated for a second. I know, in my heart, that he would take a bullet for me."

"So, what's the problem?" She asked.

"Here's my question," I said. "Can you be a great guy and a bad person at the same time?" Michelle listened intently. She curled up a bit to get closer to me and hugged a pillow with her head on my outstretched arm.

"He's a good friend, but I want to fucking strangle him half the time!" She chuckled. She didn't know I had a history of doing pretty much exactly that, so she thought I was being dramatic to make a point. "Do you understand?" I said while she was laughing.

"Of course," she said. "Don't you think I have the same situation in my office? We live in *Florida*."

"Tell me," I said.

"You have Rick. I have Pat," she said. "Pat's in the cybercrime division. Same deal. She's a well-educated version of Rick. She has two Trump stickers on the back of her car, she's knee-deep in every stupid conspiracy theory, she gets her news from Facebook algorithms . . . she's the total package."

"So how do you handle it?" I asked.

Michelle was actually kind of brilliant about it. "You know what I do? I look for things to like about her. It's like a game for me. She brought in amazing sugar cookies one day, so I asked her for the recipe. She has the cutest golden retriever. Henry. He wears a bandana. Her daughter wears pigtails in the pictures on her desk. They're everywhere. She has a silly laugh. She's a really good public speaker. I focus on those things and I'm always looking for more." She looked up to me to see if I was paying attention. "Interesting fact," she said. "You can't *really* focus on two ideas at the same time." She then went into a little philosophical debate about whether or not an idea really ever exists if it's not focused on, which I didn't follow because I was mulling over her supposedly bulletproof strategy and starting to get annoyed about it.

As she started to get metaphysical about whether ideas exist without hosts, I interrupted her and said, "What about the concept of right and wrong?" She went silent and gave me a big eye roll. "I'm serious," I said. "What about the basic tenet that there's such a thing as true and false? Their entire ideology, their entire worldview, is based on lies. Unsupported by facts or data. What about the fact that they're destroying the country?"

I was sitting up halfway and getting heated. She got off my arm so that I could sit up the rest of the way. She propped herself up next to me and pulled the sheets up to cover herself modestly. She kept the sheet in place by crossing her arms across her chest. "Would you rather be right or happy, Troy? You can't have both. If you insist on being the good guy, then they have to be the bad guys, and then you have a problem. So, which would you rather be? Right or happy?"

I was irritated by the question but considered it for a moment anyway. "I'll be happy when he agrees I'm right," I concluded.

She whistled through her teeth. "Good luck with that, buddy," she said. "You just signed on for a life of misery."

17

Nicaragua
2020

I heard the door unbolt, but by then I wasn't sure what was real, so they had to rouse me out of bed and drag me to my feet. Two guards walked me down the hall, up the stairs and through that maze of cubicles on the ground floor. On the other end of the floor were a few holding cells and then a row of offices. As they led me along, I looked in the holding cells. The first two were empty, but in the third I saw a familiar face. Andy was sitting on a bench against the wall. He held his face up so that it caught the sunlight coming through the window. His eyes were closed. He had in earphones. The cuts and bruises on his face were mostly healed. He wore fresh clothing that looked neat and clean. The cell was bare, but it was tidy. It looked like a four-star resort compared to my cell, and he looked like he was positively enjoying his stay at Chipote. By the time we reached the row of offices alongside the cells, my blood was boiling from the image of him sunbathing.

When we got to the corner office, they led me inside. I recognized the cop with the handlebar mustache and the messy hair. He was sitting behind the desk and seemed to have been waiting for me. They sat me down in a faded red plastic armchair across the desk from him. He winced and waved his hand under his nose to show that I smelled bad. The look on his face suggested it was due to a lack of personal hygiene on my part. I nodded, shrugged my shoulders and said, "Yeah. My apologies."

For the next half-hour or so, he asked me a long series of questions. He asked me all about my relationship with Andy, all the details around what I was doing in Nicaragua, how long I had been there, where I was staying, who I was traveling with, etc. He held a pen in his right hand, as though at any moment he might jot down some important aspect of my answers, but he never did. I assumed he knew the answers to all of these questions already, but I cooperated willingly and thoroughly.

Finally, he came to the point. He put down the pen and twirled the ends of his mustache in a quick, mechanical way, as though he did it many times each day and the movement was automatic. "Here is the thing. Your associate, Andrew McEwen." He looked at me when he said the name like I was supposed to react in some way. I don't think I'd ever heard Andy's last name before, but I wasn't sure that was the magic he was looking for. He looked disappointed that I didn't react to the sound of Andy's name for some reason. What reaction was I supposed to have shown?

He continued. "Andrew owes a lot of money to very important people here." He paused and reiterated, "Very. Important. Very powerful." He waited and I thought I was expected to acknowledge this, so I nodded. "We know, from talking to Andrew, that your story is not true. We know that you are his business partner and, in fact, that you are in charge of the finances . . . no, what is the right word?" He paused for a moment and my head spun. I thought of Andy sun-washed and content in the luxury holding cell. "Funding," he continued. "Not finance. You control the funding for McEwen's real estate development business."

"That's ridiculous," I said. "He's my Alcoholics Anonymous sponsor. That's it."

He twisted up his face, sat back in his seat and crossed his arms. "No, Senor Martin. *That* is ridiculous," he said and then started to chuckle.

I shook my head and closed my eyes. He wasn't wrong. "Okay, so where is all of this going? What do you want from me?"

He leaned forward and his chair let out a loud complaint. He folded his hands on his desk and tucked his chin down, looking up at me in a somber way. "Good. Now we come to the point, hmm? You have two choices." He jabbed his fat pointer finger down at his desk, making a thud on the metal surface. "One, you go back down to your cell for another week or two." He paused to see my reaction to this idea. I tried to keep a poker face, but I have no doubt there was fear in my eyes. After coming back up to the ground level and feeling the air on my skin and seeing the sunlight coming through the windows, the idea of going back down there stirred panic in my gut. "Or you do us a couple of favors and we can all shake hands and be friends."

I nodded. It didn't seem like I had a choice. I was going to have to play this out.

"Very good," he said. "Then we have an understanding. We are going to take you back to your lodge in Gigante now. On the way you are going to do favor number one. Then my men will allow you to wash up and have a meal and sleep in your own bed, and tomorrow you will do us favor number two. And then we will all be friends and we can do business together for a long time."

That last part was a curveball. I imagined that after favor number two, whatever that was, I would get the fuck out of Nicaragua and never come back. *Whatever. Let's just get out of here*, I told myself. *We can deal with this as it comes and look for an opportunity to escape.*

The two guards walked me through the cubicles and then out into the blazing sunshine. The shock of it, after a week of darkness, made my head throb. They guided me along through the courtyard in front of Chipote and out into the parking lot. I recognized the pickup truck and the two blue-shirted Nicaraguan policemen who got out. Flacco and Gordo. As much as I had learned to hate these two, the sight of them meant that I was leaving this hellhole and going back to the coast. Whatever else happened, that was a huge improvement. "Fellas," I said in greeting. "How was your week?"

The guards handed me over and Flacco walked over and pulled my hands together in front of me for cuffs. "That doesn't seem to be necessary," I complained. They walked me over to the truck and loaded me in the back, like cargo. Flacco climbed in while Gordo got behind the wheel. "Are we going to the airport?" I asked. No response.

After a few minutes of driving, I started to recognize some landmarks. It would be about two hours from there. The ride was rough, and I bounced around quite a bit, but I was happy to be outside. I was so relieved to be out of that cell. Breathing fresh air did me a lot of good. It took my eyes a while to adjust to the light, and it was a while longer before the headache went away. The truck moved along at a deliberate speed because of the condition of the road. The warm breeze felt good.

It was a strange couple of hours. I sat on the floor of the truck bed, legs crossed, with my face in the sun as the breeze moved across my body and through my hair. The sun went in and out of view behind the trees alongside the road. On the one hand, I sensed there was some terrible shit that was about to come. On the other, I was happy to be alive and strangely proud to have survived that living hell. Whatever else happened from there couldn't be as bad as that.

Flacco sat with his back to the truck cab, across from me, holding his gun pointed down and to the side a bit. He was more or less keeping an eye on me but seemed pretty relaxed. I must not have looked like much of a threat. I sat back up and watched the shadows from the trees on the road, the people passing by in vehicles and on bicycles, the villagers who were living their simple lives. Skinny dogs and wild chickens wandered around. It was good to be in the world again. I even felt connected to the quasi-militarized young thug across from me. I didn't resent him for doing his job. He was a poor schmuck from a poor country. I imagined he had a couple of kids at home with big brown eyes. *He does this terrible job to provide a better life for them,* I thought.

"Hey, Flacco," I called to him. "You know, I'm a police officer also." He didn't look impressed. "In the United States," I explained. "In Florida. I am a retired police officer." He didn't register any expression. Fair enough. "I know you're just doing your job," I said, "I respect that. No hard feelings." I left it at that.

We drove through the town of Rivas and past the police station. It was a freshly painted cinderblock building the same baby blue color as the uniform shirts of the officers. A yellow banner hung below the second-floor windows that read *Una Vida de Servicio Ciudadania* (A life of citizen service). I imagined that was where these two were stationed out of. The truck stopped at the edge of town. We were pulled over at the side of the road. I was about to ask Flacco what we were doing there, but that seemed pointless. After a couple of minutes, the afternoon rain started up. It went from a drizzle to a downpour. As far as I was concerned, it couldn't rain hard enough. It was the best shower I had had in a week.

Finally, a tattoo-covered shirtless gangster jogged across the road and jumped in the cab of the truck. My clothes were soaked through by the time we pulled back onto the road and continued toward Gigante. It was another twenty minutes of jostling around in the back of the truck before we got to the edge of town. It was the middle of the day and I realized it must be Sunday, because the streets were busy. Some people were dressed in their nice church clothes. Others were just idling around on their day off.

Gordo pulled to the side just before the main intersection into town. We were a few hundred yards from Dale Daggers, so I started to imagine a hot shower and a nice meal. I wondered if there would be other guests there. Would I walk in with my goon squad in tow and introduce them to some Australian teenagers on a surf trip? *I guess we'll see,* I figured. I couldn't imagine what we were waiting for. What was the first favor going to be? Why did they need the shirtless gangster? *Who the fuck knows with these people*, I decided.

Finally, a car pulled up behind us. It was one of the nicest cars I had seen in quite a while, a black Mercedes sedan. The driver, a uniformed soldier, got out of the car and opened the back door. I heard his voice before I saw his face. "What are we doing here?" he said. "I thought you were taking me to my house in Santana." The soldier pulled him out by the arm.

"Motherfucker," I said out loud. It was Andy. He was clean, dry and wearing his fresh clothes. He winced as the rain hit him in the face, and then he looked up and saw me, handcuffed in the back of the truck.

Gordo and the gangster got out and came around to open the truck bed. They led me down to the road. "Hey, what the fuck are you doing?" Andy yelled out from behind me. "Get off of me!" The soldier was zip-tying his hands behind his back. "Hey! I'm going to tell Omar Garcia Hufach about this! This wasn't our deal!"

The soldier pulled a blackjack from his belt and smacked Andy in the back of the head with it. "Shut up," he said, and led him out to the middle of the road.

Flacco pushed me in that direction as well, and pointed his gun for emphasis. When I got up next to Andy, he was frantic. "You motherfucker," I said. "I told you not to drag me into your shit. I can't believe I trusted you, you lying piece of shit."

"Troy, you don't understand," he argued. "They were going to kill me. I had no choice."

"Shut up," the soldier instructed both of us. I had nothing left to say anyway. The soldier got back into his car and pulled away.

The other three didn't seem entirely sure how to proceed. "Give it to him," Gordo said. The gangster pulled a box cutter out of his front jeans pocket. He walked over and handed it to me. Then he stepped back and pointed his gun at me. "Do it," he said, and then he looked at the other two.

They nodded. "Favor number one," Gordo said as he walked over to me. He unlocked my handcuffs and put them on his belt.

"No!" Andy yelled, starting to run with his hands tied behind his back. Flacco caught him across the face with his nightstick. He hit the dirt and started groaning.

"Do it now," Gordo said. He and the other two fixed their guns on me. "Favor number one, or you go back in the box."

I walked over to Andy and picked him up by the hair on the back of his head. When I cut through his throat, I could feel the blade move through the cartilage. It was a small blade, so the damage was very close to my hand. All of the subtle changes in resistance and vibration went right through to me. I thought about giving him a cursory surface cut and throwing him to the ground, pretending to have killed him so we could try to roleplay our way through this, but I knew Andy was too stupid with fear and emotion to understand what I would be doing. He would fuck it up. The only chance I had to get home to my daughters was to do it right; and honestly, after what he had put me through, I didn't even really mind it that much. I didn't want to kill him and would've been happy enough to walk away and never speak with him again, but the anger enabled me to muscle up and tear deeply through his neck, starting below his left ear, continuing under his Adam's apple, and all the way through to the other side.

I dropped his body in the road. Gordo came over and stood on his right leg, to turn him over. Andy made some gurgling noises as he bucked and thrashed like a big fish in the bottom of a boat. I looked up. All around the intersection were a dozen or so locals stopped in their tracks, watching the big hairy *gringo* bleed out in the middle of the road. Even in the country of marvels, this was something remarkable.

Flacco came over and handed me his phone. "Harfuch," he said. I stood in the road, looking at the phone and then up at the locals, who had started to continue on their way. "Talk," Flacco instructed.

I dropped the box cutter in the road and held the phone up to my ear. "Yes," I said.

"Very good," the police commissioner said. "That was favor number one. Unfortunately, now Andrew will not be able to pay the debts he owed. Since you killed him, his debts are now your debts."

I shook my head and looked down at Andy. He had stopped moving. The rain had let up and his blood had started to absorb into the dirt road.

"You understand?" Harfuch said.

"How much?" I replied.

He laughed. "Never mind that for now. We will work together, and we will be friends. Favor number two will be your first payment. Tomorrow, when the bank opens, you will make your first payment." He hung up.

As we pulled away in the truck, I watched Andy bleed out in the road. He had lived a dirty, dishonest life and he died a violent death, lying alone in the mud. I pictured Barry on the boat a few weeks earlier. "You gotta clean up your side of the street. You gotta clean that shit up, or it could kill you."

It only took a minute or so to get to Dale Daggers. As the truck pulled to a stop in front of the outer gate, the general outline of a plan started to form in my mind. The tattooed gangster got out and walked away. *That will help,* I thought. Thankfully, nobody was home when we went in. The sun was getting low across the bay, so it was probably around 4:30 or 5 p.m. Flacco followed me into the house and then into the bedroom. I pointed to the bathroom, "*Con su permiso,*" I said. He looked around the bathroom. I guess he was checking to see if there were any windows big enough to climb through. There weren't, so he waved me in with the gun. I showered and brushed my teeth. Both felt so good, they bordered on spiritual experiences.

Flacco watched me dress and then followed me to the kitchen. "*Tiene hambre?*" I asked.

Just then, Walter walked in the back door. He froze in the living room and looked back and forth between Flacco and me, his expression shifting from shock to concern to anger. Anger on that face was something to see. He looked like an entirely different person. "Are you okay, Troy?" he asked me.

"Yes, Walter. Thank you."

He turned to Flacco and yelled, "Look at what you have become! A disgrace to your neighborhood. An embarrassment to your family. You do the dirty work for animals!" These insults were personal. I was surprised they seemed to know each other. For a moment I thought that maybe Walter could shame this guy into letting me go if they had a long history together, but then he continued, "You are an evil man who came from a good family. The devil celebrates men like you. You're going to burn in hell for the life you're living. Fatima and Victor are spinning in their graves from this behavior!"

That did it. Flacco growled as he turned toward Walter and pointed the AK-47 at him. With his arms extended and stiff, his face contracted and he started to yell, "You shut your mouth...."

That was the opening I needed. I did what I do; I switched off my brain and let my body go. I smashed the barrel of the gun on the side and then drove with my legs like a lacrosse cross-check until he flipped over the half-wall that separated the kitchen from the hallway. He fired a single shot into the ceiling as he went over. I launched myself over the half-wall and got to him just as he was scrambling to his feet, driving with my shoulder, using all the force I could find. He flew into the coffee table. Fear and disbelief flashed across his face as the glass top of the table shattered on him and I jumped to my feet. A quick but accurate stomp with my bare foot snapped his head back while he was propped up on the metal crossbars of the now smashed table's base. Another shot fired before the gun dropped beside him. I stomped his face two more times—surgical, powerful blows with the heel of my foot. I had to reset a bit after the first blow because he slumped further down into the frame of the coffee table. His face came to rest directly on the frame and the second blow knocked him unconscious, and I think it also broke his jaw. I picked up the gun and fired two rounds into his chest.

I looked at Walter, who was frozen in an action pose just a few feet away. He looked like he was about to jump in, but didn't know exactly what to do. We traded "holy shit" glances seconds before the front door flew open and Gordo charged through. Walter ran toward him, letting out what I can only describe as a war cry. "No!" I yelled as Gordo fired on Walter, cutting him down. As soon as Walter dropped, I had a clear shot at Gordo, and I fired the rest of the clip in his direction. One of the rounds hit him in the side of his cheek and took him down. His Glock slid across the tile floor. As he desperately crawled for it, I ran over, picked it up and fired three rounds into his chest.

I ran back over to Walter, but he was gone. His eyes were vacant and there was a pool of blood on the floor around him. "I'm so sorry, Walter," I whispered. I marveled as I put him gently down on the ground how such a kind, sweet man could be such a warrior. "Thank you."

I ran into my bedroom and looked for my stuff. The packed bag from a week before with my cash, phone and passport were nowhere to be found. *Fuck it*, I thought. *I gotta get out of here right now.* I patted down Walter and found the boat keys in the pocket of his board shorts. I grabbed them, patted his cheek to say goodbye, and bolted for the beach. The kayak was always stored on the side of the house. I pulled it out with one hand, carrying the oar in the other hand. I dragged it across the beach and launched into the bay, less than fifty feet from the fishermen, who were pulling in their nets for the day. I paddled to the other side of the bay, where Walter always anchored the boat. There were dozens of boats out there and I started to panic for a moment when I couldn't find the black Dale Daggers surf boat.

Finally, I spotted it, paddled over and jumped on board, pulling the kayak up behind me. The anchor was heavy in my condition, but I pulled it up, hand over hand, before firing up the engine and bolting out of the bay.

At the end of the bay, I turned south. I needed to get out of Nicaragua as fast as possible. There was only one place I could possibly think to go. Barry's casita was in Salinas Bay, just over the border in Costa Rica. That seemed like my best bet. I went out a couple of miles from shore, just far enough so I could see the coastline and follow it down. Crunching some numbers in my head, I figured that the Yamaha 115 engine would probably push this modified fishing boat about 25 miles per hour at top speed. There was a little bit of wind out of the south, so maybe more like 22. Barry said that Salinas was about 35 kilometers from San Juan Del Sur, which is about 20 miles. That's a little less than halfway to Gigante, so figure 45 miles more or less. *Okay, two hours to the border.* The throttle was wide open but I instinctively pushed it down a little harder. *Let's go, baby.*

Two hours is a long time when you're running for your life. Enough time for all kinds of thoughts and plans. Even a few daydreams and fantasies. I had spent the past week laying in place and basically watching my mind, so that's what I did on the ride to Costa Rica as well. I formed the basics of a plan: find Barry, use his phone, borrow some cash, drive to the airport in Liberia, and get the fuck out of Central America.

18

Florida
2016

A few weeks after I hit the twenty-year mark with the city of Fort Lauderdale, I got a call from the Broward Sheriff's Office. One of my old captains had been elected sheriff and wanted me to come over there and run a division for them. I retired on Friday from the city and started the following Monday at the Sheriff's Office. I carried over two years of service time from my stint as a Broward corrections officer, so I only needed another three years to qualify for a second partial pension.

I retired with a bunch of guys I had come up the ranks with. My buddy Jon Adelson hosted a barbeque in his yard to celebrate. Jon and his wife Mindy had a great house on a canal in Pompano, with a big pool. It was a beautiful early spring day. The food was great and everyone seemed to be in good spirits. I got a chance to introduce Michelle to a bunch of old friends and colleagues. It was nice. To me, it felt like we were a real couple, rather than two people who were dating.

Six cups of vodka and Red Bull later, I found myself in a debate with Rick about border security. "We're a whole *nation* of immigrants," I argued. "That's literally what we do here. It's our whole fucking claim to fame since we started this thing up. Come make a better life for your family and help us build the country..."

Rick was shaking his head. "Hurt, these people are a huge financial drain on our society," he said. "Let me ask you this." He took a sip of his drink. "One of these people shows up in the emergency room in Miami. Who's paying for that? They got no insurance. Who pays for that?"

"Are you saying that *you* pay for it?"

"We all do," he said, pointing at everyone in the backyard. "They come over here and commit crimes. One of them kills your friend. Now what? One of them runs over your dog with his car. Now what? The guy's not even supposed to be here."

"Here's the difference between my argument and yours," I said to him. I had my red plastic cup in my hand and started to gesticulate violently. In my mind, I thought I was explaining something to him calmly, but I could see on his face that he was getting concerned. "My argument is based on facts. Mine is true and yours is false." I spit a little bit at that point and he winced. "You go around and repeat the same lies you hear repeated every day by FOX and Breitbart." Rick had his arms folded across his chest. He looked exasperated. His gazed down at the deck and shook his head as if to say, *I can't believe I have to listen to this nonsense.*

I put my drink down on the cocktail table next to me so that I could use both hands to emphasize my point. "Let me give you some facts. US born citizens are three times more likely to commit violent crimes. They're two and a half times more likely to commit drug crimes and they're four times more likely to be arrested for property crimes. The more immigrants we bring in the *lower* our crime rates will be. Can you understand that? Because that is the *truth*, Rick. Those are actual facts. But your boy Tucker tells you every night that *you're* the victim, so you believe it. Those evil brown immigrants are taking over and soon they're going to be ruining everything." The last point I made while stabbing him in the chest with my pointer finger. "And he makes you feel better *for being a racist.*"

"Whoa," Rick exclaimed. He threw his hands up in a stop gesture. "That's over the line, Hurt. You can't say that to me."

Michelle was apparently listening in from an adjacent conversation group. When she heard the turn things had taken, she spun around and took a few steps over to us. By now, my face was red and the veins in my neck were starting to pop. She put her arm around me. As if everything was as calm and cool as can be, she said, "Troy, is this your friend Rick? Your old friend and your patrol partner and your friend from the gym?

Aren't you going to introduce us?"

I wiped my mouth and collected myself. I nodded and exhaled and eventually looked apologetically at Rick. "Yes, Rick and I are old friends." *Well played, Michelle.*

"Rick, please say hello to my girlfriend, Michelle."

"Nice to meet you," Rick said. "You have your hands full with Hurt here."

"I prefer to think of him as Troy," she said through a wry smile. "I've been looking forward to meeting you. Believe it or not, Troy speaks very highly of you."

Before leaving the party, I went to the bathroom. Rick was walking out as I was entering. When he saw me, he threw his hands up in the air and yelled, "Truce!" We both laughed. "Easy, Hurt!"

I threw up my hands in surrender and laughed, but when I closed the door to the bathroom behind me, I realized that my friend was actually concerned when he saw me just then. *How much of a violent psycho does he think I am?* The mirror was right there, so I had a look. *So, who's the asshole in this situation, Troy? I asked myself. In fact, who was the asshole in all of those confrontations? The bar fights, the arguments . . . Was it the person who had their facts wrong? Or was it the person who acted like a savage?*

Michelle moved in with me a few months later. That's pretty much when the shit hit the fan with my drinking. It had been progressing for months leading up to her move-in, but for whatever reason it really kicked into a new gear when she gave up her apartment. She saw it. Of course she did. So why did she move in? Why did she stay? Why was she with me in the first place? These are questions I've only partially answered to this day. I was a trainwreck at that stage of my life.

To the table, I brought physical appeal, intelligence, and two amazing daughters. I also brought emotional and psychological toxic waste. I have two theories. The first is that she wanted to fix me. I don't understand it, but I'm aware that this is a motivator for some women. My second theory is that she liked dark and interesting things. This is why she joined the prosecutor's office rather than taking a cushy corporate law job. She liked the grittiness of it. With me, she may have gotten more grit than she bargained for.

I capped off my drinking career during a trip to San Francisco for her parents' fiftieth wedding anniversary. We traveled out with my girls. Michelle had family coming in from all over the world for the occasion. It had only been for the prior few weeks that I had started drinking all day, every day. For years I needed a beer in the morning or a shot before work to make my hands stop shaking and get my head straight, but that had progressed to drinking around the clock. I drank so much that I couldn't even get drunk anymore. Alcohol had stopped working. As a result, I wasn't quite drunk, but I was never really sober. I kept plastic water bottles full of vodka in my car, on my desk at work, etc. I thought I was hiding it well.

Isolation was enabling me to survive, but on vacation I couldn't hide. It was a full-time job trying to keep a buzz going so that I wouldn't start shaking and freaking out. On our first night, Michelle's mother Elaine walked into their dining room in the middle of the night and caught me swigging bourbon straight out of the bottle. I had walked by the dining room earlier that day and spotted the bar. It was stocked. I had put it off for as long as I could, but there was no way I was going to make it through the night without going back down there. *Just a few swallows*, I finally told myself at 2 a.m. Elaine looked at me with sheer sympathy. She didn't say anything. She walked over in her bathrobe and slippers and patted me on the shoulder a few times. She was too short to reach my cheek, so she reached in and kissed my shoulder. That nearly broke me. I went upstairs and cried myself to sleep, but not before I came back down a second time and drank half the bottle.

The next day, Ceci took a big swig out of one of my water bottles. She proceeded to projectile-vomit across their den. Everyone jumped up and checked to see if she was okay. They mobilized to clean up the mess. Michelle's father took a sniff of the water bottle and glared at me.

That night we were having a big dinner in their dining room. It was the night of their actual anniversary.

Elaine had it catered and there was a team of cooks and waiters working in the house. They brought in extra folding tables to put alongside their dining room table to fit the whole family. Roxy sat across the table from me, crying. She held her face in her hands while Ceci rubbed her back and tried to shush her. Michelle sat next to me. She leaned across the table and asked, "What's the matter, sweetie?"

"I don't want an alcoholic for a father," she blurted out and then cried some more into her hands.

The silence at the table was complete. The only sounds were Roxy's sobs. I tried to say something to comfort or assure her, but I had lost the power of speech by then and my words came out in a grotesque jumble. I thought about getting up and walking away, but I was surrounded on both sides, and it would've taken a lot of doing to get out of there. I had to just sit there and take it. I couldn't look at anyone else's faces. If I could've snapped my fingers and died in that moment, I would have.

The next day I swore to God that I wasn't going to drink. I was going to try to salvage this trip and restore my kids' faith in me. But I couldn't. I had no choice. It'd been a long time since I had a choice, but I couldn't even put it off for an hour. I felt like I was going to die if I didn't have a drink. "Michelle, I need help," I said to her in her parents' kitchen.

"I know, Troy," she said. "Everyone knows."

I called the employee services department at the Sheriff's Office and they arranged for me to go to rehab. There was a bed open in a place called Marworth, in Tampa. I flew out that afternoon and took an Uber to the facility. My girls stayed out there in California with Michelle and her family.

19

By the time I got to Salinas Bay there were just a few rays of daylight left. I cruised closer to the coast so I could spot the Dreams Hotel and mark where it stood on the beach. Then I headed a couple of miles straight out to sea. I felt guilty about ditching Mike's boat, but if anyone was looking for me, it would give away my location instantly.

I got the boat facing west and then tied the steering wheel to the docking cleat with straps from the lifejackets, so it wouldn't turn. I dropped the kayak off the back of the boat with the paddle tucked inside. Then I pushed the throttle about halfway down and jumped off. I swam over to the kayak and climbed in. Paddling to shore took longer than I could've imagined. I didn't have any way to mark time, but I think it was at least two hours, maybe even three. A little while after losing the last bit of daylight, I lost all concept of time. Pretty soon, I was just navigating toward the lights of the hotel. I was exhausted from my week in solitary, malnutrition and severe dehydration. The cramps traveled up my legs, starting in my toes. A little while later my calves went into terrible, painful spasms and eventually it moved up to my hamstrings. It was excruciating. I had to stop several times until the cramps subsided. A few times I really believed that I might not make it. The hotel lights just didn't seem to be getting any closer.

I had recurring fears in a loop: *Am I caught in a riptide? Maybe I'm not strong enough to fight the current. Maybe I should jump out and swim.* "These are just thoughts," I said out loud. "They aren't necessarily true. This is just my brain thinking. This is what brains do. Move the focus to your body." But my body hurt so much, I soon wanted to escape back into thought again. *Okay, let's go to fantasy: college graduation for Roxy. I am so proud. She looks so beautiful.*

By the time I got to shore I was physically and emotionally spent. I laid on the beach for a long time to rest. Finally, I dragged myself up. *Gotta move.* I needed to find Barry. There was a stone path that led from the beach up to the pool area. There were three huge pools on two levels, an outdoor restaurant, and a group of thatched huts off to the side that were probably guest suites. I stopped at the shower, took off my shirt, and rinsed the sand off my body. Then I sat on the side and used my hands to cup water from the foot wash nozzle. I must have drunk a gallon of water. It was like a gift from God. My body and mind responded to the hydration immediately. I was still exhausted, but I was able to move without as much pain, and my head cleared a bit. My sense of well-being and hopefulness leveled up too.

I walked past a huge lagoon-shaped pool that was lit from within, and shone the same aquamarine color as the ocean. There was a small set of stairs that went up to the next pool deck, where I could now see three restaurants. They were all busy. The walkway split at the end of a large rectangular pool. To the left there were three low-rise hotel buildings and to the right were another four. The ones on the left looked like they backed right up to the tree line. The ones on the right looked like they had a significant amount of space behind them. Probably a road. I followed along to the right and passed a number of hotel guests, nodding and smiling at them as I went, thinking that I must've looked to them like a trainwreck.

Sure enough, a hundred yards past the last building was a parking lot, some tennis courts and then the road. I walked along the road for a couple of minutes until I came to a guy cooking kebabs on a small makeshift charcoal grill on the side of the road. He smiled big and revealed a mixed set of teeth—some silver, some brown, some missing. "*Hola, hermano,*" I said.

"*Como estas, amigo?*" he said, looking back down to his grill and finishing up brushing his kebabs with a sauce. "*Tienes hambre?*"

I shook my head. "*Estoy buscando de mi amigo.*" He nodded. "*Conoces a . . . Barry? Blanco dude? Gringo? Tengo que encontrar su casa.*"

The guy chuckled. Without even looking up he pointed back over his left shoulder. "You found it," he said in perfect English.

20

Tampa
2016

I don't remember much from my first few days in rehab. They had me in the detox unit so I didn't die from alcohol withdrawal seizures, which I learned is a real possibility for people in my condition. I do remember freaking out because shadows and images were flying across the floors and walls. I also remember the unsettling feeling that something was crawling under my skin. I was told that these things were common and would stop eventually, but they went on for five days. After that, I moved into a room that reminded me of one of the cells in block B at the Broward County Correctional Facility. A nurse assistant showed me to my bed and handed me a bundle that included three pairs of pajamas, a bathrobe, slippers and two bath towels. "Here's your stuff," she said.

I wanted to say thanks, but it seemed too ridiculous. I laid down on the bed and felt the sheer weight of my failure on me. I had been a young man with unlimited potential. How could this have happened? My situation was so depressing and so humiliating that I didn't hear a word anyone said to me for a week. I was deep in my own head.

At the end of the first week, after dozens of counseling sessions, group sessions, AA meetings, and reading the first 164 pages of *The Big Book*, I hadn't learned a thing. I held onto two undisputed facts: 1) I was a loser; 2) These people were not going to be able to help me. Over the second week I gradually started to focus more on fact number two, probably because my ego couldn't handle being such a loser.

After a group session one afternoon, my fellow inmates filed out of the conference room and the counselor, Jose, asked me to stay. Jose was about my size, and he had a tough edge to him. He had compassion—nobody could do that job without it—but he also had a vibe that said, *Don't push me too far.* He had been patient with me for the first couple of weeks as I vented my frustrations and argued with the staff. Over the last couple of days, though, he had begun asking me to leave meetings when he felt I was being disruptive.

When the last group member stepped out of the conference room and closed the door behind her, Jose took off his wire-framed eyeglasses and put them down on the table. He stood up and put his hands together in a prayer position. "Please," he said. "Tell me what your fucking problem is, Troy." He glared at me from across the table. "I want to hear from you *what your fucking problem is*. Because I don't understand what's happening here."

I didn't understand what was happening either, but I really didn't appreciate his tone. In my experience, "What's your fucking problem?" is what you said when you were trying to start a fight with someone. I paused for a moment and decided that I was about to be attacked. So, I attacked. "You're my problem!" I yelled, pointing my finger at him. "You and your team here all suck. You're not helping me! I need real help and you hand out this boilerplate bullshit every day. My life is at stake and you people are fucking incompetent!" I was working my way around the table and toward him as I yelled.

Jose flung his desk chair out of the way. He threw it so hard that it bounced off the cinderblock wall and crashed to the ground. He walked around the table and got right up in my face. His foot touched my foot. Our noses were inches apart. *Oh yeah, he's definitely trying to start a fight with me.* I expected someone to burst through the door at that moment and break it up, but nobody came. The conference room was surrounded with windows, and a handful of staff and patients stood outside watching. I glanced over at them. Nobody was coming. I realized that they all wanted him to kick my ass. "You are here voluntarily," he said, close enough for me to smell the coffee and cigarettes on his breath. "You can leave anytime you want."

It was hard to process this statement, because I was getting ready to shut off my mind and let my body do its thing. A piece of his spit hit my cheek. I closed my eyes and breathed deep. "I can't go home right now," I said. "I need to fight. I need you to help me fight this disease. It's hurting my family. I can't go home until I beat it and I *need...fucking...help*." I was grinding my teeth now. "I'm going to fight this, and I'm going to beat it, and it'd be nice if I could get some actual fucking help while I'm here instead of your platitudes and bullshit."

Jose nodded his head and took a tiny step backward to return some personal space. "You're going to lose," he said.

The top of my head almost blew off. "What! What kind of thing is that to say? My life is on the line—my family is at stake—and you . . . you . . . you tell me I'm going to lose?"

Jose nodded. "Yep. You are," he said and then paused. He paused for too long. I turned to walk out of the room, so I could grab my few items and get an Uber to the airport. He finally called out behind me, "Because you don't *fight* this disease, Troy! That's not how you win."

"Bullshit!" I yelled, spinning around just before I got to the door. "You don't know who you're talking to. I don't lose. I'm a fucking machine! I *will* power through this."

Jose laughed out loud, and then he covered his mouth to cover up a huge smile. "Man, look at yourself. You're standing there in pajamas and slippers in a drug rehab, your hair is all messed up, you ain't showered today. You ain't welcome at your house. Your family is scared of you. You just winning all over the place, right?" He chuckled some more, and then out of the side of his mouth he sneered, "There he is, folks, the fucking machine."

My hand was on the doorknob, and I looked out the glass to the hallway on the other side. It had been a minute since I had won anything. I suddenly felt it in my stomach. I need a win so badly. Looking out the window of the conference room door, for an instant I saw a lacrosse field zipping by as I ran full speed. Sweat dripped into my eyes.

"This disease is not something you fight, Troy," Jose said. For the first time he had a bit of empathy in his voice, but it was still eighty percent irritation. "If you want to 'win,' you're going to have to surrender." I looked back at him in confusion. "You have to accept that you're powerless. That's where you have to start if you want any chance of recovering. The war is over, Troy. You lost. Time to surrender so you can get on with your life. No more fighting."

I had heard this stuff before, but this time it hit different. I finally got it. I sat down in the chair at the end of the table and my mind went back to the lacrosse field. I take the pass from Louis Strickland, our goalie in Manhasset. As I run up the sidelines to clear the ball, I spin around an attackman wearing the maroon and yellow uniform of Garden City, our rivals, and then sprint. My steps are quick and powerful as I accelerate out of our zone. As I reach midfield and top speed, I'm gliding. My stride is long and loping. I'm suspended in the air, eating up huge chunks of turf with each step. Wind whistles past the ear holes in my helmet. Sweat drips down my face as I slow down, set my feet and fire a pass to my buddy Jake, who's just curled to free himself. *Yes, this is going to work.*

I cried for a good ten minutes at the table with Jose sitting next to me. Every few minutes he said little things like, "It's going to be okay," or "you never have to feel this way again," or "you're right where you're supposed to be."

That was step one for me. Some people come into rehab already on step one. I had to suffer a little more until I got it. Jose took me through steps two and three over my remaining couple of weeks.

21

Costa Rica
2020

Fifty meters behind the kebab man's outstretched thumb was a one-room cottage. Actually, it was a stretch to call it a cottage. It was probably more of a hut. It had a rusted green metal roof that extended out over a concrete slab that was the front porch. The roof was supported by two branches of a guanacaste tree that had been jammed into the concrete while it had still been wet. The front door was painted purple. Purple and white tie-dye sheets covered the windows from the inside. The rest of the concrete block structure had a fresh coat of orange paint. I had never really thought about it, but I guess this is pretty much what I would've assumed Barry's house would look like.

There were two camping chairs on either side of the front door. I walked between them and knocked. Barry opened the door wearing just a pair of faded board shorts. "Yo, Troy!" he said. "What's up, man? What are you doing here? You okay? What's going on? Where you been?"

I didn't really know where to begin and it must have shown on my face, because he backed up and gently pulled me in by the arm, closing the door behind me. The place was a little larger than I expected inside. It was about thirty feet deep and had more of a bachelor loft feel than rustic jungle hut. There was a narrow kitchen area along the south side, a queen-sized bed, a sofa, desk and dresser. The furniture was all much nicer than I would've expected, and kind of formal. It looked like it came out of a . . . yes, that made sense, it looked like it came out of a hotel room, because it did come out of a hotel room, from the resort next door. Barry had scored a whole bedroom set, and as I looked around I saw that he had a lot of the accents as well—the mirror over the desk, the rolling desk chair, the comforter and sheets on the unmade bed. Even the pillows looked like they were hotel-quality. The room was cooled by a split unit, with the vent along the north wall. After a week in ninety percent humidity, it felt heavenly. The cool, dry air was working miracles on my skin, and I felt like I could breathe for the first time in a while. I took a deep inhale and the room started to spin a bit. "Do you mind if I sit down?" I asked.

"Yeah, yeah, of course," Barry said, walking me over to the sofa as though I needed an escort to find it. "You look like shit, bro," he added as he ambled along next to me. "Tell me."

I sat down and told him. As I told him, I wondered at each part how much I should leave out and how much to reveal. For one thing, I was probably endangering him by being there. I was probably endangering him more by telling him the story. I was also gambling over him being who I thought he was. By then, my confidence in my personal judgment about the character of my friends wasn't very high. I was obviously vulnerable to being duped, but Barry had been an open book. He had been kind and generous. He ran a good AA program and helped a lot of people ... but so had Andy, and that motherfucker almost got me killed.

As I went along in the story, the look on Barry's face, his body language and his vibe spelled concern and compassion. I didn't see judgment or self-centered fear, so I just kept telling him the next part and the next part until I was done. Barry just kept interjecting the word "fuck" every so often. He did it in different tones and lengths. At some parts it was a quick, alarmed, "Fuck!" When I was telling him about Chipote, he gave out a long, low, compassionate, "Fuuuuuck." When I finished, he added one final, quick "Fuck" that said indicated, *That was crazy.*

"Yeah," I said. "Crazy, right?"

We looked at each other for a long moment before he snapped out of his trance.

"Food," he said. "Let me get you some food and water."

That actually made me cry a little bit. "Yeah. Thank you. I'm starving."

He rummaged around in the small kitchen for a couple of minutes and brought me a bowl of granola with raw almonds and a plate with a few big slices of mango. I ate them slowly, enjoying the nuance of each flavor tone, and I imagined that I could feel the vitamins and minerals being absorbed by my nutrient-starved body. I drank half a gallon of water while I ate, and we both sat in silence. It felt almost ritualistic, the feeding of the starving man, maybe even religious. When I finished, I closed my eyes and took a deep breath. "Can I use your phone?" I asked. "I have to make some calls."

Barry took his iPhone off the night table and unplugged the charging cord. He handed it to me and said, "Use the WiFi calling app. The cell signal isn't great over here."

I knew Roxy's number by heart but not Ceci's. Over the prior few months, I had helped her fill out some online applications, and each required her to enter her phone number. I dialed the number but she didn't answer. I'm sure the caller ID was showing some weird international number and probably looked like a telemarketing scam, so I texted her: *Hi Rox, it's dad Please pick up.* She called me back before I could dial again. I didn't like the tone of her voice; she sounded frantic and scared. I was hoping to just hear concern. We had spoken more or less every day since she left for school. Eight days with no contact and a bunch of unreturned calls and texts had obviously built up for her. I got all of this just from the way she said, "Dad." You know your kid's voice. You know their tones and what they mean. I suspect it's partially an evolutionary adaptation that a parent can discern all meaning necessary from the tone of their kid's voice, but it's also just from talking to them every day for twenty years. I could picture the look in her eyes when she used that tone, and I didn't like it. It was like a cheese grater on my skin. Instinctively, the only thing I wanted to do was to assure her.

I tried to manufacture a low, calm, but deeply normal voice. I tried to be empathetic to her concern but also a little dismissive. "Hi, baby. I'm sorry I haven't been in touch."

"You're okay? Where have you been?"

"I lost my phone," I explained. "I'm totally fine. I've been visiting somewhere for the last week that was out of cell range, and then I lost the phone. I just made my way back to a friend's house now and I'm using his phone. I'll get a new one tomorrow." I was trying to keep to the truth, but it was already stretching thin.

"Where were you visiting that was out of cell range? How did you lose your phone?"

I could see she wasn't going to let this go with vague, general answers. She was scared and upset, and she needed information. She was going to demand details.

So, my horror story, where three people died by my hand, turned into a zany misadventure hiking and getting lost in the rainforest with a bunch of characters from the local AA group. All I wanted to do was to reassure her and get off the phone after a few minutes, but she needed what she needed. I sat back on Barry's couch and closed my eyes, and it felt for a minute like I was putting her to sleep at night when she was little. I was telling her a soothing story where everything worked out happily at the end. I didn't get to do this much when she was little. That was mostly Lisa's job. I was usually either working or drunk. I owed her a couple thousand bedtime stories.

Eventually, I heard her voice shift gears. I don't think she believed the story, not all of it, anyway, but she seemed to believe I was okay or at least that I was trying to make her believe I was okay, and that was a good start to me actually being okay. Again, this was not said, but I heard it in her tone when she said, "Jeez, Dad, that's some week you had." Before she let me off the phone, she wanted to know my plan for the next day. I listed some to-dos that seemed to make sense and that seemed to satisfy her. Then I asked her for Ceci's phone number.

The call with Ceci was a little bit different. She cried when she heard my voice and told me she had been scared to death. She didn't say it, but I could hear in her tone that she thought I had been on a bender. I gave her the high-level outline of the story I told her sister, but Ceci didn't ask me a million questions. She made me tell her in several different ways that I was okay and safe and coming home soon. Before I could hang up, she told me that my mom had called her a few times, asking if she had heard from me. "Michelle's been calling also. She's worried to death," she said.

I had to think hard about who to call next. I needed help, but it was a specific type of help. I had some good friends at home, including Jose and Rob, some other AA guys, a few friends from work; but who could I tell this story to and then ask them to help me escape Central America? That was a few levels up from anyone I could think of.

There was one person in the world who I knew for a fact would kill for me, help me bury a body, and swear on a stack of Bibles in court that I didn't do it. I called Ceci back and asked her to give me my mom's phone number. It was 10 p.m. in Florida, so the chances were 50/50 she'd still be awake. She picked up on the first ring and yelled into the phone, "Troy! Is that you?" As a father, I understand we never stop thinking about and worrying about our kids, but to be on the other side of the worry was a very different feeling. My mom had stood between the world and me every day of my childhood. She was batshit crazy, but she walked through every fire for me without hesitating. I could feel her gripping the phone with both hands, holding it tight to her ear in case she missed a sound. "Troy! Are you okay?"

"Yes, Mom. It's me. Yes, I'm okay."

She sighed and mumbled something away from the phone. I thought I heard something like "Gonna give me a fucking heart attack," but I could be wrong. "I've been so worried. I called the girls and they said they haven't heard from you. I got your friend Jose's number from Roxy and he said he didn't hear from you. I've called Michelle every day. She's worried *sick* about you." She moaned. "You know, you can't leave the country with your friends for a three-week vacation, not come home with them, and then not tell me what you're doing and where you are. I'm a human being, Troy. I have feelings...."

I sensed that a monologue was about to ensue, so I cut her off. "Mom, I'm in trouble." She didn't hear me because she was gaining steam on her victim rant, whipping herself into a self-righteous stupor. "Mom! Stop! Please!" I yelled.

"Why are you yelling?"

"I'm trying to tell you that I'm in trouble. Big trouble. I need your help."

I felt her gathering herself on the other end of the phone. "Oh my God, Troy," she said and I could hear her pulling out the chair in her dinette set and settling down. "Tell me. Tell. What's happened?"

I told her the whole story, leaving out the details about my week in Chipote, because I sensed that this part would be more than she could take. Me hurting other people wouldn't be such a problem for her. In fact, her only concern about me killing people would probably be whether or not I was in trouble for doing it, and whether or not I was upset about it. Me being tortured would be unbearable for her. "Mom, the problem I have right now is that I don't have a passport, money, ID of any kind, or phone."

My mom was silent for a moment. "Okay," she said. I heard her push out her chair again and I could hear her slippers flip-flopping on the ceramic tile of her condo.

"Okay," she repeated a couple more times. "You're not hurt?" she asked.

"No, Mom. I'm okay."

She started sobbing. In between sobs she kept whispering, "Thank God."

I was starting to think this was a mistake. She was a mess. I thought I better start steering the conversation and telling her what to do. "Mom, I need to get a new passport," I said. "You have some of my documents. My birth certificate and my Social Security card."

She stopped crying. "Troy," she said sharply, cutting me off. She took a couple of breaths. "Have you been drinking, honey? It's okay if you have. You can tell me."

I closed my eyes hard. "No mom. I'm still sober. I swear."

She blew her nose and seemed to be collecting herself, or she was debating whether or not to say something. "Okay, honey. That's good. Now listen to me." Another long pause followed. "As much as I hate to say it, there is one person who can get you out of this."

"Jesus Fucking Christ," I said to Barry after the long call was finally over. "This gets weirder and weirder. My dad's gonna get involved. My mom thinks he can help." I had never told Barry much about my dad. Why would I? He heard me share at the San Juan Del Sur AA meeting, but that was pretty much it.

"What's he gonna do?"

I sat back on his couch and crossed my arms. Rocking back and forth a bit, I said, "He was a drug smuggler in the '70s and '80s. I guess he has contacts in Central America. I really don't know. He got out of that business when I was a kid."

Barry's eyebrows were up in the middle of his forehead. He had just started on a drawn-out "Fuuuuuuuuck" when his phone rang. We looked at each other. "It ain't for me, dude," he said, so I answered.

"Troy? Is that you?"

"Yeah, Dad."

"You okay?"

"No, Dad, I'm not okay," I said, and then I started to cry. It came out of nowhere. Saying to someone that I was not okay seemed to release this immense, built-up grief. On my last three calls I had to protect my girls and my mom from the truth because I didn't want to worry them. I didn't want to hurt them. There was no such worry with my dad. "No, if you really want to know, I am definitely not okay." I blubbered for another minute or so. He waited silently until I said, "I need help."

"Okay, son, tell me what you need," he said. "Are you drinking?"

It took me another minute to stop sniveling altogether. Barry sat on the bed across from me with his face in his hands, watching me intently. It had to be weird to see another grown man weep like a child in his house. I felt badly again that I had to bring him into this. He was a good guy, and he didn't deserve this.

I caught my breath. "No, Dad, I'm not drinking," I said, and told him an abbreviated version of the story.

He asked where I was at that moment, he asked all about Barry, he asked all about Andy, quantities of questions and a level of detail that were surprising and eventually irritating. He grilled me for a solid half an hour, and I heard him scribbling on paper the whole time. I imagined him sitting at his kitchen table with his glasses on, writing down everything I said. He tapped his pen a few times and whistled quietly. "Okay," he said. "It's going to be okay. Don't worry, Troy. I'm going to take care of this." Then he went silent for a minute. Was he crying? No way. "Just let me take care of everything," he said. "Please."

We were both silent for a little while and then it hit me. Was it finally going to happen? *Was my dad going to rescue me?* "How?" I asked. "What are you going to do?"

We stayed on the phone for another hour. My dad looked up the process for lost and stolen passports on the State Department website. It said that the process takes about two weeks if you have all the correct documentation. It also says that special cases should call for assistance. We interpreted that to mean that the process could be sped up if you plead your case with the embassy staff. Since I didn't have a coherent story I could tell, we agreed that this would be tough.

"Two weeks isn't so bad," I said. I could hang out in Tamarindo while they processed the new passport. Barry and I exchanged glances and he seemed to agree. He shrugged his shoulders as if to say, "Sure, why not?"

"I don't think that's a good idea," my dad said. "You killed two police officers, Troy. Even if they were corrupt, they're not going to let this slide. They're going to come for you."

I stood up and carried the phone over to the kitchen area and put it on speakerphone so that Barry could listen in. "Whoa, whoa, Dad, hold up. They can't just roll into another country, grab an American citizen, drag him back to Nicaragua and kill him. That'd cause an international incident." I looked at Barry again for support. He just stared back. I was still woozy and needed to get another opinion.

"Oh no?" my dad responded. "First of all, we don't even know who *they* are. For all you know, your friend Andy could owe money to President Ortega, or any number of powerful, influential locals." Barry pointed to the phone and nodded, as if to say, *Listen to that guy.* "Secondly, who's going to stop them, Troy? The security guard at your hotel? The Costa Rican police? They'll look the other way for a couple hundred bucks. You're saying that this guy Andy was into them for a lot of money. You think people don't go missing in Costa Rica too?"

Barry was pacing the room and rubbing his scruffy beard. "What do you think, Barry?" I asked.

"I think your dad is making a lot of sense, bro. These people are pissed off, they're super motivated, they're super violent, and they're operating out in the open like they're not too worried about anybody stopping them. Not encouraging signs. You could be a sitting duck in Costa Rica in a day or two."

Those words hung in the air for a moment before my dad continued. "Troy, listen to me," he said. "I have friends in that part of the world. I never told you about this part of my life, but I know people who can step in here and help us. Let me work on it and I'll get it figured out. I want you out of there tomorrow." Barry gave me a *holy shit* expression. "Sleep at Barry's tonight. At first light tomorrow I want you to head toward Tamarindo. Stay out of sight. Keep the lowest profile you possibly can. Wear a hat to cover your face, and plain, simple clothes—nothing that draws attention to you." He paused. "Are you listening to me? Do you understand what I'm saying?"

Barry and I were looking at each other. We both shrugged our shoulders. It sounded like he knew what he was talking about, but something deep inside me told me not to trust him, that he was going to fuck it up and I was going to get hurt again. But this time I could get killed, not just collect another emotional scar. I muted the phone and asked Barry, "What do you think?"

He nodded and closed his eyes. *Yes*, he seemed to say. *Do what he says.*

"Okay, Dad."

He exhaled deeply into the phone. "Good boy. You just keep your head down and I'll call this number tomorrow with the rest of the plan."

"Okay, Dad," I repeated. "Thanks."

"Thank you for letting me help you, Troy," he said. "I love you, buddy." He hung up.

—

The next night, Barry parked his truck in the empty lot of Santa Clara de Guapiles Airport. The airport, which was just an airstrip in the middle of a huge pineapple plantation with a terminal the size of a suburban gas station minimart, was closed for the night. The last flight had left hours earlier. We walked up to the terminal building, which had a green awning with yellow letters that said *Aeropuerto*. The lights were off and the doors were locked. There was a ten-foot-high chain-link fence that ran in both directions as far as we could see.

We walked along the fence until we spotted the hangar my dad had described.

We walked down for a couple more minutes until we found a gate. I checked the handle, and it was unlocked. A chain with a lock laid on the ground. We looked at each other and shrugged. It seemed too easy. We walked through and headed toward the hangar. We both broke into a jog after a few steps because it was dark, the place was closed, and we were trespassing, so it just seemed like we should hustle in case anyone saw us.

"This is crazy," he said as we got to the hangar and instinctively walked over to the opposite side, away from the moonlight, where we could hide in the shadows. We stood there for a few minutes, the only sound our breathing and the wildlife in the surrounding tree canopy. Barry checked his phone. It was 11:35. We had a little time to kill. "Do you think I should hide the truck?" he asked. He had parked It in the lot, right in front of the terminal. It was the only vehicle in the parking lot.

"That's probably not a bad idea," I said. "It's kind of conspicuous."

"Yeah," Barry agreed. He jogged around the building and back the way we came, leaving me standing there by myself. The tarmac extended from the hangar, out about fifty yards to the landing strip. There was a truck parked at the end of the tarmac. Relative to where I had been for the past week, this was not a strange or scary situation, but my heart was beating out of my chest. I could feel it pulsing in my ears. It wasn't really stress or anxiety, per se. It was more like just intense anticipation.

A howler monkey or two belted out some screams that filled the air and echoed across the landing strip. Some birds chimed in. On the third or fourth monkey scream Barry touched me on the shoulder and I almost shit myself. "Jesus!" I yelled out.

"Sorry, bro," he said. "I didn't mean to sneak up on you." We stood in silence for a while, absorbing the weirdness of the situation. "Don't worry," Barry whispered. "He'll come. He'll be here."

Moments later, the lights flashed on along the landing strip. It was startling and we both instinctively stepped back against the building. We searched the sky and moments later, a small business jet dropped out of the darkness and turned on two strobe lights. It skidded twice on the landing strip, hit the brakes, reversed the engines and came to a stop about fifty yards from where we were standing. We watched the door fold out and down. My dad climbed down the steps and stood on the runway, scanning the area. His silver hair was buzzed in a tight crewcut, and his gray chevron mustache was trimmed and caught the light from the runway as he searched back and forth. Joe's jeans, t-shirt and construction boots were all black. He looked as wiry, athletic and fit as ever, as though he could have played right field for the Cardinals that afternoon. He spotted the hangar and waved his arms in our direction.

"Holy shit," Barry said. "Your dad's a fucking badass."

I chuckled. *If you catch him at the right moment, I guess he is*, I thought. "I gotta go, brother. I'll be in touch." I hugged Barry for a long while. His head was buried into my chest, so I whispered "Thank you" many times into the top of his head. "I owe you everything," I said.

"No, man. Just have a great life," Barry said, pushing me away. "Go ahead, buddy. Get home safe."

I stepped out of the darkness and waved to my dad as I walked toward him. He bolted to me and grabbed onto me tightly. He held the back of my head and squeezed me into him. "You okay?" he asked.

"Yeah, Dad," I said with my face buried into his shoulder. "I'm gonna be fine."

Finally, he turned me around and walked me toward the plane with his arm around me. When we got to the airstairs he pushed me ahead and followed right behind until we were both on board. The door closed right behind him. The only other person on the plane was the pilot, a chubby middle-aged Latino guy with a big bushy gray beard. "Pacho!" Joe yelled as they walked onto the plane.

"*Sí!*"

"Say hello to my son."

"Hello, Troy," the pilot said as the door closed behind us. "Your dad has told me all about you for many years. I'm glad to finally meet you."

I didn't know what to say to this—there were too many questions to ask, and I was emotionally not up for a conversation, so I just sat in the seat across from my father in the cabin and put on my seatbelt.

"I'm gonna gas this bitch up and we'll be out of here in less than half an hour," Pacho said. *Who's gassing up this plane in the middle of the night in a closed airport?* I wondered. Pacho sent a text message from his phone and, almost immediately, two headlights turned on from a truck parked alongside the tarmac. The lights flashed twice. Pacho taxied the plane over to meet the truck on the side of the runway, alongside the hanger. He got up and grabbed a crumpled paper grocery bag that was on the floor next to him. He opened the passenger door, put down the stairs and carried the grocery bag down with him.

I looked at my dad.

He smiled and patted my knee. "We have a long trip back," he said. "I'll explain everything."

We walked up to the cockpit windscreen and watched Pacho as he waited for the man from the truck to climb down and meet him on the runway. It was dark and the man was wearing a faded old red baseball hat. He wore overalls and I guessed that he probably worked at the airstrip during the day. They shook hands and Pacho handed over the bag. The man walked around to the driver's side of the truck and opened the door, which caused the light in the cab to turn on. We could see him open the bag and inspect the contents for a moment before stepping down and walking back around to Pacho. He left the door of the truck open so that the light stayed on.

Pacho walked under the plane as the guy disconnected the hose from the side of the truck and came to meet him. From inside the plane, we heard the chinking and turning of the metal as they secured the nozzle. When he flipped the switch to turn on the pump, it was startlingly loud. It sounded like a gas generator firing on. "How long do you think this'll take?" I asked. I was getting nervous. I felt very exposed sitting on the runway in the middle of the night with the lights from the truck illuminating us and the generator roaring.

My dad rubbed his forehead. "About ten minutes." He went and sat down in the front row of seats. He patted the seat next to him, so I joined. We looked at each other. I studied him unself-consciously for maybe the first time since I was a kid. He was an old man. His face was still handsome, but deeply lined. The creases by his eyes reminded me of the ruts in the Costa Rican dirt roads. Many monsoons had left their grooves. I wondered how good of a man he was. At that moment, he was doing a good thing in rescuing his son. He was breaking several international laws and associating with known criminals in doing so, but it was still a selfless gesture. Wasn't it? Or was he still working on some selfish, self-centered version of personal redemption at any cost?

I'm not a young man. I understand now that it doesn't have to be one or the other. Both things and many others can be true at the same time. I guess the point is that I still didn't know him. Certainly, I was grateful to be saved. I would've preferred he had rescued me thirty years earlier, but he wasn't this man then. And the truth was that I didn't need rescuing. I was just fine. I just didn't feel good in my skin, and that was what I wanted to be rescued from. No father can do that for his son, no matter how much he wants to.

I looked back and forth from the window to my dad. I'd have to get to know him. I'd have to give him a chance. The thought was scary. That had not gone well for me in the past, but I was willing and open-minded. And I'd have to treat him fairly, not expecting perfection, not expecting a savior. I think by that point I was ready to try to have a relationship with him as a human being, as whoever he really was. I didn't need him to be anything. I didn't need to protect myself from him, because I was okay. I didn't need to hurt him back anymore because I wasn't afraid. That was gone.

"I got all of your documents yesterday from your mom," he said as he looked out the window. "I have your birth certificate, Social Security card, and even some utility bills she took out of your post office box." He explained that I would stay with Pacho's family in Mexico City for a week while they worked on a replacement passport so that I could get back into the U.S. legally.

I nodded as he went. It all made sense. "How was Mom?" I asked. "Is she holding up okay?"

"Yeah," he said. "She's fine. Obviously worried about you, but she's a tough lady." He hesitated for a minute and searched out the window as if he was trying to find the right words. "She was telling me about these frogs that spray venom from their eyes. She said they can kill small dogs with the poison. . . ." He trailed off and focused back on the action out the window again. "You know, she's fine. She's a tough lady."

After a few minutes, I asked where we were going, and my dad explained the plan that he had been working on for the last 24 hours. We were heading for Ixtepec Airport in Mexico. It's a small commercial landing strip in the province of Oaxaca, roughly five hours flying time. He explained that Pacho was an old friend from his drug days in Miami, although I had already guessed that part. Pacho and his brothers used to fly planes like this Hawker Siddeley HS-125, which looked like standard business jets, back and forth between Mexico and Miami. Pacho himself had an interesting story. He had retired after a career of some distinction from the Mexican Air Force (*Fuerza Aérea Mexicana*). He had flown hundreds of combat missions during the Mexican Dirty War, which was an internal conflict and basically Mexico's theater for the Cold War, killing left-wing guerrillas for the PRI government.

After leaving the military with a chest full of medals he joined his family business, trafficking cocaine and marijuana out of Sinaloa. Joe was his main contact in Miami and eventually he was the best man at Pacho's wedding and godfather to his son. Pacho had checked himself into a drug rehab in Florida and gotten clean a decade before Joe. He stepped out of the family business and tried to follow Joe's path to going legit, but he wasn't a smooth-talking bullshit artist, so he used his ill-gotten gains to open car washes and burger joints. For the last six years he and my dad had traded cryptocurrency together and made fortunes. I had no idea. I guess this was now the fifth or sixth time Joe had made a fortune.

The Hawker Siddeley that Pacho was flying was on loan from his brother-in-law, Federico Gonzales. The plane had been customized for narco smuggling. There were two sofas, side-by-side along the starboard side of the cabin. My dad unbuckled his seatbelt and walked over to one of them to demonstrate. He unhinged three latches that were hidden beneath the seats and folded the sofa down into the aisle. I got up and looked inside. Both of the sofas opened into a padded hull capable of holding hundreds of kilos of drugs, or two to three people comfortably. The cargo holds were ventilated and even had reading lamps installed. I was going to be smuggled into Mexico.

I was imagining what it would be like to sit in that hole when I heard my dad murmur, "What the fuck is this?" The hair stood up on the back of my neck. I joined him in the cockpit and watched an old Humvee driving toward us with a spotlight shining. It pulled past the hanger and blocked the plane. It was open in the back, and I could see some figures, maybe three or four seated. Everyone froze and waited as a man in the passenger seat shined the searchlight back and forth. He shouted a command and four militarized Costa Rican police officers climbed down from the rear.

The passenger and the driver climbed down and they all gathered between their Humvee and the gas truck. The passenger seemed to be in charge. He was a short, stocky man who wore a black button-down, short-sleeved uniform shirt. His white undershirt was visible beneath the open first button. He wore black pants, combat boots and a thick military belt with a sidearm. In gold letters his cap read *POLICIA*. The rest of the officers were better armed and equipped. They wore bulletproof vests and had machine guns strapped across their shoulders and hanging in front of their chests. Their vests had double yellow horizontal stripes across the bottom and said *POLICIA* in thick white letters above.

"This is not good," my dad whispered as the officer in charge addressed Pacho and the man in the overalls. My dad got up and walked back a few rows. He grabbed and unzipped a backpack, pulling out a black Glock 19. He racked the slide to put a bullet in the chamber and pushed down the safety. He waved the gun toward the sofa and said, "Jump in. Don't come out until I come back."

It took me a few seconds to understand that he was telling me to hide in the cargo hold. "Are you serious?" I asked.

"Don't fuck around, Troy," he said. "We don't have time to argue. I have to get you home safe. Please. Get in there."

It was so ridiculous that I had to laugh. This old man was telling *me* to hide. "Dad..." I didn't even know where to begin, but he was right, we didn't have much time for a debate. "I have twenty-five years of firearms and martial arts training, Dad. I've killed three people *this week*." If we had more time, I would have added that two of them were militarized police officers and I didn't even have a weapon. Not to mention three decades of being a violent psychopath in virtually all phases of my life. Just as I was getting ready to say, "Give me that gun and you fucking hide in the cargo hold," I took a quick breath to gather myself and asked, "Are there any other weapons on the plane?"

Joe nodded. I took this as a double affirmative: Yes, you can sit at the grownup's table and yes, there is another gun. He brushed past me in the aisle, opened a cargo box in the cockpit and grabbed Pacho's Springfield XD .45. He spun around and held it out for me. I advanced a round but chose to keep the safety engaged. I stuck it in the back of my pants. I didn't need to shoot myself in the ass if I had to draw it quickly.

Moments later, Pacho called out, "Joe!" He waved his arm. "Come out."

My dad and I looked at each other. I said, "You go down to the first step. I'll stay at the top so we can triangulate if we need to." He nodded.

Joe walked slowly and casually down the stairs, yelling to Pacho as he went,

"*Que paso hermano*?"

"These officers are concerned that we may be smuggling illegal goods out of their excellent country," Pacho explained.

"Hands up!" one of the officers yelled at us.

Joe and I looked at each other and then back to the officers. We both shrugged our shoulders and put our hands up. "Why?" I yelled. "Relax. There's no harm here. No need for concern."

"Joe," Pacho called. "I tried to explain to the captain here that we have already paid for the use of this runway tonight."

"Who did you pay?" the driver of the vehicle challenged. His voice and body language was the most hostile of the group. He walked alongside the officer who seemed to be in charge and leaned forward aggressively. He seemed to be younger and was the designated tough guy for the group. "Who?" he repeated.

Pacho hesitated for a beat and then leaned forward. "You know who."

The aggressive young officer took hold of his weapon. "Who!" he yelled.

In rapid-fire Spanish Pacho yelled back, "All the right people, and they're going to fuck you up if you fuck with us, you silly little boy."

My blood started to boil. I could hear my heartbeat in my ears. Violence was near. My breathing slowed down and I started to focus acutely on targets. I later learned that it had been over twenty years since Pacho had had a contact in Costa Rica. He couldn't remember any of their names on the spot. Even if he could, they would all probably be retired or irrelevant by then.

"*Hoy*," my dad yelled out. "Who told you we would be here?"

"That's none of your business," the young officer yelled back.

Joe pressed, "How did you know we would be here? You don't sit on closed runways every night waiting for a lottery ticket to show up."

The man snickered, and the rest of the men followed suit, chuckling and murmuring to each other. "You shut the fuck up, Clint Eastwood," the man yelled.

"You're not asking the questions here, old man."

"Who's your supervisor?" Joe asked. He seemed to want to stay on the offensive. "Tell me your name and rank. I'm not going to put up with this shit."

"Hey!" He seemed to have gone from amused to angry to concerned and back to angry in the course of a few questions. They had the machine guns and the badges and the power. Why did this old *gringo* seem so confident? Why wasn't he afraid? Just the opposite; he was getting pissed off. The young officer had no way of realizing that he had come face-to-face with one of the great liars of his era. When it came to bluffing, bullshitting and arguing, he had brought a knife to this gunfight.

The captain in the button-down shirt put his hand on the aggressive kid's shoulder and whispered something to him. They took a few steps away and had a quiet consultation. The other officers took this as an opportunity to discuss the situation quietly among themselves, as well. I heard an engine roaring in the distance and the sound of music. Everyone turned to watch a pickup truck slam through the airport fence at high speed and tear across the lawn of the infield. The truck barreled out onto the runway and turned to charge toward them. They could hear the engine from the truck roaring and music was blaring out the windows. Was that Metallica? It took me a moment to recognize the truck. It was Barry. "Holy shit," I murmured. He was bearing down on them and blasting "Ride the Lightning" at maximum volume.

The officers all took hold of their weapons and pointed them at the truck. When he got to within fifty yards, he slowed down and veered off the runway, driving back across the infield and barreling through the chain-link fence behind the hanger.

The captain barked an order and pointed at two of his men. They jumped into the Humvee and took off to chase Barry, who had stopped in the parking lot momentarily. *Is he waiting for them? Yes.* As soon as he saw that the Humvee was in pursuit he took off, accelerating through the parking lot and down the service road, staying a football field ahead of the military vehicle.

When they were out of sight and we could no longer hear James Hetfield's guitar solo, everyone on the runway seemed to take stock of the situation. The remaining officers were rattled. They were all gripping their weapons and pointing them back and forth between the men on the runway and the men on the stairway of the airplane. "*Tranquillo,*" Joe said. "Calm down. Nothing bad has to happen tonight."

"Come down here!" the captain commanded. He pointed his handgun at Joe and waved it toward Pacho and the man in the red cap, who still stood alongside the gas truck. "Now!"

"First I have to tell you something," Joe answered, putting his hands up in surrender. He paused for a moment so that everyone could take a breath. "We all have guns. I am not threatening you. This is just a fact."

"Throw out your guns!" the man commanded.

Joe laughed. He shook his head. "No," he said. "There are three of us and three of you. You have guns and we have guns." He paused for a moment to let this sink in. "Are you with me? This means that some of you will probably die if we start shooting."

He held his hands forward in a stop gesture. "But there is no reason for that. We're rich Americans and we're willing to pay you officers the tribute your authority deserves."

"Where is the money?" the captain barked, extending his arm with the gun now, pointing rigidly at Joe.

"Not so fast," Joe said. "I need two of you to put your guns on the ground first."

"No!" the captain yelled. "You give me the money or I fucking kill you."

Joe shrugged and smiled. "Maybe you will," he said. "Listen, sir, I'm an old man. I probably shouldn't have lived this long anyway, so that wouldn't be such a tragedy. But maybe right after you kill me, maybe my son or my friend kills you." I couldn't believe what I was seeing. He looked as calm as a man trying to negotiate with a housewife at a farmer's market. He smiled again, this time broadly, showing his teeth. "Now that would be a tragedy." *Was he enjoying this?* I wondered. *Was he showing off for me?* "But there's no need for that," he concluded. "I'm going to show you how everyone here can get what they want, and everyone can go home and sleep in their beds tonight. Nobody's family has to cry tomorrow." There was a long pause. "*Si o no?*"

The captain nodded. "Go ahead," he said. "Show me." His gun was lowering down bit by bit as he focused on Joe's words. All three officers were now totally focused on Joe. I could shoot them all from where I stood, but my father would probably get hit.

"*Muy bien,*" Joe said. He walked down the last two steps and onto the runway.

He was within thirty feet of the captain and the other two were ten feet further. *What is he doing?* I wondered and then I realized, he was walking to a spot where all three were unobstructed. If he had to, he could get a shot at any or all of them from there. "Here's the situation," he continued. "There's 75,000 dollars in a bag nearby. We were going to give it to this piece of shit right here," he said, nodding his head at the man in the overalls and the red trucker hat. "The greedy asshole was probably the one who tipped you off." He paused for a moment to try to read the captain's reaction. "Okay, so now we know how you ended up here tonight. Now let's get you home safe and rich." The captain nodded. "These two are going to put their machine guns on the ground. You're going to keep your gun on me. I'm going to get the money for you."

"How do I know you won't kill us if we put the guns down?" the captain asked.

"Simple," Joe answered. "We were getting ready to leave when you arrived. I was going to leave the money here, one way or another. Why would I care if this piece of shit gets it or you?"

The captain nodded. That seemed to be good enough for him. He turned and told his men to lay down their guns. Both seemed glad to be rid of them as they slung them off their shoulders and placed them on the ground.

"Over there," Joe pointed. They walked over and put their guns twenty feet away and then returned to their original places. Joe turned and looked at me. He nodded. *What does that look mean?* "*Muy bien,*" he said. He started to walk around the truck, but realized something and changed course. He came back and walked around the gas truck in the other direction. He went the long way around, which made the captain turn his back to me as he followed Joe with his gun. For ten to fifteen seconds, I had an open shot at him and the other two. Pacho looked up at me to see what I would do.

I could have easily killed all three of them right there. I never considered it for a moment, because I decided I'm not that kind of person anymore, but I wondered if that was what Joe expected me to do.

He took the crumpled paper grocery bag down from the driver's seat and carried it back to Pacho, where the searchlight was still shining brightly. He opened the bag up and showed it to the captain. The captain nodded. "Now what?" he said.

Joe turned and told Pacho to collect the machine guns. Pacho walked briskly around the truck, picked them both up and jogged back. He looked like he was worried that they might change their minds. "Now take the gun from the captain, please."

"Hey, wait a minute," the man in the overalls complained loudly. "You can't do this. You can't give them my money!"

Joe held up a finger to the police captain as if to say *Wait one moment, please, while I take care of this*. He dropped the bag on the runway and grabbed the gun from the back of his pants as he walked over to the airport attendant. He stepped in with his right foot and backhanded him across the face with the Glock, knocking his hat off and sending him down to the runway in a heap. The man shouted out in pain. Joe climbed over him and jammed the gun into his open mouth.

As he pulled the hammer back with his thumb Pacho stepped forward. "Easy, brother," he said. "We

don't behave like this anymore. *Lo siguiente correcto.*"
Joe kept his gun in the man's mouth and looked in his
eyes. "*Lo siguiente correcto*, Jose," Pacho repeated. "It's
just money, brother. Do the next right thing."

Joe got up and tucked his gun back into his jeans.
"Take the pistol from the captain, please," he said to
Pacho, wiping some froth from the corner of his mouth.

We got onto the plane without any further delays,
and Pacho taxied down to the far end of the runway and
made an adept three-point turn. He lined us up with
the centerline and then punched it. "Here we go," he
said as we accelerated down the runway and he pulled
us up into the night sky. I watched out the window and
seemed to finally exhale as the landing strip accelerated
away from us. I wondered what happened to Barry.

"He's a good man," my dad said. I nodded. After a
moment, he added, "Thank God for him."

We both dozed off after a meal of beef jerky, raisins,
and seltzer. Five hours later, we approached Ixtepec.
My dad patted my leg to wake me up and pointed out
the window. At 4:15 a.m. the airport and the industrial
area around it were almost entirely dark, except for a
strip of lights down the runway.

"Okay, guys," Pacho said. "Making our descent."

My dad popped open the sofa and I climbed inside.
I sat down on the padded floor with my legs out in front
of me and my back up against the side. My dad switched
on the reading light, which illuminated on the opposite

side of the cargo hold. He gave me a thumbs-up and a little smile of reassurance. I gave him a thumbs-up back. Before he folded the sofa closed on top of me, he held his finger up to his lips and made a "shhh" sound. I laughed and he winked at me, closing and latching the hold. Other than bouncing around a bit when the plane touched ground, I was perfectly comfortable there. After spending a week in that dungeon in Nicaragua, this little cell felt like Shangri-La. I was a bit nervous about the customs inspection, but I imagined that this abandoned landing strip in the middle of the night on Pacho's home field would probably be fine. I assumed that another rumpled shopping bag full of money would change hands.

I heard the murmurs of voices in the cabin but couldn't make out the words. The cargo hold was sealed tightly, so the only sound that I got was through the ventilation shaft, and that was drowned out slightly by the faint white noise of cool air flowing through. I imagined a customs agent asking them where they were coming from and what the purpose of their trip was. A couple of minutes later I heard the sound of laughter and then shortly thereafter the door closed. We were moving again. I lost track of time at that point. I was doing a concentration meditation where I focused on my breath, made different breathing patterns, and focused on the sensation of the breath in different parts of my body. As I was feeling the air hitting my nostrils for an inhale, I heard the fasteners being opened again on the sofa.

We deplaned in a small metal hangar. As I walked down the stairs, my mom stepped out of the back door of an old green Ford Explorer. She ran over and threw her arms around me. "I'm here," she said as she squeezed me and then started to weep. "It's okay, baby," she said as she sobbed. "It's okay. I'm here." Pacho and my dad walked over to the car and got in while we stayed there for a while. Her cheek was buried in my chest and she held on to me behind my back like her life depended on it. This is how it's always been. Her holding on to me, no matter how crazy things got . . . no matter how crazy *she* got . . . she did everything for me, and everything she did was for me.

I put my face on the top of her head. "Thank you, Mom," I said. "I never would've made it if it wasn't for you."

She let go and looked up at me. "Come on," she said. "Let's get out of this place. I've been in this *farshtinkener* hangar all day." We walked hand-in-hand toward the truck. "Oh, I've got a surprise for you," she said and hurried her pace a little bit so that she could get to the back door before me. She opened the door and said, "Ta-da." Sitting in the back seat, with a wary smile, was Michelle. I have to confess, I wasn't that surprised.

She climbed out and checked for my reaction before stepping in for a hug. She stepped back and looked me up and down. "You look like shit," she said.

"Yeah," I replied. "It's been a rough week." I held on to the sides of her face gently and bent down to kiss her. "I'm so happy to see you," I said.

"I hoped you would be," she answered.

Pacho yelled from the driver's seat, "Let's go! It's six hours to Mexico City from here!"

We piled into the back. As we pulled out of the airstrip and into the streets of Ixtapa, Michelle pulled out her phone and started texting. I looked over and saw that she was in a group text with Ceci and Roxy. *Got him. He's ok. Everything ok.* I kissed her head.

We drove for hours along the highways of central Mexico. I fell asleep for a while. When I woke up, my mom was describing a scene that had played out weeks earlier in her hair salon in Boca Raton. There was a misunderstanding about the style of cut she wanted. She brought in a picture of someone's hairdo that she clipped from a magazine, and her stylist apparently assured her it could be replicated. There was a lot of debate and discussion during the haircut. Other ladies in the salon got involved. There were several layers of misunderstandings and hurt feelings. There was enough dialogue for a three-act off-Broadway play, and there were a couple of lengthy tangents about the characters involved. My dad and Pacho exchanged glances and I started to worry that this story would take up the whole rest of the ride. I felt the familiar dread of these crazy stories begin to churn in my gut. I turned to

Michelle, and she smiled and patted my hand. I decided to reach into my toolkit and take out the one I'd been working on for this situation. I shifted my focus to my inventory of my mother's positive attributes.

At the top of the list of things that I liked about my mother was that she cared more about me than anyone else ever had or ever would. At the age of forty-six I was finally ready to feel gratitude for that. She had given up her life for me. She had worked two jobs and raised me the way she thought I needed to be raised. She was always my number one fan, and let's be honest, she was my only fan for most of my life. No matter how insane, violent, drunk, ungrateful, unkind or selfish I was, I couldn't make her leave me. I could never make her stop loving me. I was finally ready to like that about her.

It was impossible to think about this and feel irritation for the crazy story at the same time. When these thoughts wore thin and her story threatened to pull me back into irritation, I had a long list of other positive attributes about my mom I had memorized. I went through them in sequence and even thought of a couple more. When she reached the end of the story and said, "So then Gloria turns to me and says, 'Copper hair is the exact same thing as burgundy.' Can you believe that *schmendrick*?"

I said, "Yeah, Gloria's a real *schmegeggy*."

She got a good laugh out of that, and we held hands for the rest of the ride. For better or worse, we were in it together.

—

Eight Weeks Later

My dad's home group in Delray Beach met in a clubhouse on Jog Road. It was in a strip mall, next to a barber shop on one side and a nail salon on the other. As soon as we walked in, there were twelve rows of armchairs, all facing left towards two folding tables and a lectern with a microphone. The kitchen and bathrooms were in the back.

We all sat in the front row. It was Pacho, my mom, Grandma Leticia, Roxy, Ceci, Michelle and me. The meeting was well-attended, and by the time the chairperson started things off, there were only a handful of empty seats. Rather than try to shush people, he turned on the microphone and said, "Hi, my name is Charlie and I'm an alcoholic."

"Hi, Charlie," the group replied in unison, and everyone's conversations trailed off.

"This is the anniversary meeting of The Great Escape Group. Tonight, we have just one celebrant, our friend Joe, who's celebrating twelve years of sobriety. Before we ask Joe to come up and say a few words, is there anyone here who has any AA-related announcements?"

My mom looked like she was going to raise her hand, but she looked at me to check. I shook my head.

"Okay, then without further ado, here to celebrate twelve years of continuous sobriety is Joe. Joe, come up and get your coin and let's see what you have to say for yourself."

My dad stood up and walked behind the lectern. He shook hands with Charlie and took the coin while his group and his family applauded. He looked sharp in jeans, a white button-down shirt, and a blue blazer. "Thanks, Charlie," he said, looking down at the coin in his palm. He went over to the microphone and looked up at us. He took a deep breath and rested his hands on the sides of the lectern. "The promises," he said. He looked down at Pacho. "My friend here used to read these to me all the time. He got sober before me and he used to tell me that he had all these things and I could have them too, if I would just do what he did. I used to know them by heart, but I brought a cheat sheet with me just in case."

He reached into his jacket pocket and pulled out an index card. "These are the ninth-step promises of AA. 'We are going to know a new freedom and a new happiness. We will not regret the past nor wish to shut the door on it. We will comprehend the word serenity and we will know peace. No matter how far down the scale we have gone, we'll see how our experiences can benefit others. The feeling of uselessness and self-pity will disappear." He paused and looked back at Pacho. "You want to finish these out, *hermano*?"

Pacho laughed. "Our whole attitude and outlook upon life will change," he called out. Then he turned to face the rest of the group. "Everybody!" he called.

A handful of people chimed in. "Fear of people and of economic insecurity will leave us. We will intuitively know how to handle situations which used to baffle us. We will suddenly realize that God is doing for us what we could not do for ourselves." Pacho let out a woot, which got a big laugh and some applause.

"Nice," Joe said with a big toothy smile. "Thank you. That was great. I used to be—still am on a bad day—a real bullshit artist. I thought I knew a sales pitch when I heard one, and that's what this sounded like to me back then. But it didn't matter. I did the program anyway. I had no choice. I was going to die if I didn't, and I decided for whatever reason that I didn't want that to happen yet. And what do you think happened? It worked. Just like it had for millions of other people. Not that shocking to you people, I know, but I went through the twelve steps honestly and I had what they call *a spiritual experience that was sufficient to overcome my obsession.* Just like a lot of you did.

"By the time I was done with the steps and my first year, almost all of these promises had come true for

me. In fact, all of them but one had come true. I went
to tons of meetings, worked the steps every day, did
all the readings and the praying and the meditation.
I had service commitments, I had a sponsor. *Everything.*
You name it. I took every suggestion. But there was
one promise that remained outside my grasp for many
years." Joe let go of the lectern and held up a finger. He
twisted up his face for a moment and then took a deep
breath. "I never had a moment where I could honestly
say that I did not regret my past."

His eyes welled up and he took a couple of deep
breaths before continuing. "My past is . . . regrettable.
I did a lot of bad things and I hurt a lot of people. It took
me a year to even make a dent in my amends, but I kept
at them. But no matter how well I lived, it didn't seem
possible that I could ever get to the point where I no
longer . . ." He blew out hard and took a break. He wiped
his eyes. "Sorry," he said. "No matter what, I regretted
what I did to my family."

Joe balled up his fists and tucked his chin as though
he was going to charge through this. "But *you* people
told me to keep going. You told me that if I kept working
these steps . . ." he turned around and pointed to the
shade hanging on the wall to the right. "These steps
right here. . . . I would live a life beyond my wildest
dreams. *You obviously don't know me,* I thought. I have
some pretty wild dreams. . . . But never in my life would
I have dared to dream something as incredible as this."

He turned his palm up and gestured across our group in the front row. "This is really beyond my wildest dreams. So, you fucking people were right again." That got a good laugh and it gave Joe a break.

"Celebrating with me tonight, I have my mother, Leticia." He looked at her. "My God, what I put her and my father through. . . . But my parents have forgiven me and they never stopped supporting and loving me. Thank you, God."

He looked over at my mom. "My ex-wife is here," he said. "Amazing. This is a woman who I lied to every day of our lives together. I abandoned her to raise our son alone. I probably *still* owe her some child support payments. This amazing woman has forgiven me and now we can live the rest of our lives as friends. Thank you, God."

He looked at my girls. "I have my beautiful granddaughters, Roxy and Ceci, who I've never had a chance to know." He paused for a moment and seemed to study them. "I missed it all," he continued, but had to quickly step back and cover his eyes with his hand. He shuddered a couple of times and took a few deep breaths. Wiping his eyes, he came back to the lectern and looked at them. "Thank you for coming, girls."

Joe looked like he was concentrating on his breathing. His chest rose and fell a few times as he stared off at the back of the room. "And my son Troy is here with his fiancé, Michelle." He didn't look at me. I felt badly for him. It was too hard, and it wasn't necessary. I shook my head. He should have just taken his coin and said a few words and then we could all go out to dinner together. He didn't have to go through this. I couldn't really hear what he said next. It sounded something like, "What does it mean to be forgiven by my son," but it took him out. He turned his back and got hysterical. With his face in his hands, he cried like someone who doesn't know how to cry. It was fitful and it sounded like he was suffocating.

Michelle pushed my shoulder. "Go rescue him," she whispered.

So, I got up and walked behind the table. "Come here," I said to get his attention. We hugged for a minute, but I could see that he wasn't going to stop. "Come on," I whispered to him, "Let's get out of here." I led him out the front door of the clubhouse into the warm night.